YOUR PLACE OR MINE?

PORTIA MACINTOSH

Boldwood

First published in Great Britain in 2023 by Boldwood Books Ltd.

Copyright © Portia MacIntosh, 2023

Cover Design by Debbie Clement Design

Cover Photography: Shutterstock

The moral right of Portia MacIntosh to be identified as the author of this work has been asserted in accordance with the Copyright, Designs and Patents Act 1988.

Every effort has been made to obtain the necessary permissions with reference to copyright material, both illustrative and quoted. We apologise for any omissions in this respect and will be pleased to make the appropriate acknowledgements in any future edition.

A CIP catalogue record for this book is available from the British Library.

Paperback ISBN 978-1-80426-655-7

Large Print ISBN 978-1-80426-651-9

Hardback ISBN 978-1-80426-650-2

Ebook ISBN 978-1-80426-648-9

Kindle ISBN 978-1-80426-649-6

Audio CD ISBN 978-1-80426-656-4

MP3 CD ISBN 978-1-80426-653-3

Digital audio download ISBN 978-1-80426-647-2

Boldwood Books Ltd
23 Bowerdean Street
London SW6 3TN
www.boldwoodbooks.com

For Joe – who is very easy to live with

1

Your wedding day is *the* most special day to ever occur... just like everyone else's.

Ellen certainly believes hers is. She's sitting opposite me, talking relentlessly about her upcoming wedding, as well as trashing supposedly terrible weddings she has attended previously, and all the while, she's making me taste cake after cake after cake. I never thought *I* could get sick of cake, but here we are.

If people knew before they agreed to be a chief bridesmaid for the first time exactly what it was going to entail, it's hard to imagine anyone would say yes. And I seriously struggle to believe anyone would do this twice. I suppose there's a mutual element, between best friends, where you are one another's chief bridesmaids on your big days, but god help the person who marries first, because, after months on end of all of this, the second person to tie the knot won't just want all the usual bridesmaid duties carrying out, they'll want revenge too.

'It's supposed to be fruit cake, isn't it?' Ellen asks as she uses her fork to rifle through a vanilla sponge, as though she's going to find the answers she is looking for inside it.

'It's a tradition, but one that more and more couples are turning their back on,' I reply. 'Fruit cake is supposed to be a sign of fertility. The idea is that you would serve it in the hope that it would bring you lots of kids in the future. In fact, they say that the reason you have a cake with three tiers is so that you can serve the bottom tier on the day, hand out the middle tier to guests to take home, and save the top tier in your freezer – to eat at your first child's christening.'

'You save it?' she replies in disbelief.

'Yeah, you preserve it in the freezer,' I say, in no way keen to do so, just relaying the facts.

'But what if you don't have kids?' she asks. 'Or if you wait a really long time to have them, when you're old, like when you're in your thirties or something?'

I decide not to unpack her remark about people in their thirties being old. I can't have that on my plate right now, not when it's already piled high with cakes I don't want to eat.

'Some people eat it on their first anniversary,' I say. 'But obviously you don't have to save it at all.'

Ellen puffs air from her cheeks.

'I don't know, cake that gets you pregnant and can survive for a year – it makes you wonder what on earth they're putting in them.'

She says this with a real look of horror. Then she narrows her eyes at me almost accusingly.

'I'll stick to sponge,' she says eventually. 'Vanilla, lemon or chocolate – what would you do?'

'I would probably do a tier of each,' I admit. 'So that there's something to please everyone.'

'Ah, but see, it would be *your* wedding day,' she reminds me.

'Forget what the guests want. You're supposed to please yourself and no one else.'

'And the groom, of course,' I point out.

'I guess, a bit,' she says begrudgingly. 'But everyone knows it's all about the bride, right?'

Ellen gives me a wink. It's probably best I don't say anything in reply to that.

'We've not tried that one, with the pink frosting,' Ellen says. 'Come on, let's compare it to the vanilla.'

A single hiccup escapes my lips. I only had lunch – including dessert – less than an hour ago, I'm so full, I can't possibly fit another bite of cake into my mouth. I hesitate and Ellen notices.

'Please,' she pleads with me. 'It's hard enough being a bride, I can't do this on my own. This is why brides have a chief bridesmaid, to help make decisions like these.'

I use a fork to cut the tiniest piece of cake from the edge of a slice. As it hits my tongue, the sugar in the strawberry frosting attacks my mouth, provoking my saliva glands into overdrive to try to dilute the sweetness.

'I like the strawberry frosting the most,' I reply.

'You ought to let your face know,' she ticks me off. 'You don't look like you're enjoying it.'

I can't help but massage my left temple with my free hand. I grip the fork tightly in my right. Be polite, Serena.

'Sorry, I'm just so full, I had a big lunch,' I reply.

'But you knew we were doing this today,' she snaps back. 'We've had the appointment for months.'

I don't feel like I owe her an explanation. Still, I give her one.

'The guy I'm dating took me out for lunch, to celebrate his promotion at work,' I reply. 'I ate way too much – and then I had a huge dessert. They're all gorgeous cakes, I just can't physically fit any more food in my body.'

'All right, it's not all about you,' she reminds me through an unamused frown.

However I'm feeling right now, I feel even more sorry for Ellen's poor fiancé, because she's really starting to seem like the bride from hell.

'If we can just try the chocolate one...' she starts up again, ignoring every word I just said.

Ellen doesn't get to finish before we're interrupted by Arnold, the longest-serving host at Diana's Tearoom. He's just made his way through the busy tea room, weaving in and out of gorgeously laid-out tables, crowded with ladies who lunch, sitting under chandeliers while a pianist plays ambient music. He has a frazzled-looking, petite brunette with him. She plonks herself down at the table with us.

'I know, I know, I'm late,' she babbles as she kicks her bags under the table. Then she turns to me. 'Who the hell are you?'

She's talking to me. Arnold gives me a sympathetic smile before returning to his post.

'I'm Serena,' I reply.

She briefly widens her eyes, as if to command more information from me.

'She's the baker,' Ellen replies. 'Well, you stood me up, and I needed someone to taste cakes with me.'

My life isn't interesting enough – and I don't have nearly enough friends – for me to be someone's chief bridesmaid. I was just a placeholder cake tester, until Ellen's real friend got here.

Ellen turns to me.

'You can go now,' she says casually. Pah, and after everything we just went through together.

By the time Ellen finishes her sentence, something appears to switch off in her brain. I am officially out of her orbit. Her friend shoos me away with a jerk of her neck.

'I wondered what you were doing hanging out with one of the maids from *Downton Abbey*,' Ellen's friend teases her with a snort.

I run my tongue across my front teeth as I stand up, keeping it busy so I don't accidentally speak my mind. Speaking your mind only ever gets you in trouble, doesn't it? Fair enough, my black knee-length dress with the lacy white apron isn't the coolest, and with my long blonde hair pulled tightly into a low bun (garnished with a dorky frilly white headpiece), it doesn't do my round face any favours, but come on, cut me some slack, I'm at work.

To Ellen, I might be nothing more than a placeholder friend and 'the baker' but my role here at Diana's is more varied than that. I'm somewhat of an up-and-comer in the kitchen, learning to make all the fancy cakes and delicious sandwiches in the iconic 'Diana's style' that people travel for miles to try. It's a step up from when I started working here as a waitress, but alongside working in the kitchen, I'm also overseeing some aspects of the wedding catering we offer.

Diana Atwood, the brains behind the tea room, said she was giving me extra responsibilities so that I could work out where exactly in the business I thought I might be the happiest. Wait-ressing was never the plan, but Diana gave me a job when I needed one, so I really appreciate her letting me stretch my wings like this, to try to find something I enjoy. I have to say, after meeting a few too many brides like Ellen, I'm starting to lean more towards working in a role that isn't customer-facing.

'Another happy customer?' Maël asks, seeing the look on my face.

Maël is our resident French patisserie chef. Well, he's French on his mum's side. His last name is Smith and he was born in Halifax and raised in Horsforth, but he thinks his heritage lends him an authenticity you can't put a price on – I just think he's great at his job.

'Another bridezilla,' I correct him. 'Honestly, I thought they were only creatures that existed in fiction. I'm peddling a theory that something early in the wedding-planning process possesses women.'

'Perhaps it's the pressure of throwing a party spectacular enough that you can make peace with the idea of being with one man for the rest of your life,' he wonders out loud.

I scoff.

'You've been with Martyn since Year 11,' I point out.

'Don't remind me,' he replies, although I know he doesn't mean it. 'His latest big idea is moving to Edinburgh to live closer to his sister and her brood.'

'You don't fancy it?' I ask curiously.

'Not really,' he replies. 'Mostly because I love this job so much – put the kettle on.'

I do as I'm told. We probably drink just as much tea behind the scenes here as we serve in the tea room.

'If he keeps pushing me, we might need Serena the scam artist to rear her head again,' he says with a laugh.

'Scam artist?' Clare asks after barging through the double doors, bum first, dragging a trolley loaded up with dirty dishes.

Clare is one of the servers here. She's got decades of experience on me. I feel like I've learned so much from her in the year I've been working here, and given that it was Maël – my old school friend – who alerted me to the job in the first place, we feel like a family. Diana always describes us all as her children, but lord knows her actual children are nothing to brag about.

'When we were at school, Serena just had this way of working people – with a Robin Hood kind of vibe, though,' Maël explains to her. 'She knew exactly how to make things happen – to get the class out of a break-time detention they didn't all deserve, or for the bleep-test cassette to go mysteriously missing so no one had to do it. People would even go to her for alternative relationship advice too. She would only use her powers for good, as far as I know, but if you had a boyfriend you wanted rid of, Serena would tell you exactly what to say, depending on whether or not you wanted to stay friends or scorch the earth. My favourite thing of all, though, was if you didn't want to be the bad guy in the break-up, she seemed to know just what a person needed to do to get dumped – without actually doing anything awful, though. It was genius. You loved a good scam, didn't you?'

'Serena!' Clare laughs with a roll of her eyes before heading back out into the tea room with a trolley piled high with after-noon teas.

'I would never break you and Martyn up,' I inform him. 'If you're still together at thirty-one, you're not going to call it quits now. Anyway, I'm far too grown-up for antics like that now.'

'That reminds me, your lunch with your boyfriend... or is he your fiancé now?'

I place Maël's cup of tea down next to him with a controlled thud. He's definitely teasing me.

'Dean is just the guy I am dating – not my boyfriend – and anyways, the special lunch to celebrate something turned out to be him getting a promotion at work,' I inform him.

'I thought you were going to be our next bridezilla,' he says, winking at me over his teacup. 'Do you think you would be any different to the customers?'

'It's not even worth thinking about,' I tell him. 'Marriage is definitely not in my immediate future.'

It's not that I'm against the idea of marriage, or even marrying Dean, it's just way too soon to be thinking about anything like that. We've only been dating for a few months, we're not even official yet.

Clare reappears.

'Whatever he's saying, ignore him,' she insists. 'At thirty-one, you're still young, everyone gets married older these days.'

'See, everyone gets married old these days,' Maël adds cheekily.

I stick my tongue out at him.

'Excuse me, everyone, if I can have your attention for a moment please,' Arnold interrupts us as he enters the kitchen with – as far as I can tell – every staff member on shift at the moment. 'Please, this is important. I have some news.'

'Here we go,' Maël whispers to me, thankfully quiet enough that Arnold can't hear him. 'Watch him mention how he's worked here the longest and blah blah blah.'

There's something about Arnold's face that rattles me. There's no emotion, no colour in his cheeks. I know it sounds silly, but Arnold's job as a host almost verges on an acting gig. He wears his black suit without so much as a speck of fluff on the back. Genuinely, I've never seen a gram of mess on him, and a work experience girl once crashed into him with a lit birthday cake – we all joke that he treats his suit with all kinds of chemicals to ensure it repels disaster (I wish I could get me some of that). Not only that, though, the way he carries himself is exactly as you would imagine, so poised and controlled. But right now, his shoulders look low, his body language is all wrong, he's breaking character.

'As the longest-serving team member here at Diana's...' he starts.

Okay, so he's not fully breaking character. Maël can't help but snigger as his prediction comes true.

'Take something seriously for once in your life,' Arnold practically screams at him. His lack of colour disappears as red surges through his cheeks. It disappears as fast as it comes, as Arnold recomposes himself, but now I know something is seriously wrong.

'All right, calm down,' Maël insists. 'It's not like someone died.'

Arnold dusts himself down, as though briefly losing his temper may have messed up his suit in some way.

'That's where you're wrong, dear boy,' he replies. 'Now, please, everyone listen...'

2

―――――――

'Which side?' a fifty-something vicar asks me through a frown.

'Which side?' I repeat back to him.

He nods towards the empty pews behind him.

'Oh, sorry, I think I might have got the wrong church,' I reply, embarrassed because aren't we all always so quick to accept that we've messed up? Picking a side doesn't seem right, I'm supposed to be attending a funeral, not a wedding.

I'm a slave to the bus timetables, which usually means I get to choose between arriving early or late – late didn't feel like the right call for a funeral. At least I have time to find the right church now.

The vicar reads my mind.

'No, you're in the right place,' he tells me. 'Left is the brother's side, right is the sister's side.'

My eyes widen. Suddenly it makes sense.

'Oh, neither, I guess,' I reply. I don't know what else to say.

'Sorry, I must confess, I'm not in the best mood today,' he says as he runs a hand over his balding head. 'I'm anxious about the service. How did you know Diana?'

'She was my boss,' I say, but then I smile. 'Actually, she was so much more than that.'

'You were close?' the vicar says. At first, it seems like a question, but as the look on his face softens, I realise it's more like he's confirming a fact.

'We were really close,' I reply. 'I owe her so much.'

'Listen, you're quite early, how about I make you a cup of tea?' the vicar suggests. 'Although I do have an ulterior motive. If you help me, I'm sure I can scratch your back too.'

'Oh?' is about all I can reply.

I'm worried, like I'm about to make a deal with the devil, although I suppose making a deal with a vicar couldn't be more the opposite.

'Well, there's the tea,' he starts. 'And I could let you sit in the good seats for the service, so you don't have to pick a side and, of course, helping out a vicar looks really good on your CV at the Pearly Gates.'

I'm pretty sure it's going to take more than a good reference from a vicar, but it's a nice thought.

'Church has good seats?' I reply.

'Yep,' he says proudly as we head into a back room. 'Please, take a seat, I'm really at a loss today.'

I can see the desperation in his eyes. Of course I'll help him – if I can.

The vicar introduces himself to me as Ken as he makes our cups of tea in what I can only describe as a staffroom with a small kitchen – of course churches have staffrooms, you just don't think of it, do you? Eventually, he sits down next to me at the shabby wooden table.

'I take it you know Andrew and Agatha Atwood,' he starts as he pushes a packet of chocolate digestives towards me.

'I do,' I confirm.

Andrew and Agatha are Diana's children – well, I say children, Diana was almost eighty so they must be in their forties now. As is the case with many children who grow up with rich parents, Andrew and Agatha are spoilt, entitled and greedy. Diana always told me she didn't know where she went wrong with them, for them to turn out the way they did. I think she had always imagined them growing up and working in the family business, but neither of them wanted to work. When Diana's husband – their dad – died, and they got a chunk of inheritance, that only sealed the deal on their lifestyle. But being so similar puts Andrew and Agatha completely at odds with one another for some reason – hence having a side of the church each.

'I asked them both for information about Diana, because I always like to talk about the person individually – anyone can say a few words and knock out a few hymns,' Ken explains. 'It means so much to me, to honour a person's life, to talk about who they were, the effect they had on the world, and what they'll leave behind.'

'That sounds lovely,' I reply.

'Except neither Andrew nor Agatha could tell me much about their mum,' he continues. 'Andrew sent this. See...'

Ken hands me a folded-up piece of paper which reads:

Name: Diana Atwood.
  Died: 14:02 20/01/2023.
  Cause of death: heart attack.
  Place of death: LGI.

My jaw drops.

'Not exactly eulogy material, is it?' Ken says. 'And while Agatha sent more, it turned out to be Diana's biography from her website. I was hoping you might be able to tell me all about

Diana. Start with how you met, anything she loved, what she was like as a person, what her business meant to her.'

How awful that her own children can't even think of anything to tell the vicar about her. Not that I'm surprised, they never visited her.

I take a deep breath as I find the words to begin with.

'You said you owed everything to her,' Ken prompts me. 'Why don't you tell me all about that – if you don't mind?'

'Well, my dad moved abroad when I was little, so it was just me and my mum,' I explain. 'When she died, I was not only devastated but I was in a real mess. I gave up my job to look after her, near the end, so things were tough after she passed. I was frantically looking for any job that would have me, not expecting to land anything special – or at all, to be honest – but one of my old school friends shared a post advertising for waitstaff at Diana's, so I submitted my CV and got an interview with Diana herself. My friend told me everyone got an interview because that's the kind of person Diana was, but when I sat down with her, and explained the gap in my CV, she sprang into action – in a way that reminded me of my mum.'

'She gave you a job in your time of need,' Ken says with a smile.

'Not just that,' I reply. 'She gave me somewhere to live too, in the flat above the tea room, and even though she said my wage reflected a deduction for rent, I don't think that was true. She took me in, showed me the ropes – we became really close.'

My voice wobbles, just a little, so Ken changes tack.

'What did she like?' he asks. 'What made Diana who she was?'

'She loved Elvis,' I say with a smile. 'Like genuinely, truly adored him. And murder mysteries were her favourite thing to watch on TV – those and *The Great British Bake Off*. I always told

her she should enter and she would always say she wasn't interesting enough to be on TV. I think she was, though, and she
would have crushed the competition in any series, but nothing
could take her from her tea room. People were always offering to
buy it but there was no number high enough, and retiring was
never going to be an option for her. She just loved her job – and
her staff – too much. She always said we were like a family and,
with a family like hers, who can blame her for making a new
one?'

I've been so upset since I got the awful news about Diana that
it's been impossible not to feel sad whenever I thought of her.
Right now, I can't help but smile. It's nice to remember the good
things, the things she liked, the things that made her the amazing
person she was.

'Serena, I am truly sorry for your loss,' Ken tells me. 'And I
can't thank you enough for giving me some genuine things to say
about Diana, to give her the send-off she deserves.'

'It's the least I can do,' I insist. 'I'm going to miss her so much
and, with her passing so suddenly, and so unexpectedly, I never
got to say any sort of goodbye. It's comforting to know I can help,
even in a small way.'

'Well, people should start arriving soon,' Ken says. 'I'm going
to very quickly put together some notes, so that I don't forget
anything, but if you head through that door there, and down the
aisle, Diana is already there, if you would like a moment to say
goodbye before anyone else arrives.'

'I thought people usually arrived in a hearse?' I can't help
but ask.

'Andrew and Agatha couldn't agree,' he says before pursing
his lips for a second. 'I imagine this was the compromise.'

'I see,' I reply. 'Well, I'll do that, thank you.'

I make my way down the aisle to where Diana is waiting to be laid to rest.

When I was younger, maybe eight or nine, and my grandma passed away, and I saw her coffin – the first coffin I'd ever seen – I was terrified of it, but Mum told me not to worry, that my grandma wasn't in there, it was symbolic. At the time, I took this quite literally, and for a good few years I thought coffins were just empty boxes. Now that I'm older, I understand what she meant. Diana isn't here, in this box – not really. She's gone. Still, I can't stop myself from running a hand over the smooth wood and whispering: 'Goodbye. Thanks for everything.'

I hear a bang, and then...

'How many millions do you need?' I hear a woman ask angrily.

'You think getting little more than a mil each from the house sale is going to last us forever?' a man replies. 'Delusional as ever, sis.'

'You're being a wanker in church,' she snaps.

'Well, that's a matter of opinion, but you just said wanker in church, and that's so much worse,' he claps back.

I sigh. My heart feels even heavier, watching Diana's grown children bicker as they walk down the aisle together. Do they have to do this right now?

Andrew is the spitting image of his dad. Diana had lots of pictures of her late husband, Armand, around the place and looking at Andrew is like looking at a contemporary reboot. He's tall and slim with a neat beard – the kind you don't get without a comb and fancy beard oil. His dark hair and dark eyes give him a sort of mysterious vibe, but his general unapproachable demeanour doesn't make you want to know the answer to any of your questions. Agatha, on the other hand, looks just like her mum. Well, a version of Diana that had been run though a machine that creates Disney villains. Her facial features are tight – almost as though she begrudges using the muscles (well, that plus the Botox she's using to try to suspend her looks in time, but they're really just suspending her face in the miserable state it must have been in when they injected her).

I catch Agatha's eye.

'Erm, who are you?' she asks me. 'And what are you doing with our mum?'

'Sorry, I was just saying goodbye,' I reply. 'I'm so sorry for your loss, I loved your mum, she was amazing.'

'Shit, you're not a love child, are you?' Andrew asks me. 'If you are, you're not getting any money.'

'Oh, no, I worked for your mum,' I explain. 'And she let me live in the flat above the tea room. My name is Serena, we've met a few times before.'

Clearly, neither of them remembers me.

'Great, can you tell my thick sister that the business is booming, please?' Andrew asks, not quite nicely, but at least he says please.

'Oh, yeah, definitely,' I confirm.

'Okay, fine, we can push for more,' she reluctantly gives in.

'More what?' I ask without thinking.

'Not that it's any of your business,' Agatha starts. Then she thinks for a moment. 'Then again, I suppose it is, we're selling the place. The business, the building, the lot.'

'You can't do that,' I blurt.

Andrew laughs.

'Why not? Mum left it to us...'

'The one thing your mum was always adamant about was never selling up,' I remind him, trying to keep my own emotions in check, but I feel passionately about this, because Diana felt passionately about this, and they both know it.

'She would hate this,' I add as calmly as I can.

'She's not exactly around to run it, is she?' Agatha points out. I don't understand how she can be so flippant with her mum's coffin a matter of feet away from her.

'Who are you selling to?' I ask.

Of course, it's none of my business, but countless people have tried to buy the business, the building or both over the years. The best I could hope for is for them to sell to one of Diana's competitors.

'You're so nosy,' Andrew says, amused. 'If you must know, it's all being bought by a pub chain. What they really want is the building, so we're making them buy the business as well, and over the odds too, even though they don't want it – it's genius, really.'

'Guys, honestly, your mum would be horrified by this,' I tell them – I feel like I'm duty-bound to, not just out of loyalty to Diana, but because she was their mum, and they can't realise what a mistake they're making.

'Wait, are you just annoyed that you're going to have to find somewhere else to live?' Agatha asks me, sounding only mildly irritated as she misses the point completely. 'This isn't about Mum at all, is it? Wow, using Mum to keep a roof over your head. That's so low.'

'That's not what I'm doing,' I insist, keeping my voice strong but losing my nerve more and more by the second.

Agatha isn't having any of it.

'It was more of an informal thing, right? You don't have any sort of tenancy agreement?' she checks.

Oh, god. I don't. Diana was pretty much letting me live there rent-free. My face must tell Agatha everything she needs to know.

'Right, well, in that case we need you out of there by the end of the week,' Agatha tells me plainly.

'But it's Friday,' I point out.

'Oh, she knows,' Andrew tells me casually, with a look that confirms he's aware of exactly how horrible Agatha can be, but he doesn't actually mind all that much.

'Fine, fine, you can have Monday and Tuesday too, to clear out the flat. And, you know what, we'll still pay you, but don't work your notice,' she adds.

'Really?' Andrew asks her in disbelief, as though it's so unlike her to do anything nice.

'We don't want her tanking the sale, do we?' she says under her breath.

I stare at them both for a moment. Realistically, is there anything I can do? Diana and I may have been close, but I have no say in anything, I can't do *anything*. All that's left to do is walk away.

There is a growing crowd outside the church, with clusters of mourners scattered around, everyone wrapped up as best they can to fight off the cold, dark January day. I scan an eye over them until I spot someone I know.

Maël, who is looking sharp in a skinny-fit black suit, looks almost excited when he sees me.

'Serena, quick,' he insists.

I head over as quickly as I can before anyone sees him beaming.

'You're looking awfully chipper considering you're at a funeral,' I point out.

'Obviously I'm really sad,' he says, not sounding it, but I know he is deep down. 'But look around, this place is crawling with Yorkshire royalty. There are even a couple of Leeds Lions players here.'

'I hear they're dirtbags,' I tell him. 'Not the kind of boys you want to mourn with.'

'Anyway, what were you doing in the church, getting us the good seats?' he asks.

I laugh.

'Erm, yes, actually,' I reply. 'I had a run-in with Andrew and Agatha while I was in there.'

Maël pulls a face.

'I'll bet that was unpleasant,' he replies. 'Andrew is a poor man's Patrick Bateman just, you know, without a job, and Agatha is vile.'

'They told me something,' I start. I pause for a second. 'Can you keep a secret?'

'No,' he replies with a completely straight face. 'But I'll make an exception for you.'

'They're selling Diana's,' I tell him, cutting to the chase, but keeping my voice low.

'Diana's what?' he replies.

'The tea room!'

'No!'

Maël is as shocked as I was.

'Selling was the last thing Diana wanted,' he says. 'Bloody hell, she'll be spinning in her grave. Bloody hell, she's not even in it yet.'

'They're not even selling it to someone who will keep it open,' I say with a sigh. 'They're selling to *that* pub chain who have been trying to get their hands on the building for years.'

'Diana's is going to be a bloody Old Duncan's?' he replies in disbelief.

No amount of rugby players in suits could make Maël smile now. Somehow the look of absolute devastation on his face seems to intensify.

'Oh, god, I've just realised something,' he starts. 'I'm moving to Edinburgh.'

'What?'

'I'm losing my job,' he replies. 'There's no way I'll get my way to stay in Leeds now.'

As sad as it is to say, Maël and Martyn are my two best friends, and I don't have many close friends otherwise. It's just one of those things, when you're in your thirties, and your friends start overtaking you as far as life steps go. My married friends are all either too busy, or too happy being in their own little couple bubbles, to be bothering going on nights out with their single friend. I'm not sure I blame them, really. If I had a partner at home, I'd probably want to spend all my time with them too. I don't suppose giving up work to look after my mum helped either, it really wiped out my social life – not that I'm complaining, I would do it again in a heartbeat. That's why I was so happy to end up working with Maël. Of course I would be gutted if he moved away, but I would never, ever hold him back. I have to be supportive.

'At least you're going to have a home,' I reply. 'And a boyfriend who cares about you.'

'This might work out for you, you know,' Maël says. 'Once Dean hears about this, he'll probably let you live with him.'

'Do you think?' I reply. 'It's too soon, surely?'

'Emergencies trump "too soon",' he informs me. 'Oh, look, we're all heading inside.'

I link arms with Maël and head for the church.

'This is going to be all the more heart-breaking now,' Maël whispers.

'Edinburgh is nice,' I tell him, but I know what he means.

I'm not going to say Diana loved her tea room more than her children, but it was definitely like one of them to her, and it probably gave her more back than Andrew and Agatha ever did. Not only selling up but closing down is definitely against her wishes. I should be saying my final goodbyes to a woman I loved like a relative and now all I can think about it is how wrong they are doing by her. Oh, that and the fact I'm not going to have a home or a job in a few days.

Perhaps Maël is right, maybe Dean will invite me to go stay with him, even if his grumpy flatmate has a strict 'no girls' rule. I know it's too soon to move in together, after casually dating over the last few months, but I like to think we've been seeing each other long enough that he'll have my back.

I guess we'll see later...

3

As I sit on the sofa in the flat, I glance around the room. I've called this place home for a year now – I can't believe I have to leave.

Most of the furniture isn't mine, it was fully furnished when I moved in, but I've found ways to make the place feel like my own. Diana liked pastels and florals, so I made the most of the colours by adding my own items like plants and cute bits of art.

Dean is sitting on the sofa next to me. He has one arm around me, lovingly massaging my shoulder, while the other rests on my thigh. It means so much to me that he came over to meet me, within minutes of me arriving home from the funeral, to make sure I'm okay, and to try to cheer me up.

'Those bastards,' he says when I'm done telling him all about Andrew and Agatha, and their plan to sell the tea room against their late mum's will. 'People can be absolute scumbags.'

'Always, whenever I think I've met the worst person living on planet earth, someone will find a way to prove me wrong,' I say with a sigh.

'You want to try working in finance,' he says. 'Everyone is a scumbag.'

'Diana would be devastated if she knew what was happening,' I tell him.

'I know I only met her that one time, briefly, and I could tell she didn't think much of me, but you clearly adored her, and she adored you,' Dean reassures me.

'Yeah, she was usually a pretty good judge of character, but she did only meet you for a minute or two,' I remind him. 'She was just doing the overprotective-mother-figure thing, making sure you were good enough.'

'And what do you think the verdict would've been?' he asks with a smile.

'She would've loved you if she had got to know you,' I reply.

'Ooh, careful, throwing around the L-word like that,' he teases me.

'I said *she* would've loved you,' I remind him. 'I'm even harder to win around.'

'Duly noted,' he replies through a smile.

'The icing on the cake is that, as well as losing my job, I'm also going to lose this place,' I tell him. 'They want me out of here in a few days.'

'Well, that's unreasonable,' Dean points out, snapping into business mode. 'What does your tenancy agreement say? Do you want me to have a look?'

'That's good of you but I never had one,' I admit. 'I know, it sounds stupid, but even though Diana says my wage was minus rent, in reality, I don't think she took any money at all. She was letting me live here for free, so no rental agreement. She was only thinking of me, giving me somewhere to live while I was working for her, neither of us had an ending like this in mind.'

A tear that has been building up in my lower lid for some

time now finally escapes and speeds down my face. I quickly swat it away.

'Well, that's why I'm here,' Dean tells me. 'I'm here to make you feel better. I brought pizza, those awful premixed cocktails you like, I'll even sit through one of your mafia movies, even if you've tried to make me watch it before.'

I feel the weight that has been crushing me all day slowly starting to lift.

'I've never met anyone who could fall asleep during *Goodfellas*,' I point out, allowing myself to smile. 'You're lucky you're still here.'

'Well, that might be something to do with the first step in my plan of action,' Dean says as he leans closer.

As he places his lips on my neck, he fumbles for the zip on the back of the black dress I wore to the funeral today – my only smart black dress.

Dean is a handsome guy. You can tell he loves to go to the gym from his muscular physique, although somehow his muscles seem more like they're for show, rather than for being strong. He has a very neat, strait-laced look – a by-product of working in a serious industry like finance, I'd imagine, so he keeps his dark hair short and slicked back, and his clothes are always smart and stylish, like he could join in on a board meeting at a moment's notice (I don't know if he has actual board meetings, but you know what I mean). He's definitely good-looking... but no one is good-looking enough for this fresh from a wake.

As his kisses get more passionate, I shrug him off as politely as I can.

'Sorry,' I tell him. 'It's just... hard to be in the mood right now.'

I can tell from the look on his face that I'm the only one who feels that way.

'To be honest, my living situation – or lack thereof – is playing on my mind,' I tell him.

'Yeah, yeah, I'm not surprised,' he says, backing off a little, both his body and his enthusiasm retreating.

Come on, Dean, tell me I can stay with you. Even if it is only for a couple of nights while I find something else, please, please. Don't make me ask.

'Why don't I grab us those cocktails?' I suggest, mostly just to fill the awkward silence.

'Yeah, that will help,' Dean replies with a smile.

It's an open-plan flat so the kitchen is only a matter of metres behind the sofa – far enough for me to walk away, but close enough for the silence to still feel like a thing.

I grab a bottle of strawberry Bellini from the fridge and two glasses. Wow, he's gone all out, this one has a cork instead of a screw top. Pathetic as it sounds, I hate popping corks because I never quite seem to have control of the situation. The last thing I need is to smash a window or damage a wall – awful Agatha would think I'd done it on purpose.

As I approach the sofa, I can't help but notice that Dean is looking at a picture of a woman on his phone. I recognise it as Instagram straight away. Dean is one of those men who has Instagram but never posts on it. He's just there to look. He is seriously lingering on this photo, though, so I edge closer to get a proper look.

A petite brunette is sitting in front of a large cake with 'Congratulations Lacey' iced on the top. She has her hair in space bunches as she pouts and flashes the peace sign. She's very pretty, and he seriously is staring.

Dean must be able to sense me lurking behind him because he turns around. He looks at me, almost accusingly. Rather than awkwardly trying to style it out I decide to casually own it.

'Who's that?' I ask him. 'I love her hair.'

I walk around the sofa and hand him the bottle to open before sitting back down.

Dean locks his phone casually.

'Oh, she's just an ex,' he says.

Wow, that was honest. Is that a good thing or a bad thing? If it was bad, he would have lied to me, surely? But can it ever be good, to catch the guy you're seeing drooling over a photo of his ex-girlfriend? I tell myself off. I was behind him, I don't know that he was drooling, but he was certainly lingering.

'She's pretty,' I tell him, trying to sound casual – the crazy jealous type isn't the kind of girl who gets invited to stay for a few nights. 'Anyway, yeah, so my living situation...'

I start back up again, as naturally as I can, giving Dean the chance to save the day. Ordinarily, there would be something about a man saving the day that rubbed me up the wrong way but I'm too desperate to be choosy when it comes to, you know, not being homeless right now.

He quietly and effortlessly pops the cork. Staying at his place while I get back on my feet might be a much bigger ask, but I'm all out of options. He must see that.

'I know, it's really rough,' he says, handing me a drink before shifting away from me slightly. 'And I feel terrible because I can't be more help. I'd invite you to stay with me in a heartbeat, but you know what my room-mate is like when it comes to the house rules about no girls staying the night. But if I break the rule, then he'll break the rule, and then it will be like there's a revolving door on the place – with his girls, obviously. I just feel like my hands are tied, you know?'

He isn't holding eye contact with me, he must feel so guilty, but not guilty enough to break the rules. I haven't even been invited to his place yet, we always hang out here seeing as I don't have any annoying flatmates to contend with, so it's a big ask to be allowed to stay there. You can't rush the stages of a relationship just because you're in need, right?

'Yeah, I get that,' I reply.

I suppose I do, in theory, but this is an emergency. Dean knows I don't really have any close friends (even if I could ask Maël, he's certain he'll be moving away now) and I don't have any family left around Leeds. So, unless I want to go to Norway, to see if the dad I haven't seen for years will let me crash there, I'm pretty much out of options. It's not that I don't have friends generally, but I feel like you have to be pretty close to a person to just turn up on their doorstep with your bags like, hey, I'm homeless, can I sleep on your sofa, please? I can't imagine any of my happily married friends being all that jazzed about taking in an unemployed lodger.

'Look, you've clearly had a rubbish day, you're grieving, you've got problems you need to sort out,' Dean starts as he edges away from me. Then he stands up. 'I'm going to leave you with your thoughts, you don't need me here, annoying you all night.'

'You don't have to leave,' I insist. 'Sorry, I know I can't be much fun to be around right now.'

Am I stupid for apologising? I know that something as huge as a death this early into a relationship is a challenge. I guess I thought he was stepping up to the mark. Now I feel like I'm driving him away. I suppose I just need to back off. I'm clearly making him uncomfortable with my grief, and if he tries to put the moves on me again, I'll probably just cry on him.

'It's fine, I have tons of work to do,' Dean says, leaning forward to kiss me on the forehead. Then he grabs his coat from the chair. 'You need a long bath and a good night's sleep. Call me when you're feeling up to it and we'll do this whole night again, okay?'

'Okay,' I say, stifling a sigh.

Some company would have been great but perhaps he's right, maybe I do need a night alone with my thoughts.

With Dean gone, I sip my drink as I wonder what to do with myself. I'm hoping it's just my morbid thoughts, but I can't help but wonder: did he just not want to be around me? Is he just worrying about me essentially moving myself in too soon? Was that lingering look at his ex – Lacey – a sign that he's still hung up on her, or even just that he's looking around? God, I do sound crazy, no wonder he doesn't want me shacking up with him, I must be coming across as so intense right now.

A wave of relief washes over me when my phone rings. I don't care who it is, it could be someone trying to sell me double glazing or someone trying to get into my bank account, I don't care, whoever it is, I'm chatting to them.

I'm thankful when I look at my phone and see the name of someone I know: my friend Taylor. She's another friend I have thankfully been able to keep a relationship with since we were at school together, but since she got married and bought a house that needed a lot of attention, I haven't seen all that much of her.

'Hello,' I say brightly. 'How are you?'

'I am doing great, thanks,' she replies. 'You?'

'Yeah, I'm good,' I lie.

'I am calling because: when was the last time we saw one another? Was it that Halloween fundraiser thing?'

'I think it was,' I reply. It's hard not to sound disappointed, given that we're in January now.

'I can't thank you enough for coming, by the way,' she adds. 'I was worried no one would show. I told Tim it was a mistake, taking on a gig making bloody bankers look ethical and charitable. I hope you didn't have a totally terrible time.'

'I met a guy there,' I admit. 'So it wasn't all bad.'

'Well, I can't say I know any of them personally yet, but if it's a guy who works with Tim, I can only apologise,' she says with a laugh. 'My Timmy is definitely an odd one out there. He's not as cut-throat as the others – I keep telling him he needs to kiss more butts, to play the game, or people will walk all over him.'

One of the things I love about Taylor and her husband, Tim, is the way they got married. They got engaged, sent out the save-the-dates, and started putting money away for their big day and their honeymoon, travelling to a few places, fitting in as much as they could. They never really explained why (although it makes perfect sense to me) but they then decided that instead of throwing a bunch of money into a big, fancy wedding, they would tie the knot in a more low-key way, and use their savings to buy a house. They bought a fixer-upper, had a very simple wedding, and the plan was always to flip the house for a profit and go on the trip of a lifetime with it. I guess life just got in the way of their trip.

'Hopefully you've found a good one, though,' Taylor adds, filling the brief pause.

My mind darts back to Dean. I hope I haven't put him off.

'Serena, are you... are you okay?' Taylor asks, filling the silence. 'I was calling to see if you wanted to go out with us tomorrow night but that can wait. It's just some crazy, silly last-minute thing one of Tim's friends suggested, and you know what Tim is like, he's so easily led.'

'I'm okay, sorry if I'm being weird,' I say. 'Diana, my boss, passed away suddenly, and if that's not bad enough, her kids are selling the tea room so I'm losing my job and my flat. I would love a night out, but I can't really afford it, and I need to spend the weekend finding somewhere to live.'

I want to say it feels good to tell someone but it's painful to get out. It's almost as though it takes a sharp tool to remove it. Even after it's out, it still stings.

'Serena, I'm so sorry, that's all so awful,' she replies. 'Listen, hear me out, because this is going to sound bad before it sounds good.'

I laugh. I feel a little better just for hearing her voice.

'Okay...'

'The reason I'm calling is to invite you on a "going away" night out,' she explains. 'Tim and I have had enough of DIY, we need a break, so we're going to go travelling for a couple of months. Tim is going to be working remotely, I'm taking a break from teaching, we just thought, screw it, you only live once, right?'

'I'm so happy for you,' I tell her sincerely. 'I'm so pleased you're finally getting your honeymoon.'

'It's only a scaled-down version of what we wanted to do,' she explains. 'Obviously we can't afford that until we finish and sell the house. The master bedroom and en suite are done, the lounge and kitchen diner are finished and, well, we've got a lot of plans – Tim and I were only talking last night about hiring someone to check in on the house while we were away. So I'm thinking we need someone to watch the house, you need somewhere to live – why don't you move in, while you find somewhere?'

My breath catches in my throat.

'Oh, my god, Taylor, are you serious?' I blurt. 'Are you sure? That would be just...'

'You're the one doing me the favour,' she says. 'And I'm not just saying that. You can water the plants, and if we had any spare money, we were hoping that, if we left a key with a neighbour, they might let workmen in to do the messy jobs while we were away. But we don't even know our neighbours, so this is way better.'

'I would happily do that,' I tell her. 'Of course, just leave me a list of jobs, anything. This is a real lifeline.'

'Hey, it's nothing,' she insists. 'Tim will be delighted we don't have to ask a neighbour, or his mother. He's worried she'll go in and douse the walls in magnolia – she hates the grey.'

I laugh.

'Thank you,' I say again.

'How about you come over in the morning?' she suggests. 'I can show you around, tell you everything you need to know.'

'Sounds great, thank you,' I reply. 'Thank you, thank you, thank you. You don't know what this means to me, at the end of a seriously crappy day.'

'Hey, what are friends for?' she says. 'See you tomorrow.'

I've no sooner hung up the phone when everything I've been bottling up all day surges to the forefront and I cry and cry and cry. Grief, worry – even relief. It's all coming out.

Living at Taylor and Tim's will give me a moment to take stock of my new circumstances, and to find a way to move forward. Things might be bad – really bad – but there's always good in the world if you want to see it. That's what I need to focus on tonight and tomorrow, tomorrow I get to go see my new home for the foreseeable. I don't believe in anything spooky... I don't think... but if Diana is somehow watching all this play out from beyond the grave, then I know she would be happy that I've got this life-line from my friend. It's just such a shame I can't keep her legacy living on – her name in lights above the door of Diana's meant everything to her – but no one will forget her, least of all me.

4

If you've ever been a student in Leeds, then the chances are you have lived in Headingly at some point.

Just a couple of miles north of the city centre, the suburb is a strange mixture of students and families. One minute, you're walking past a massive old house in absolutely pristine condition with a fleet of expensive cars parked on the driveway, the next, you're passing the house down the street which has been converted into lucrative student flats, with a drunk girl dressed as a Minion screaming in the garden because she lost her keys on an Otley Run.

God, I used to love an Otley Run. I don't think I'd have the stamina for it now. If you're a student in Leeds, then the legendary fifteen-stop pub crawl is practically a rite of passage – always in fancy dress, of course. Luckily it's a downhill route to the city centre. It's unlucky for me this morning, though, huffing and puffing my way up the road, looking for Taylor and Tim's house.

Eventually, I happen upon the red-brick semi tucked away at the end of St Andrew's Crescent, a cute little cul-de-sac with a mixture of family and student houses. It isn't hard to tell which is which.

Taylor and Tim have done a great job prettying the place up, having the brickwork cleaned, a new lawn laid, and they've got plenty of evergreen foliage, so the garden looks great all year round. The house next door is most definitely a student place, with its scruffy yard, tired old windows and general griminess. It really brings out the *everything* in Taylor and Tim's place.

Taylor greets me at the door. She's wearing a floaty summer dress, even though it's winter – she's clearly more than ready for her holiday, although I don't know how prepared she is, she looks a bit stressed out. The first thing I do is grab her and give her a big squeeze.

'You are my hero,' I tell her. 'Anything I can do for you while you're away, please, just let me know.'

'It's great to be able to help you,' she says, but... is it?

Perhaps I'm just being my usual overthinking self but, I don't know, I'm picking up on something in her voice. Has she changed her mind? Was all that stuff about them looking for someone to water their plants just something she was telling me to make me accept her offer? I hope I haven't caused any problems between her and Tim. Imagine them starting their holiday on a bad note because of me.

As we step into the hallway, I'm blown away by how much progress they've made. The walls are white and the floor is covered in what I could describe as fancy patterned Victorian tiles – although I don't know anything about flooring, or Victorian-era décor, so I could be way off the mark. If I'm right, I have no idea where I've pulled that from.

'Ooh, you look nice,' Taylor says as she takes my oversized pink puffa coat.

'Aw, thanks,' I reply.

Her shift in tone is another red flag. Is she buttering me up? I'm not wearing anything special. Jeans tucked into a tired pair of Ugg boots and a black Bardot jumper. I probably feel more dressed up than I am because, in the tea room, make-up was to be kept to a minimum and nail polish was an absolute no – I get it, it was to match the desired aesthetic of the place, but now that I'm not working there any more, I've layered on the black nail polish and liquid eyeliner. I'm like a rebellious teenage girl today, that's what it's come to.

Either way, I'm sure she's buttering me up, but why?

The banister is painted black, which looks super-stylish, and they've got one of those trendy gallery walls made up of lots of black-and-white photos from holidays, their wedding, family parties and so on.

'Let me give you the tour,' Taylor suggests. 'This first room is the living room, back there is the kitchen/diner. Let's, erm, head upstairs first, though.'

She seems to change course quite quickly. Something is up. I am definitely picking up on a vibe, I just can't work out why. Whatever the reason, this can't be good.

'Okay, sure,' I say, all smiles. 'Well, the hallway looks fantastic.'

'Yeah, I'm really pleased with how it came out,' she replies. 'Tim said he hated the tiles, but I think he's come around to them now. I won them in a compromise because I hated the ones in the en suite.'

Taylor pauses at the top of the stairs and leans in close.

'Just between us, I don't hate the tiles in the en suite, Tim picked out the exact ones I wanted, but I realised that if I pretended to hate them then I could use them as a bargaining tool.'

'Wow,' I blurt with a smile. 'That's a move even I would be proud of.'

'I've learned from the best – you should write that one down,' she jokes. 'So, on this floor we have one bedroom we've not done any work on yet, although we've been using it as an emergency guest room. Then we have another bedroom absolutely full to the brim with junk from the move that I can't even begin to process, the old house bathroom that still needs modernising, and the box room which we've killed off to turn into a staircase up to the loft conversion. Follow me.'

Sure enough, the box room has little more inside it than a staircase that leads up another flight of stairs.

'Oh, my gosh, Taylor, what?' I squeak as I admire her bedroom. 'This is just... wow.'

The large loft room is super minimalist, with those stylish wardrobes that fill an entire wall, crafted in the exact shape of the room – all of her stuff must be hidden in those because it's so tidy in here. My own bedroom (ha!) is a real tip, with discarded clothes all over – usually because I tried them on, decided I didn't want to wear them, but didn't put them back away after – but this is like a boutique hotel. A large super-king bed sits at the heart, with contemporary panelling behind it. I'm loving the colours – they've got a chic Scandi vibe going on, with muted tones and walls that are painted just about green. Everything is so subtle and soft.

'I think I need new people to look at it every now and then to remind myself that it looks great,' she reasons. 'When you look at it every day, you forget how much work you put into it, and how well it turned out. I did the modern panelling behind the bed myself, and Tim did the fitted wardrobes on the other wall. We're getting quite good at this stuff now. All the more reason to have a break, though. Oh, and through here is the en suite.'

I follow Taylor into the bathroom.

'Oh, yeah, these tiles are hideous,' I joke. 'Just awful, and the rainfall shower and free-standing bath are just...'

I pretend to stick my fingers down my throat.

'Good girl,' she says. 'The underfloor heating is a *nightmare* too. I might get a boiling water tap out of it, if I keep laying it on thick. For the kitchen, obviously, not the bathroom.'

A pile of dirty clothes unsuccessfully stuffed behind the washing basket catches her eye.

'Honestly, my bloody husband,' she says with a sigh. 'Surely it's as fast to put the dirty washing in the basket as it is to hide it behind it?'

I laugh, leaving Taylor to clean up after Tim as I head back into the bedroom. I can't believe this is going to be my room. Sleek, modern, spacious and with bags of storage and a super-king bed with... a man on it? He definitely wasn't there when we walked through a moment ago.

I cock my head as I stare at him. He does similar – I'm not sure who goes first but the other person is like a perfect mirror image. Well, almost. One of us standing here like a lemon while the other lounges on the bed. Either way, he's as surprised to see me there as I am him.

Even lying down, I can tell he's tall because his black skinny-jean-clad legs reach almost to the end of the bed, and the size of his feet in his eye-catching red and black stripy socks give up his size too. So to speak. An aged black T-shirt for a band I am either not old enough or cool enough to recognise clings to his slender frame. He's got great cheekbones – laid back on the bed like this, he's got a real statue vibe about him, like he's been freshly chiselled, just for me – imagine if he came with the bed! His dark hair is long on top and perfectly blown back, with the sides short and neat.

He runs a hand through his hair as he narrows his big brown eyes at me curiously. As he smiles, the deepest dimples become visible on his face. Instantly I feel some kind of connection with him, even though I'm pretty sure I've never met the man before in my life.

'Hi,' he says, still smiling.

'Hi,' I reply, struggling not to smile myself.

Taylor runs out of the en suite just as Tim arrives at the top of the stairs, clearly flustered. They both have that same look in their eye – a look that confirms something is definitely going on here.

'You said you'd stay downstairs,' Taylor ticks him off. 'And that you'd stop jamming your dirty boxers behind the washing basket, but I can park that one until later.'

'Sorry, sorry,' Tim says breathlessly. 'He's a slippery one – I only turned my back on him for a minute. Did you tell her? Hi, by the way.'

That last part was directed at me.

'Oh, hi,' I reply, confused.

'Not yet,' Taylor tells him. 'Have *you* told *him*?'

'Told me what?' the man asks, sitting up, smiling curiously, confirming that the answer is no.

Taylor fills her cheeks with air, holds it for a few seconds, and then lets it all out.

'We had a conversation about trying to find a last-minute house sitter, and we both thought it was a good idea,' Taylor explains. 'But while I was asking you if you wanted to stay, Tim was doing something similar with one of his friends, and, well, now you're both here.'

My eyes widen. Shit, I should've known this was too good to be true.

'Are you comfy there?' Taylor asks the man, narrowing her eyes at him.

'Very,' he replies with an impressive confidence considering he's in Taylor's bed right now. 'It's a great mattress.'

He flashes her a smile before taking the hint and standing up.

'Serena, this is Ziggy, Tim's football friend,' she says, reluctantly making the introductions. 'Ziggy, this is my friend Serena – one of my oldest friends, from school.'

'Why, were you held back a year?' Ziggy teases me.

'Ziggy is his actual name,' Tim informs me proudly. 'His mum met his dad while he was roadying for Bowie.'

It's almost as though Tim is trying to market Ziggy, to make him seem like the cooler friend, I just can't understand why. Taylor rolls her eyes.

'And Serena is Serena's actual name,' she adds mockingly. 'Just so we're all up to date on the important details.'

Tim frowns.

'So...' I start, but I don't know where I'm going. I just shift my weight between my feet awkwardly.

'Technically speaking, as best we can tell, I asked Ziggy first,' Tim explains. 'The words actually left my lips first.'

'Yes, but I didn't know that, and Serena has nowhere else to live at the moment,' Taylor reminds him through gritted teeth.

'Neither do I,' Ziggy chimes in. 'My housemates were driving me mad, none of us are getting on, things are really difficult. So, when Tim asked if I wanted to move in, I jumped at the chance.'

'So you do have somewhere to go back to?' Taylor asks, although I suspect she's saying it to make a point.

'Oh, no, definitely not,' he replies. 'I scorched the earth on my way out.'

'Fantastic,' Taylor says with a sigh. 'Well, there's only one option: why don't you both live here?'

'Really?' I say.

'Yeah, why not?' she replies. 'We've got loads of space, you both need somewhere to live, there will be two of you here so less responsibility on either of you. We only have the one nice bedroom and the one nice bathroom, though. Someone is going to have to make do with the old ones downstairs.'

'I've technically already claimed this bed,' Ziggy says playfully.

'You could come up with some sort of way to decide who gets which room,' Tim suggests diplomatically. 'That would be fairer.'

'Are you sure this all okay with you?' I ask Ziggy.

Please say no, please say no.

'Sure,' he replies. 'You can't be as bad as my last housemates.'

'I didn't have any,' I tell him.

'Great, you'll have nothing to measure me against,' he jokes – god, I hope he's joking.

'Well, we're off early tomorrow,' Taylor says. 'Drinks tonight are a low-key thing. Are you sure you can't come?'

'I wish I could, I need to head home and pack,' I reply.

It's true, but I also worry about the financial implications of going out with other people. When money isn't great, there is nothing worse than someone suggesting everyone buys a round.

'I can tell you all about it tomorrow,' Ziggy says before adding: 'Roomie.'

'Okay then,' I say. 'I'd better go.'

Taylor follows me downstairs.

'Are you sure you're okay with this?' she asks as she helps me on with my coat.

'I mean, beggars can't be choosers,' I reply with a friendly smile.

'He's okay, you know,' Taylor reassures me. 'He's a lot of fun –

he's got the same crazy energy as you on a night out. And he's pretty hot, which helps.'

She says this last bit in hushed tones.

'Thanks,' I laugh. 'Honestly, it will be fine. I can't thank you enough.'

Taylor gives me a big hug.

'In case I don't see you before we set off in the morning,' she says.

'Have an incredible time,' I demand. 'Take lots of pictures for me.'

'I'll bring you back some souvenirs,' she replies. 'It's the least I can do to say thanks for looking after my money pit.'

As I walk in the direction of the city centre, wondering whether or not to catch a bus or save some money by walking, two girls dressed as cheerleaders practically shiver past me as they head for the pub.

It's going to be different, moving back out here. I'm hoping it's going to be good for me, a nice change of pace, a change of scenery, new cafés and old favourites to revisit. But it's like I told Taylor, beggars can't be choosers. With nowhere else to live, I'm just going to have to make the best of it.

5

The beauty of having basically no material possessions is that when you need to move house, you can fit almost everything you own in the back of an Uber.

This is the last box for today. I'll pick up the last couple of bits tomorrow.

The tea room is still open, for now. It's just me who has been shown the door prematurely, so I stick my head in to say goodbye to Maël.

'I'm going to miss you,' he says as he hugs me tightly. 'If it doesn't work out at your new place, promise me that you'll come and stay with us in Edinburgh for a while.'

'Oh, yeah, Martyn and his family would love that,' I joke. 'A friendly neighbourhood spinster.'

Maël and Martyn are going to go and stay with his family for a while, to look at houses up there, and to see if Maël can find a job. They're going for a month, to begin with, but I can't imagine him not loving it there. I'm jealous. I would love a change of scenery right now.

'Don't give up on Dean yet,' he tells me. 'It's early days. He probably didn't want to freak you out by asking.'

'Maybe,' I say with a sigh. 'Anyway, I'd better get going.'

'Come on then, give me a hug, in case I never see you again,' Maël insists.

I laugh.

'We'll see each other again,' I tell him. 'I'll be back here tomorrow to collect the last of my things, so there's that, but I'll definitely visit you in Edinburgh.'

Maël tightens in my embrace. That's not the usual reaction when you tell someone you'll visit them.

I follow his gaze to the serving hatch that looks through into the dining room. It's awful Agatha, weaving between tables of oblivious customers, closely followed by two men in suits.

'She's despicable,' Maël tells me – not that I didn't already know that. 'They're selling everything, and I mean everything, they're going to gut this place. Honestly, it's going to be like Diana never existed.'

I do my best to swallow away the lump in my throat, say my goodbyes and then head out to find my taxi before Agatha spots me. I can't face her today.

At the side of the road, where I last saw my taxi, sits a pile of my things instead. The driver must have grown impatient, emptied my belongings out of his car, and driven off. I can't have been more than a few minutes, and the driver knew I was getting more things. Fantastic.

I um and ah about what to do before I decide – screw it – I'm going to call Dean. He works in the city centre and it is almost lunchtime. I'm sure he'll help me out.

Sure enough, after swapping a few messages back and forth, Dean eventually pulls up outside the tea room in his black Tesla

Model S. More than the lift, it feels good to see a friendly face right now.

He greets me with a kiss before loading what little I have into his car.

'Thanks for doing this,' I tell him. 'Sorry to drag you out of work.'

'I'd just finished a meeting anyway, it's no trouble,' he replies. 'Headingly, yeah?'

'Yes, St Andrew's Crescent, please,' I say. 'If you head up Otley Road, I can tell you where to turn.'

'Should I be jealous that you're moving in with some guy?' Dean asks – he sounds like he's joking, but I'm detecting a hint of insecurity in his voice.

I wasn't even sure Dean was listening to me when I explained about Taylor letting me stay in her house while she was away. It was only when I mentioned Ziggy living there too that his ears pricked up.

'Hardly,' I say with a snort. 'Ziggy is your exact opposite, so not exactly stiff competition.'

'Good,' Dean replies. 'I won't worry then about the two of you playing house together. No man wants to hear about the girl he's seeing shacking up with a guy called Ziggy.'

The girl he's seeing. I'll save overthinking his choice of words for another time. Instead, I smile and focus on Dean's preoccupation with Ziggy's name. Is a Ziggy more like to steal your girl than a Dean?

'Why don't you come in and meet him?' I suggest.

'I don't have time, I've got to get back for a work lunch,' he replies. 'But we're still on for dinner tonight, right? Let me take you somewhere nice, for a sort of moving-in present. Somewhere nice, like Tattu or Fazenda.'

Tattu – an ultra-fancy contemporary Chinese restaurant – and

Fazenda – a uniquely cool Brazilian steakhouse – are pretty much the only two restaurants Dean will eat at. I've never quite got to the bottom of why, and they're both amazing places, so it's never really been a problem, but it's certainly taken the element of surprise out of our dinner plans.

'That would be great,' I tell him. 'Thank you.'

It's strange to be leaving the city centre again. I can't help but feel like I'm going backwards. Growing up in Horsforth, even being a short train journey from the city felt like the first hurdle I wanted to jump. I wanted to be cool and cosmopolitan and live it up in the city centre. Fair enough, I was living in a one-bed flat above a tea room, but I was in a stunning 1900s brick building with high ceilings and a huge living room window looking out over Vicar Lane. Sitting between the Victoria Quarter and Victoria Gate shopping centre, I felt like I was in the heart of something beautiful. Moving back to Headingly feels like I'm not only leaving the city, but also returning to my student state – in fact, if you take the train from Leeds city centre to Headingly, the next stop is Horsforth, so it feels like I'm well on my way back to square one. It's only a matter of time.

'It's this one here,' I instruct Dean as he crawls up St Andrew's Crescent.

'Wow,' he blurts as he claps eyes on the red-brick semi-detached house that is going to be my home for the foreseeable future.

'Good wow or bad wow?' I ask.

'Don't get me wrong, your friends' place looks all right, I can tell they're working on it, but next door is a bit of a shithole,' he says.

'It's a student rental,' I explain.

'There's a bath in the garden,' he claps back.

'It's boujee to have a bath in your garden these days,' I reply.

'Yeah, plumbed in,' Dean replies, rolling his eyes, clearly not getting my joke.

'You sure you can't pop in and see the place?' I say as we unload my bags and boxes onto the driveway.

'I'll be late if I do,' he replies. 'But I know where to pick you up later.'

Dean snakes his arms around my body before leaning me back against his car to kiss me passionately. When he finally lets me back up for air, he glances back at the house, almost as if he's checking to see if anyone was watching. Was that for Ziggy's benefit? Was Dean marking his territory?

'See you tonight, beautiful,' he says as he makes a move for the driver's side.

'See you tonight,' I reply.

A combination of me running late and the taxi running off meant I didn't make it here on time to say goodbye to Taylor and Tim, so I had to wish them a safe journey (and thank them another thousand times) in a message. Ziggy is already here, though, and Taylor and Tim have shown him the ropes and given him the keys, so they said to just knock on the door and he would bring me up to speed.

My hand hovers in front of the shiny teal front door. I'm nervous – why am I nervous? I'm being silly, I just need to knock.

Ziggy opens the door before I get the chance.

'Hello,' he says through a wide, welcoming grin.

'Er, hi,' I reply. 'I didn't even knock.'

'The cameras,' he points out. 'There's one at the front and one at the back. They ding a tablet in the kitchen when they detect motion.'

'Wow,' I blurt. 'I don't know if I feel safe or spied on.'

'There's none inside, I double-checked,' Ziggy says through a laugh. 'Come in, let me help you with your things.'

'Thank you so much,' I reply.

I hover in the doorway for a second.

'Go through to the living room,' he instructs.

I do as I'm told. Wait, this isn't his house, it's both of our homes for the time being. I don't need to be so awkward.

'I didn't get to see this during the world's strangest house tour,' I say as he joins me.

'It's nice, isn't it?' he replies. 'I love the walls.'

The walls are painted a very light shade of sea-foam green. A TV sits on the wall above an old fireplace with a wood-burning stove underneath.

'They said not to use the fire,' he tells me. 'There's something wrong with it apparently. The TV works just fine, though – and it's the only one in the house.'

Ziggy raises his eyebrows, as though this is something he finds odd. I get where he's coming from, because I'd have a TV in my bedroom if I could justify having two TVs for my single self, but I doubt it's uncommon for families to only have one in the living room.

As I smile at him, he places a hand on the back of his neck and looks down at his feet for a second. I maintain that Dean has nothing to worry about; however, there is – and I say this in an objective, observing kind of way – something very attractive about Ziggy. He's just got this... thing about him. He's so effortlessly cool, and I kind of get the feeling he knows most girls will fancy him, but it isn't coming across as obnoxious. Yet.

He's wearing another black-skinny-jeans-and-band-T-shirt combo but this time the T-shirt has a purposeful slash across the abdomen, which forms a sort of letter box for his abs. You can't quite see inside, but it teases you with a peep.

'Are you a fan?' Ziggy asks me.

Oh my god, he just caught me trying to look inside his shirt. And now he's asking me what I think.

'I, erm, yeah... yeah, not bad,' I mumble awkwardly.

'I don't know many Alex Cameron fans,' he replies with a smile.

I can't help but widen my eyes as the bullet I just dodged flies past them. He thought I was looking at the band T-shirt he's wearing, not his abs – imagine if I'd said more than I did. Obviously now I'm going to have to keep that lie going. Shit. Is Alex male or female?

'Love 'em,' I say, letting my accent do the heavy lifting, hopefully hiding the fact that I'm oblivious.

Ziggy smiles.

'Let me show you the kitchen,' he says.

I follow Ziggy through to an impressively modern kitchen diner, with perfectly clean white cupboards topped with sparkling black worktops. Everything looks unused, it's that new and clean, I'll be terrified to use it. It's lovely, though.

Ziggy takes me through all the need-to-know information, showing me where everything is, opening all the cupboards.

'...and they said we could help ourselves to any of the food. There's lots of dry stuff, tins, and enough long-life almond milk to flood the place,' Ziggy jokes.

'I can't believe they're letting us stay here,' I say with a contented sigh. 'It's stunning. Everything is perfect.'

'Well, there is something not quite right in this room,' Ziggy starts. 'The elephant, over there.'

He points behind me and I stupidly follow his finger before realising he doesn't mean it literally.

'Oh?' I say to try to prompt more information out of him.

'So, the bedroom on the top floor, the one we met in,' he starts. 'That bedroom and bathroom are perfect. However, the guest room and guest bathroom haven't really been touched yet... meaning they're not quite so nice.'

Taylor didn't show me the guest room, during the tour – here's hoping it's not too bad. Nothing could be as nice as the master bedroom, but there are varying levels of worse.

'Oh,' I say again, with a different tone this time. 'So, what do we do?'

'We could let fate decide, I suppose?' he suggests. 'That seems fair.'

'What, like tossing a coin?' I reply.

'Yeah,' he says. 'That's as good as any method. Shall I do it?'

'No, no way,' I insist. 'That's not fair at all.'

'A coin toss isn't fair?' he checks through a frown.

'Not at all,' I reply. 'They're easily rigged.'

'How do you rig a coin toss?' he asks in bemusement.

'I dated a magician who showed me how,' I tell him. 'He showed me how easy it was. You just place the coin down on top of your thumb, with the side you don't want facing upwards, always flip it with the same force, and when you catch it and slap it onto the back of your hand, it will always show the same result.'

'I've never dated a magician,' he tells me. 'So, why don't I do the flipping?'

'Because I just taught you how to rig it too,' I point out.

Ziggy laughs and rolls his eyes.

'Rock, paper, scissors?' I suggest.

'Very mature,' he teases. 'But okay. Ready?'

I nod.

Ziggy counts us in. One... two... but then something happens. I go on three, making the shape of scissors with my hand. Ziggy, however, was clearly planning of going on the beat after three, meaning he still had his hand in a fist shape when I showed my hand. With a fist being so close to the shape of a rock, he's clearly trying to style it out as intentional.

'Rock destroys scissors,' he announces as he lightly bops my hand with his.

'Nah, I'm not having that,' I reply angrily. 'You clearly hadn't done your move yet, you thought we were going after three, not on three.'

'Everyone goes after three,' he informs me.

'Well, let's go again then,' I suggest. 'And this time I'll go after three.'

'Not happening,' he informs me. 'Now I know you're going to pick scissors again, *or* you're going to pick something else.'

'Yes, that's generally how this works,' I reply.

'Which means I don't just choose rock, paper or scissors,' he explains. 'It means I have to overthink what you're going to choose or not...'

'Wow, you're giving me a headache,' I say. 'Can we just do something else?'

'There's a pack of cards in the cupboard with all the board games,' Ziggy suggests. 'High card wins?'

'Sure,' I reply.

God, I just want to get this over with. It's turning into a whole thing.

'I've never dated a magician, but I can shuffle a deck,' Ziggy informs me, as though I'm giving him a look, although I didn't realise I was.

Ziggy takes a card before handing the deck to me so that I can draw one at random too.

'Okay,' he says, instructing us both to look.

My heart skips a beat of joy and I can't resist a smug grin, but then I look up and see that same look on Ziggy's face and I'm confused.

'Why are you smiling?' I ask him.

'Because I'm pretty sure I've won,' he says. 'Why are you smiling?'

'Well, unless we've got the same card, then I know I've won,' I reply. 'Turn them around on three?'

'On three or after three?' he asks through a smarmy grin.

'*On.*'

I'm delighted when Ziggy shows his card to be the king of clubs. But wait, why is he looking at my ace of hearts in the same way?

'So, I win,' I say, making sure we're both on the same page.

'How do you reckon?' Ziggy replies.

I massage my temples for a second.

'An ace is higher than a king,' I point out.

'Aces are low,' he replies.

'You're genuinely driving me mad,' I blurt. 'Aces are always high.'

'Apart from when they're worth one...'

Oh, my god, I want to strangle him. He might look good, and he might seem cool, but he's a first-class clown.

'Are you messing with me?' he asks seriously.

'Am *I* messing with *you*?' I reply.

He nods.

'Wow, no, I'm not messing with you,' I reply. 'Look, we just need a foolproof way to do this, with no room for interpretation. Or you could be a gentleman and let me have the nice room.'

'Ha, good one,' Ziggy says. 'I have an idea. Unless you want to share the room?'

I roll my eyes.

'What's this idea?'

'We draw straws,' he suggests. 'Except I'm not sure they have any straws, so we'll have to use spaghetti. We take turns drawing pieces until one of us picks the single short one. That person gets the crappy room.'

'It's a crappy room now, is it?' I reply. 'Okay, that seems fair. I can't see any room for interpretation there.'

Ziggy is careful to do everything right in front of my eyes. He snaps one piece of spaghetti shorter before placing it in this hand with a bunch of long strands.

'Ladies first,' he instructs.

'Now he's chivalrous,' I say, mostly to myself.

As I pull a piece of spaghetti from Ziggy's hand, I feel nervous. Why is this so tense?

I sigh a small burst of relief when I pull out a long one.

Ziggy goes next, then me, then Ziggy again. All long pieces.

With only three pieces left in Ziggy's hand, I take a moment to think about which piece to take. For some reason, I have a good feeling about the piece I reach for but, by the time it's in my hand, I realise it's shorter than the other pieces.

'Oh, there we go,' he says proudly.

'Fair is fair,' I say reluctantly. 'The room is yours.'

'I'll have to tell you about all the quirks with your room,' he says. 'Taylor told me them all before she left.'

'Wonderful,' I reply.

Ziggy places the last bits of spaghetti down on the worktop and I notice something. I furrow my brow as I take a closer look.

'Erm, hang on a minute,' I say. 'That's the short piece, there. The piece I pulled must've snapped as I pulled it out, look, there's a small piece there.'

'Serena, come on,' Ziggy says with a sigh. 'You're clutching at spaghettis.'

I'm in no mood to laugh at his jokes right now.

'If you want that room so much, and to see me in the "crappy room" then fine, have it,' I insist, trying to sound like the bigger person.

'Cheers,' he replies. 'I'm going to go unpack my stuff, I'm out tonight. But if you have any questions about anything in the house just shout, yeah?'

'Yeah, great,' I say, my tone betraying my words.

As icebreakers go, this hasn't exactly been a roaring success. I can't believe I'm going to have to live with this guy. Perhaps now he's got what he wants, Ziggy will be easier to live with.

Right now, I don't think he could be worse.

6

I thought that Ziggy was exaggerating when he described what is now my bedroom as the 'crappy room' but, boy, he wasn't wrong.

It's easy to start with the décor because it's the first thing that strikes you when you walk through the door. This room hasn't been decorated in decades. Think the Overlook Hotel from *The Shining* – dark oranges, shades of brown, everything but a pair of creepy twins and a tidal wave of blood, although the latter could be arranged if Ziggy is as irritating as he seems.

Worse than the room being ugly, it's impractical too. For starters, it's January, and for some reason only the bottom one-sixth of the radiator gets even remotely warm, and it's not even like you can curl up nice and warm in the double bed because the mattress must be older than me – it's lumpier too.

And then there's the icing on the cake, the iconic avocado-green bathroom, fresh out of the seventies.

So Ziggy gets all the modern comforts and I'm left with Artex ceilings, woodchip wallpaper and the world's thinnest curtains that I sincerely hope were bought in this shade of brown.

By the time I got home from dinner with Dean last night,

there was no sign of Ziggy. I'd like to say that, if I'd known, I would have invited Dean in but, truthfully, I'm embarrassed to have been landed with the crap room. Dean would hate it.

After an uncomfortable night alone in a bed from a haunted Disney World attraction, the plan was to loosen up by walking into the city. But screw that, my back is seriously aching, I'll get the bus instead.

I know what you're going to say, beggars can't be choosers and all that, but I thought being given an entire house to live in rent-free was going to be a dream come true. Now I'm starting to think it's going to be a nightmare and it's all because of Ziggy, and it's not just because of his metal rocker look – although he never quite seems like he turns the look off. Even now, where I've just found him sitting at the kitchen island, hunched over a guitar while he eats his toast, he's still got his naturally dark eyes, his undercut hair, plugs in his ear piercings, and skulls all over his pyjama bottoms. The black vest he's wearing reveals some of his tattoos, but I can't quite see what they are. It's hard to take in the details of his sleeves, without getting close, but I don't want him to think I'm remotely interested in him.

He must be around my age, and his accent is definitely local, but Leeds and all its suburbs cover quite a lot of ground. Despite what an eighty-something Londoner once implied when I served him in the tea room, most of us don't know each other, and we do have more than a handful of surnames between us.

On paper, he seems like he should be a fun guy – and he must be nice, and not a creep, because there's no way Taylor would have suggested I live with him unless she could vouch for him. She would never roll the dice on her friend's safety or sanity like that.

And yet he seems so annoying, so selfish, so... so annoyingly dreamy-eyed – why is he staring at me right now?

'Morning,' he says, his hands still on his acoustic guitar, but his eyes firmly fixed on me. 'Sleep well?'

In that horrible, cold, ugly bedroom? I certainly did not.

'Really well,' I lie. 'That mattress is just...'

For some bizarre reason, I do a chef's kiss. I'm such a dork sometimes, it's as though I'm not happy unless I'm making things weird.

'Tim said that one was like sleeping on a bag of spanners,' Ziggy replies through a mouthful of toast. 'He said whoever wound up in that room was getting the short straw. Or the short spaghetti, I guess.'

He laughs.

I ignore him, popping the kettle on before placing a teabag in a cup, and heading to the fridge to grab the milk. I reach to pull it out but it's so much heavier than I was expecting it to be. Upon closer inspection, I realise it's frozen solid.

'Have you had any milk today?' I ask him.

'I had some oat milk in my coffee, why do you ask?' he replies.

'There's something wrong with the regular milk,' I explain. 'It's frozen.'

'That's unusual,' Ziggy says. 'Do help yourself to my oat milk.'

'I've tried it before,' I say, pulling a face. 'I don't like it in tea, or on cereal, which is what I was going to have for breakfast, so...'

'Give the milk a bit of time, it'll thaw,' he says with a casual shrug. 'And help yourself to my bread, if you want to have toast instead.'

'Thanks,' I reply. 'But I've got somewhere to be. I'm going to miss the bus if I don't get a move on.'

'Are you going into town?' he asks.

'Yeah, Vicar Lane,' I tell him.

Ziggy puts down his guitar and dusts off his hands.

'Sit down, have some toast, and then I'll give you a lift,' he says.

'Oh, that's okay,' I reply.

'Come on, I'm not doing anything,' he replies. 'I'm between jobs at the moment. It will give me something to do with myself, and it will give us a chance to get to know each other a little better.'

'I didn't realise you had a car,' I reply. He definitely didn't have one yesterday.

'I don't,' he replies. 'But the bandwagon is on the drive, I told Otto he could park it here so he dropped it off this morning. I thought it would be safer than the street parking near where he lives. People break into it, just to see what's inside.'

'Bandwagon?' I repeat back to him.

'Yeah, for driving to gigs, transporting the gear,' he explains. 'We all put together and bought it last year, had it all fitted out with everything we needed, loads of storage, seats for us all plus guests.'

I don't know what my face looks like right now, but Ziggy reacts to it.

'Come on, it can't be as bad as the regular bus,' he points out.

In the interests of house relations, I should probably accept his lift. This might be what we need to get on friendly terms, after all the hostility surrounding the games to decide who got which bedroom yesterday.

'Okay, thanks,' I reply.

'Grab some toast and try to thaw out your milk,' he insists. 'I'll go grab a hoodie and some trainers.'

Not clothes then? Skull pyjama bottoms it is – let's hope we don't get pulled over.

I hold the bottle of milk over the warm kettle to try to speed up the process. Come on, I only need a little for my cup of tea. I make myself some toast and then wait for Ziggy to return.

'Right, let's go,' Ziggy says, jangling his keys at me.

I suppose if he's going to make an effort then so will I.

'Let's do it,' I say.

I follow him out to the 'bandwagon', only to find the world's oldest converted minibus. Actually, it's a bit bigger than a minibus. It's like one of the small buses you see driving seriously limited routes every eight hours in remote villages.

'What do you think?' Ziggy asks proudly. 'Cool, eh?'

'It's... wow,' I say. 'It's like a makeshift tour bus.'

'It's not makeshift at all,' he insists. 'Hop aboard and I'll show you.'

It really is just like an old cream-coloured bus (I mean, it was probably white, back in its day) with some kind of faded cluster of shapes on the side (most likely from the bus company's logo being removed). The very back windows are completely blacked out but the ones at the front of the bus have blackout curtains covering them.

I step aboard. You know how 'van life' is big right now? People are buying all sorts of old vehicles and turning them into those spectacular tiny houses with a finish that would put most Leeds semis to shame.

This isn't like that.

There's the driver's seat, and then one of those lone passenger seats you often find next to the door because what else can you fit there? Next, it's still so far, so bussy, right down to the worn yellow handrails dotted around everywhere. There are four seats on each side of the aisle, made up of two facing each other, but then the rest of the seats have been ripped out. In their place is a structure, made from what looks like old pallets, creating six sleeping bunks – three lots of two stacked on top of one another. When you stand in the aisle, you're basically facing the bottom of them, which makes them seem a bit like the drawers they have in morgues.

'Cool, right?' Ziggy says. 'It was a bargain.'

'Yeah,' I reply, my voice betraying me. 'So, you sleep in those?'

'Yeah, it sleeps at least six,' he explains. 'And there's a big space behind it so we can load all our gear into the back.'

'Is it strong enough?' I wonder out loud.

'Oh, yeah, it's definitely strong enough,' he insists confidently. 'We've really put it to the test.'

Ew. I hope that doesn't mean what I think it means.

'So, do you have a toilet and a shower?' I ask.

'No, nothing like that,' he says. 'Is it not up to your standards?'

There's a detectable tone in his voice – I think he's annoyed I'm not more impressed.

'Hey, no bathroom is only one step below my current bathroom,' I point out.

'Still salty about that, eh?' he replies. 'I can't blame you. Come on then, let's go.'

Ziggy heads for the driver's seat so I take a seat in the one by the door – perfect for a speedy exit.

'Good shout,' Ziggy tells me. 'Locate the emergency exits. You should be fine, though. Things like fires and wheels falling off only seem to happen when you're on the M1.'

'So long as the wheels only fall off on the motorways,' I say with a sarcastic relief.

Ziggy looks around at the various controls. It takes him a few seconds before he starts the engine, and begins making moves to pull out. He stalls it pretty much instantly.

'You can drive, right?' I ask, because I feel like it needs asking.

'Of course I can drive,' he insists. 'I passed my test in 2011.'

He starts the engine again, successfully this time.

'When was the last time you drove?' I ask him.

'I passed my test in 2011,' he says again.

Oh, god.

'I can just get the bus, you know, this really isn't necessary,' I tell him.

'Don't you trust me, Serena?' he asks, feigning offence. 'I'll be fine, once I get going, gears just take me a minute.'

The bus judders. Bloody hell, is he driving badly on purpose? Surely no one with a licence can be this bad?

'I take it you don't usually drive it,' I say.

'No, Otto does,' he replies. 'Don't worry, though, I'm insured.'

'I'll rest easier now,' I reply sarcastically. 'Thank you.'

Once we're on Otley Road, it feels like we're plain sailing.

'So, where were you living before?' Ziggy asks me.

'In Leeds centre,' I reply.

'Why would you want to leave the centre?'

'I lost my job,' I tell him. 'And the flat came with the job.'

'You'll be looking for a new job then,' he confirms. 'Are you going to find one with accommodation?'

I can't help but feel like he's trying to get rid of me. Perhaps I should turn the tables on him.

'What about you, what are your plans?' I ask. 'Your long-term plans?'

'I haven't even planned to put real trousers on yet,' he laughs. 'So I'm not going to be able to give you my four-point plan for the rest of my life.'

I resent the way he's teasing me. I hardly have a life plan, do I? If I did, I'd be royally shagging it.

'I don't have a life plan, but I wasn't intending to crash at Taylor and Tim's for the rest of my life,' I reply. 'This is temporary, while I find a job, and a place of my own.'

'And how long you do think that will take?' he asks curiously.

Wow. He really does want me to leave so that he can have the place to himself. Obviously the plan was never to stay here long-term, only while I get back on my feet, but the day I leave can't come soon enough. I'm not sure how long I can stand living with this guy.

Why didn't I just take the bus?

7

I still had Ziggy drop me at the bus station because, for some reason, I don't want him knowing anything about my life. Thankfully it isn't a long walk from there to Diana's. I've got maybe two bags for life left at the flat and then that's it, that's me done there. I'll never step foot through the doors of Diana's again – not just because I'm banished, but because Agatha and Andrew are bringing about the end of an era by closing the place down. I still can't believe they are letting their mum's legacy go, just like that, for what? More money.

I grab my bags and leave my keys inside the flat. It's been nice, living here. I can't resist resting my head on the door frame for a second – like a crazy person – while I say goodbye in my head. I suppose it's not only the flat I'm saying goodbye to, or my job, it's Diana herself. I'll never be able to repay her for what she did for me. Sometimes, something as simple as a leg-up is all you need to turn things around, the hardest part is finding someone willing to give you one.

At the bottom of the stairs, you can go left, towards the staff exit, or right, through the staff corridor towards the kitchen. I make a move to turn right, to say one last goodbye to my friends, until I see Agatha marching towards me. I quickly turn left but, of course, she's seen me.

'Oi,' she calls out.

'Serena,' I offer, because it seems like she might have forgotten my name.

'Keys?'

'They're in the flat,' I say. 'On the table, through the door.'

'Right then, thanks,' she replies. 'Hang on, wait a second.'

I stop in my tracks again.

'What's that?' she asks me, nodding towards one of my bags. 'Is that Mum's? Are you stealing it?'

I look down at my bag to see the teal neck of a long, skinny ceramic vase sticking out of my bag.

'That *is* Mum's,' she confirms to herself. 'It's from that godawful pottery painting afternoon tea thing she had here years ago – we told her she couldn't keep it in the house because it wasn't exactly a Gordon Baldwin, you know what I mean?'

I have absolutely no idea what she means. What I do know is that Diana was so proud of the vase she painted, and she told me all about how her kids made fun of it, so she kept it in the flat. She was so happy with it, even though she said she'd done a pretty dodgy job. I think that's why I used to admire it, it was unique, just like Diana was.

I remember the night she gave it to me like it was yesterday. We had a long chat about anything and everything, drinking tea, eating cakes she'd brought up from the tea room. She told me she wanted me to have it, that she wanted it to go to a good home. She said her kids couldn't care less about it, and that they would probably throw it in the bin if anything ever happened to her – I guess she was wrong about the first part.

'Your mum gave it to me,' I tell her honestly. 'It was one of my favourite things in the flat, she really wanted me to have it.'

'Right, well, that's the first I'm hearing about it,' Agatha informs me. 'And her will reading was this morning, and you weren't in it – unsurprisingly – so, as the property of the business, I'm afraid this needs to stay here, and be sold along with the rest of the property, plant and equipment. Oakwell Auctioneers are handling it – you're welcome to buy it when the time comes, if your pockets are deep enough, but, for now...'

Agatha places the vase on the nearest windowsill.

'...it stays here. Is there anything else, before you go, do I need to check any of your other bags?'

'No,' I reply, gritting my teeth. 'Thanks.'

I know it sounds stupid, but that vase was my last little bit of Diana – my something to remember her by – so I'm going to have to find a way to get it back, one way or another.

I head for the staff exit and leave for the last time. I can't believe it all ends like this.

I walk around to the front of the building and back in the direction of the bus station. As I pass the front of Diana's, I notice Arnold, the host. When he spots me, he beckons me over. I have no idea what he's going to do when he loses his job, because Diana's is such a huge part of his identity.

'Serena, there was a man looking for you earlier,' he tells me. 'I've been keeping an eye out for you, to pass on the message.'

'Sorry, I walked in through the back door, and Agatha threw me out of it,' I explain. 'A man is looking for me? A man-man?'

'I wasn't under the impression he was here to ask for your hand in marriage,' Arnold explains with just a little bit of snark. 'But he was a man, and he was looking for you, and he didn't want to talk to Agatha or Andrew.'

'No one wants to talk to them,' I reason out loud.

'That's certainly true,' Arnold replies. 'The man left his contact details for you and asked that you give him a call ASAP.'

He takes a piece of paper from his pocket. I unfold it to see the name 'Stephen Gates' and a mobile number.

'I guess I'll call Stephen Gates, then,' I tell Arnold, careful to say his full name, just in case the authorities need to know anything at any point.

I'm not the kind of girl, adult or human generally to have other grown adults seeking them out for conversations, no one ever wants or needs me for anything.

So what on earth does Stephen Gates want with me? I guess there's only one way to find out...

8

Stephen Gates is a man of very few words. Still, as long as he isn't a serial killer who only targets foul-mouthed fuck-ups with chipped nails and over-processed ends, then I'll be okay.

He gave nothing away on the phone – other than confirming that it was in fact me he needed to speak to, and this wasn't some kind of mistake. He said that his office was nearby and that he could meet me in half an hour, so I went for a wander while I wondered what he wanted with me.

I'm not far from where I started now, just down the road from Diana's, walking past Leeds's famous Corn Exchange. It's funny, when I was a teenager, the Corn Exchange was a very different place. These days, the grade I listed Victorian building is home to an array of ultra-trendy shops. It's a truly stunning place, inside and out, but in my day – hello, I'm old as hell, I say things like 'in my day...' – it was so different.

The building was exactly the same, but the shops and the clientele were a whole other thing. The Corn Exchange (unofficially, at least) used to belong to the subcultures of Leeds. Whatever you called yourself – a goth, a mosher, an emo – it didn't matter, the Corn Exchange was the place to be. With kooky shops inside selling the baggiest jeans with the longest chains hanging from them, the darkest lipsticks and the brightest eyeshadows that were not that popular on the high street at the time, and posters of everyone from Slipknot to Blink-182. In the 00s, the weird and wonderful youth would gather outside the old building in their PVC platform boots, their best piercings on show, with their Korn dolls and their attitude and I was there with the best of them. It felt like such a safe space to be an odd teenager. At school, you would be picked on for daring to be different, but here you had an army. Of course, it was eventually bought by someone who wanted to turn it into something more upmarket.

I check my watch. Time to meet Stephen Gates, a man of few words and many secrets. I'm getting a vibe from him, like this is something covert, something sensitive... I'm secretly hoping he's my long-lost real dad who also happens to be a very generous millionaire on close personal terms with Jake Gyllenhaal and, by the way, if only he could meet a nice girl like you – perhaps I'll introduce you.

Shit, I'm going to be gutted when I get murdered.

I walk around the back of the building and weave through a couple of backstreets until I spot him, standing out like a sore thumb, Stephen Gates in his suit, carrying his briefcase, bearing absolutely zero family resemblance to me, and you can just tell he doesn't know Jake Gyllenhaal.

'Serena Ross?' he checks.

'That's me,' I say cautiously.

I definitely got the sense, when I called him, that this was some sort of official business, I'm not trying to put myself in danger. I do still have that sixth sense all women have, though – being ready for danger at any time.

'You may or may not know that Diana Atwood's will was read this morning,' he begins.

'I'd heard something,' I reply.

'Mrs Atwood unsurprisingly left the bulk of her estate to her two children,' he explains. 'She also left a series of donations to charities and organisations – although the room did clear as the instructions went on.'

'I can't say I'm surprised to hear that her kids cleared off after they found out what was theirs,' I reply, because Stephen is clearly too polite to say it. 'But what does any of this have to do with me?'

'I knew Diana,' Stephen admits. 'She buried something – if you'll pardon the phrase – in her will. She knew her kids wouldn't stick around for the boring part – namely the money not going to them. To make a long story short... Diana left you something: a business.'

I gasp.

'Diana's?' I blurt. 'The tea room?'

Stephen quickly shoots that one down.

'No, no, no, not the tea room,' he says. 'Diana's was left to her children. Dirty Di's was left to you.'

My jaw falls.

'What was?'

Stephen clears his throat.

'Dirty Di's,' he says again, this time gesturing at the building next to him.

I turn to look at the tired old building. It has a large glass-window display, and while you can't see inside, you can see the black PVC-clad male mannequin in the window. I look back at Stephen for an explanation.

'This was Diana's other business,' he informs me. 'Let's head inside.'

What is going onnnn?

I follow Stephen through a corridor with what I can only describe as retro-porn Polaroid pictures all over the walls. I want to say they're not hardcore or anything but I'm not exactly an authority on the matter – they're nothing too explicit, they're sort of arty, really.

By the time we reach another set of doors and walk through them, everything becomes crystal clear.

'This was Diana's other business venture,' Stephen says. 'A...'

'A sex shop,' I squeak.

'I think you'll find we call them an adult store,' a woman corrects me in a light-hearted way. 'A sex shop sounds like somewhere you go to buy sex.'

I turn to my left to find myself face to face with the biggest purple penis I've ever seen in my life – and I'm not talking, like, a big size. I mean it's six feet tall.

'Don't mind him,' the woman insists.

I stop gawping at the penis and look at the woman. My jaw has dropped so low it's starting to ache.

'Sorry, just...' I turn to Stephen. 'What is happening right now?'

'Diana left Dirty Di's to you,' Stephen confirms.

'Diana owned *this* place?' I blurt in disbelief.

'Oh, no, you're not a prude, are you?' the woman says with a roll of her eyes. 'Are you one of those who thinks places like this are dirty and we're all going to hell?'

'Don't get me wrong, I've robbed my TV remote batteries like the best of them,' I insist. 'I just can't believe Diana owned a place like this and no one knew – and that she left it to me.'

'Di never told anyone about this place because she thought they would judge her,' the woman says.

'She left a letter of wishes explaining that she wanted you to have it,' Stephen explains. 'I have a copy here, if you want to read it, but Diana left something addressed to you specifically to give you more of an idea of why she made the decisions she did.'

'I just can't believe it,' I say. My mind should be racing but it's closer to being empty right now.

'Believe it, boss,' the woman replies. 'My name is Jen. We've also got Kit, but he only fills in for me when I take time off, and then there's Oliver, who manages the business side of things – he tries not to come in, now he *is* a prude.'

Jen is probably in her late thirties. She has enviable curves and she flaunts them well in a purple corset dress. Her hair is jet black, complimented by her dark eye make-up and her plum lips, but her most distinguishing feature has to be her confidence. You can see it from a mile away and it's so attractive – we would all do well to be more like Jen.

'I need to go, I have a meeting,' Stephen tells me. 'I'll leave you to talk with Jen but feel free to call me with any questions. Oh, and I'll be in touch about the paperwork.'

'I'll walk you out,' I tell him. 'Back in a sec, Jen.'

'Yeah, take your time,' she calls after me. 'We're not busy.'

'Just one question, before you go,' I say to Stephen once we're out of earshot. 'Diana left this place to me? As in, I own it?'

'That's correct,' Stephen replies.

'Can I just sell it?' I ask him.

What I need right now is money – what I don't need is an adult store.

'You could sell the business,' Stephen says. 'However, it's not worth much. It's a leasehold property, the business isn't thriving... Look at it as more of an opportunity. However, if you want to try and sell the business, I can pass you on to someone who can help. Diana was passionate about this place going to you. See what you think.'

'I'll do that,' I reply. 'Thank you.'

'Oh, I almost forgot.' Stephen rifles through his bag. 'Diana left her message to you in the form of a video. It's on VHS, unfortunately.'

'Wow, thank you,' I reply. 'I'm sure I can get my hands on a player somewhere.'

'Diana was old-school,' Stephen says. Then he looks back at the shop behind me. 'Well, in most senses.'

I sigh, thank Stephen and head back inside. I'll have to find something to play this on but it can live in my handbag for now. I can't quite bring myself to watch it yet.

'So, Serena, right?' Jen says.

'That's me,' I reply.

'I like your outfit,' she replies. 'I like people who do their own thing.'

I wonder if that means she thinks I look strange. I'm wearing oversized denim dungarees over a white crop top, keeping the cold out with my trusty oversized pink puffa coat and a black beanie hat.

'I think when you're a weird teenager you're never quite able to let go of it,' I explain. 'Plus, working in the tea room, we had to look a certain way, so now that I've been... relieved of my duties... it's nice to just wear whatever I want.'

'Di talked about you all the time, you know,' Jen says. 'You were like her honorary daughter. She would always wonder about showing you this place. It's a shame she never got the chance.'

'I've never heard anyone call her Di,' I confess.

'This place was so special to her,' Jen continues. 'But I don't think she felt like she could be Diana *and* Di. People can be funny about adult stores. Di was working hard to make this place a success. Things have been quiet. Perhaps you can help with that?'

'Perhaps,' I reply.

What do I know about running an adult store? What I need is to sell it, but if the building is rented, and the business is failing, would anyone even buy it?

'You can start with this,' Jen says as she places something in my hand.

'Erm... what is it?' I ask.

It's a matte black something, with rose gold details, and various shapes and textures. It looks like the Millennium Falcon – Han Solo's spaceship – if I'm being honest, although this doesn't seem like a place you would come to buy *Star Wars* memorabilia.

'Your homework is to find out,' Jen replies. 'Obviously, it's some sort of sex toy but, try as I might, I can't work out what it does, how to turn it on – nothing.'

'Does it not come with instructions?' I ask.

'Honey, that thing isn't coming with anything,' she jokes. 'We bought these cheap pallets of miscellaneous stock. They're a bargain but you get what you get. So take that thing home with you and figure it out. Oh, and here are some batteries, just in case. Save your TV remote.'

I laugh as Jen tosses me a packet of AA batteries. I place them in my bag before examining the toy. There are no obvious places to open it up, no buttons to push, nothing.

I place it in my bag, to take it home, as instructed. I have no idea how I'm going to figure out what it does but it's the least of my worries. Never mind the toy – I need to figure out what I'm going to do with the shop. Right now, I'm not sure what is going to be harder.

9

You know that feeling after a long day when all you want to do is make some food, curl up in front of the TV and then get a good night's sleep? That's my plan for this evening. Sadly, I don't think that's going to happen, though.

The smell of cooking – admittedly a delicious smell – hits me as I walk through the house door. I follow my nose into the kitchen. I would only be expecting to find Ziggy there, were it not for the volume of noise pumping out of the room.

'Here she is,' Ziggy says excitedly from behind the hob on the island. 'Everyone, this is Serena.'

Everyone shouts hello.

The room is busy with people, mess and general chaos.

'Hi,' I reply. 'Erm...'

'Let me introduce you to everyone,' he insists. 'That's Benji, at the dining table, and Koby sitting across from him.'

Benji is messing around with an electric guitar – thankfully they don't make much noise when they're not plugged in, but it's the only quiet thing in the room.

'And this is Kira,' Ziggy says.

The leggy brunette sitting on the kitchen island leans over to hook her arms around his neck playfully as she smiles.

'Hi,' she says.

'We just had a band practice, and everyone really wanted tacos so, long story short, here we are,' Ziggy explains. 'Were you wanting to cook? We're almost done with the oven, Kira is just using it to make nachos.'

I'm still hovering in the doorway with my shopping bags. I could go have a bath, I suppose, then come back down and make some dinner and watch TV. It will be quieter when they've gone.

'I thought I might go have a bath first anyway,' I say. 'I can use the oven when you're done.'

'Well, you might want to take that bath later,' Ziggy says. 'Otto is having a shower in the house bathroom.'

'The house bathroom?' I repeat back to him. 'You mean my bathroom?'

'No, my bathroom is my bathroom,' Ziggy clarifies. 'You use the house bathroom – where else would guests go?'

'Guests who have showers?' I reply in disbelief.

I don't have the space in my brain to deal with this tonight. Forget a hot meal, I'll make myself a sandwich and go watch TV in the other room.

Kira hops down from the worktop. She's wearing a pair of seriously tight black skinny jeans and a long-sleeved almost luminous green cropped top that says 'pocket rocket' across the chest. She's a lot shorter than me, and that's in her super-high-heeled boots, so that's checking out.

'Trust me, you want Otto to shower,' she tells me. 'Drummers stink after they've played. You would not want him stinking up the sofa, watching a movie in the living room like that.'

'Oh, are you guys using the TV too?' I blurt.

'We're going to watch a movie,' Benji tells me.

'I can give you a shout when it's free,' Ziggy suggests as he squirts barbeque sauce into the pan in front of him. It splatters everywhere. I can't believe what a mess the kitchen is.

'We're watching the extended cut of *The Two Towers*, it's almost four hours long,' Benji reminds him.

'Yeah, okay, don't give me a shout in four hours,' I say. 'I'll just get a sandwich and take it to my room.'

'We're doing *The Lord of the Rings* trilogy,' Kira tells me with a roll of her eyes. 'We have these movie nights where we just binge-watch different franchises. I want to do Bond.'

'No, you want to do Daniel Craig,' Ziggy points out.

'Literally,' Benji joins in.

'They're all insecure about their skinny rocker bodies,' she tells me, clearly in an attempt to wind them up. 'They get uncomfortable around jacked men.'

'Erm, I'm shredded,' Ziggy jokes, although you can tell that he takes her teasing on board, just a little.

'Gothmog is pretty jacked,' Benji says under his breath.

'You could join us?' Kira suggests. 'Couldn't she?'

'Er...' Ziggy doesn't rush to say yes.

'Oh, I don't want to intrude on your band time,' I insist.

'I'm not in the band,' she tells me, sounding almost offended. 'Ziggy is vocals and guitar, Benji plays guitar too...'

'Just better,' Benji adds.

'...Koby is the bassist and Otto is the drummer.'

'Kira is sort of a Neon City Split groupie,' Benji informs me.

Neon City Split, that must be the name of their band.

'Oh, I'm more of a WAG than a groupie,' she tells me.

Ziggy laughs so Kira grabs him with her legs and pulls him close to play-fight him.

Hmm. I wonder if she's Ziggy's girlfriend. It makes sense. They're both cool, beautiful people.

'What do you say, do you want to join us?' Kira asks again.

I look over at Ziggy. He keeps his eyes on his pan.

'That's okay,' I insist. 'I'm pretty tired. I'll make my sandwich and take it upstairs.'

'Do you want me to grab some anti-bac wipes and clean you some space?' Kira asks helpfully. 'Ziggy, you're making a right mess.'

'Can you just use kitchen roll?' he asks. 'I hate the smell of cleaning products.'

'It shows,' I can't resist saying. I turn to Kira. 'Honestly, it's fine, I'll just make it on the plate.'

I grab the bits I need to make my dinner and attempt to clear myself a space on the island.

'Perhaps we need a rota, for the shared rooms?' Ziggy suggests to me quietly as his friends continue to be loud with one another.

'Yeah, that sounds like a good idea,' I reply.

We continue to prep our very different meals in silence – silence from one another at least.

I should have known that being given somewhere free to live was going to be too good to be true. I can't believe I've been saddled with someone so selfish.

10

Today is not a good day.

I didn't get a very good night's sleep, which never helps things, but on top of being absolutely shattered, I am also bloody annoyed. The reason I didn't sleep was because Ziggy and his friends were being noisy all night, way into the early hours of the day, and with my room being above the living room, I found it impossible to get any sleep. Even when the noise died down a little, and I probably could've slept, I still couldn't get to sleep because I was having fantasy arguments with Ziggy in my head. I was thinking about going downstairs and screaming at him to shut up, and him feeling so bad he agreed to swap bedrooms with me, or even move out and leave me here to live happily alone. Of course, I didn't do that, I just lay in bed, seething.

I was unsurprisingly up and out before Ziggy this morning, so at least I didn't have to face him over breakfast. I also wasn't shocked to discover that he had left his cooking mess untouched, so I had to work my way around that to make my tea and toast. I was adamant that I wasn't going to tidy so much as a crumb, not even to make space, nor by accidentally knocking bits onto the floor, and I'm delighted to say that I was successful. It's amazing how petty I can be sometimes, but I do like to think that I'm a moral kind of petty – if such a thing can exist.

This supposed moral pettiness is the reason I am where I am right now, lurking at the staff door behind Diana's Tearoom, psyching myself to go in. The reason I'm here? To steal a vase, obviously.

Maël messaged me to say that the tea room is shutting down as early as next week, with all of the stock, the furniture, and everything else inside the building being imminently sold off. I took that as my cue to sneak into Diana's and take back what's mine. I know, it's just a painted vase, worth absolutely nothing, but Diana gave it to me, it's worth a lot to me. I can't even imagine anyone else buying it, without the sentimental attachment I have. Awful Agatha is just being awful. That's the only reason she's clinging on to it, and why I don't feel remotely guilty for taking it back.

I take a deep breath and walk through the staff door with confidence, like I have done a hundred times, and stroll along the corridor to where Agatha placed the vase. Pathetically, my plan is simply to grab it and run. This isn't *Ocean's Eleven* – although if George Clooney wanted to drop by and help me out, that would be much appreciated.

By the time I reach the last place I saw Diana's vase, I realise it's not there any more, and because I didn't take the time to come up with a contingency plan, I don't know what to do other than stand frozen on the spot.

'Serena?' a male voice calls out.

I glance down the corridor and see Andrew standing there. Agatha and Andrew never spent any time here when their mum was alive. Now it's their meal ticket, they can't keep away. It's almost as though they want to watch it slowly stripped for parts, the layers of history their mum spent decades building up being stripped away one at a time, until all that's left in the rubble is a pile of money for them to promptly stuff into their pockets and walk off with.

'I thought you'd gone?' he says.

'I had – I have,' I correct myself. 'I just came back to get something.'

'It's not a vase, is it?' he asks.

The fact that he knows exactly why I'm here briefly floors me, but I do my best to keep my poker face firmly in place.

'A vase?' I repeat back to him as blankly as possible, cocking my head curiously, potentially overcooking it, but I wasn't prepared to be interrogated.

'Aggy said you were trying to steal one, and that she wouldn't be surprised if you came back for it,' he tells me through narrowed eyes. 'If I'm being honest with you, she doesn't want you to have it, and she doesn't want you to buy it either. It's probably something to do with your relationship with Mum but, hey ho, I promised I wouldn't let you take it.'

It's the most surreal thing, looking into Andrew's eyes, and seeing Diana's looking back at me. It gives me a pang of... something. I don't know if it's good or bad.

I do know that, even though both Atwood siblings are horrible people, Andrew doesn't seem to have the evil streak his sister has. I also think it's hilarious that he calls her Aggy, because aggy is exactly how I would describe her.

'I'm here for brownies,' I blurt.

'Brownies?' he repeats back to me.

'Yeah, well, you're closing down, and the brownies here are my favourite,' I say. 'So, I thought I'd better come and buy a box.'

'You're here for a box of brownies?' he says, once again repeating my words back to me in disbelief. 'Okay, sure.'

Fantastic, he's calling my bluff.

'Come with me,' he insists. 'And, in the future – although I suppose the place won't be open for much longer, so it won't matter – please use the customer entrance. That door is for staff use only.'

'Got it,' I reply.

Andrew orders a box of brownies for me. He then stands over Wilma, the girl working behind the counter, while she takes my payment.

'Right, so is that all?' Andrew checks.

'Yep,' I reply.

'Okay then,' he says, glancing over at the door, then back at me.

I guess that's my cue to leave. I'll just have to think of some other way to get my vase back. If it's not here, I wonder if perhaps it might be at the auction place already? I'll have to give that a go.

I step outside the shop, my cute Diana's paper bag in my hand, with the box of brownies that I didn't technically want but, also, I would always want. I could have done without paying £15 for four, but there you go.

'Excuse me, do you work here?' a petite brunette with a west coast American accent asks me.

I stare at her for a second. Say something, Serena. Don't be weird.

'Yes, no, I did, I *used to*,' I babble, hopefully reaching a clear answer by the end. 'It's closing down, unfortunately.'

The brunette bursts into tears.

Oh, god, please don't do this – do this with anyone but me. This is so beyond bizarre. Girl code kicks in before I can stop it. I place an arm around her and usher her toward the nearest bench.

'Is everything okay?' I ask her.

'No,' she blurts. 'No, it isn't okay at all.'

I watch her fill her lungs with air, ready to tell me – a stranger – all about it. But while she might not know me, I know her. It's Lacey, I recognise her from the photo I saw – it's Dean's ex-girlfriend.

'Sorry, I just need to get a grip,' she says, sniffing hard. 'It's just... I just got engaged, and – it's a long story – but I need to sort the catering for the party kinda last minute because the company we were supposed to be using has let me down, and someone at work recommended Diana's... it was my last hope. I called up earlier, they said they weren't taking on any new bookings, I was hoping I could come down here and appeal to someone's better nature...'

'Oh, no, I'm so sorry,' I tell her sincerely.

'It's not your fault,' she says, batting her hand, sniffing again. 'I just so want this engagement party to be perfect and everything is going so wrong. My family can't come over from the States, the person doing the balloons has billed me twice, and now this. I said I could handle the planning on my own and I so wanted to, for my fiancé, because I told him I would and... he's... he's my Teddy, you know? He's my support, always there for me, always solving my problems and I just wanted to show him that I could handle this one. I feel like I'm screwing it all up and I'm going to lose him.'

I still can't believe that Lacey is here next to me, in the flesh, crying her eyes out to me. More than anything – and it's an awful thing to say – it's such a relief to hear that she's moved on with her life and that she's getting married. I know, all I did was catch Dean looking at a photo of her, but there's a pathetic comfort that comes from knowing he isn't looking at her photo because he's trying to get her back. Wow, that is tragic. It's almost like the difference between your boyfriend not cheating on you because he doesn't want to versus him not cheating on you because he's in a room on his own. A victory by default – although I know I'm just being crazy, and I do really feel for Lacey. You can tell she doesn't want to let Teddy down, and while I'm sure he wouldn't love her any less for not sorting out the party food, she seems like a nice girl, and I think I can help her.

'It's not Diana's, but I do know a catering company who can help you out,' I tell her. 'They only cater for events, so they'll be better equipped for what you need, and if you're flexible, they can probably do it at pretty short notice.'

'Oh, my god, do you think so?' she replies, her eyes widening with hope.

'I could call them for you if you like,' I say.

'That would be awesome,' Lacey replies. 'Thank you. You seem like you know your stuff – how are you with wedding planning?'

'Well, I've never planned my own,' I confess, pulling a funny face as if to laugh off my own unmarried status. 'But I've met my fair share of brides recently.'

'This is kinda weird, but I don't have any close female friends in this country – not who are old enough to be even thinking about marriage, at least – and I have no idea what I'm doing,' Lacey confesses. 'Maybe you can give me a few pointers?'

Perhaps it's because Lacey seems so nice, maybe it's because I feel sorry for her, because I know what it's like to feel like you're struggling, or maybe it is just because I'm happy she's not going to be my love rival. Whatever it is, it's the reason I say...

'I can do that.'

'You're a doll,' she says, instantly perking up. 'How about I give you my number, we could hang out sometime? You can tell me where the second-best place to get a cake is.'

I smile.

'I'm sure I can figure that out,' I tell her. 'But, for now, would you like a brownie?'

I take the box from the Diana's bag and pop the top.

'Oh, my god, I shouldn't, but I can't resist,' Lacey replies. 'I don't suppose they're vegan?'

'The two on the left are,' I reply. I'm glad I got a mixed box now.

She takes a bite out of one and her eyes roll into the back of her head.

'Wow, it's a real shame they're closing down.'

'It really is,' I say with a sigh.

I hand Lacey my phone so that she can put my details in, and I promise that I'll call her, to help her figure out her catering problem.

Well, when you've already got a million problems, why not throw befriending the guy you're dating's ex-girlfriend into the mix, hey?

11

I am beyond irritated (although still not at all surprised) when I get home to find out that while Ziggy has attempted to clean and tidy the kitchen, it does not feel clean at all, leaving muggins here to reach for the kitchen cleaner and the kitchen roll to clean the place properly.

I've treated myself to a pizza – a supermarket one, but one of the fancy, hand-stretched, wood-fired ones – but, before I can put it in the oven, there is one more thing I need to do.

I reach into my bag, to grab a pen, only to feel my hand hit something large and unexpected: the Millennium Falcon of sex toys. No, I haven't been able to figure out how to make it work or what it even does. Yes, I am still carrying it around in my bag. My worry with leaving it in the house is that Ziggy somehow gets eyes on it – I would never live it down, or be able to live with him, if he caught me with a sex toy, never mind one I can't even work.

I quickly stuff it deeper into my bag and take out a pen. Next, I use a box of Frosties as a ruler, to draw a grid on a piece of paper. I'm putting the finishing touches to my masterpiece when Ziggy walks in.

His hair is all wet and sweaty, which bizarrely suits him, as it's brushed backwards and held in place with a headband. He's wearing his dark green parker coat – well, it is bloody cold out there this evening – but he's also wearing shorts. I think it's safe to assume, from his muddy shins, that he's been playing some kind of sport.

He smiles at me as he dumps a bag containing a takeaway (although I can't tell what from the smell alone) on the newly cleaned island. His face quickly falls.

'Whoa, what's that horrible smell?' he asks, his face contorted.

'You, I'd imagine,' I reply.

I don't intend it to be as mean as it sounds but he is the one that's all sweaty and covered in mud.

'It's not that,' he says. 'It's... it's cleaning products?'

'I cleaned the kitchen,' I tell him. 'You'd... missed a bit. You're welcome.'

He had, in fact, missed a lot.

'Oh, sorry, I'm really sensitive to smells,' he tells me.

'You're allergic to cleaning?' I ask in disbelief.

'No, not allergic, I just really don't like strong smells, like cleaning stuff and nail polish – things like that.'

'How does that work out for you?' I ask.

He ignores me.

'I'm going to go for a shower – can you stick this in the oven for me, to keep it warm, please?'

'Sure,' I reply. 'Before you go, I did as you said, and I came up with a rota for the lounge. Here we are.'

'You have it tonight,' Ziggy points out.

'Well, yeah, you had it last night,' I remind him. 'So I thought it was fair.'

'It's fair but Leeds City are playing tonight,' he says. 'Can we trade a night? If I'd known, I would've gone to the pub to watch it or something but I've got my food now and...'

'Oh, my god, fine,' I say. 'I'll just take the next two nights, but then that's it, right? We stick to the rota?'

'Yeah, yeah, of course,' he insists. 'Could you do me one more thing, please? Can you just give the room a wipe with a damp cloth? It's just the smell...'

Ziggy doesn't wait for an answer, he dashes upstairs, clearly eager to get in the shower because the football is about to start.

I can't believe that he expects me to put his food in the oven, and for me to give up my night with the TV for him, and for me to clean the *clean* kitchen that he should've *cleaned to begin with*. Bloody hell, it's almost as though he's trying to drive me away.

Wait! Is he trying to drive me away? Is that what all this is, a thinly veiled attempt at being so difficult to live with that I'll pack my bags and leave?

If Ziggy thinks he can play games with me then he needs to think again. I've been playing games like this since I was at school.

He might think he can play dirty, but I can go even dirtier... or perhaps that should be cleaner.

I grab the packet of antibacterial wipes from the cupboard under the sink. First, I pop Ziggy's food in the oven for him, then I head into the lounge and start cleaning.

Well, if Ziggy is going to take my night in front of the TV, then the least I can do is get the room cleaned up for him. Make sure everything is all nice and clean and smelling it too. Really smelling it.

Game on, Ziggy.

12

Oliver Thomas has a very straight face for a man sitting on a box of novelty dildos.

I can see the names and photos of a couple of different ones, peeping out from the box, just about visible between his legs – which is a hilarious coincidence, and all the more reason for me to stop staring. It's just I've never seen a Squildo or a Megalodong before.

I twirl anxiously in the room's only desk chair as he taps away on his laptop. Oliver is the sort of accountant, business manager something or other at Dirty Di's – my god, I still can't believe this place exists. I definitely can't believe that it's mine now.

'I feel so thick,' I confess.

Oliver has seemed so far so serious, but he allows himself to smile at this.

'Not everyone knows spreadsheets,' he says. 'We all have the skills that make our job our own. Spreadsheets might be my thing but yours is...?'

'Unemployed!' I announce, complete with jazz hands.

Oliver smiles a little wider.

'You're a business owner now,' he replies, in an attempt to make me feel better, I'd imagine, but then he taps the screen. 'Just not a very successful one. So these are the outgoings, and these are the incomings,' he says.

'Wow,' I blurt.

'This is what the business is worth,' he continues.

'Wow,' I say again.

'But this is what you'll probably get for it,' he says, showing me one final number.

'Oh, god, wow, okay, so it's a pretty bleak situation,' I confirm. 'So...'

'Well, Di was trying to make a success of it,' he says. 'Everything is all paid up for this month, which gives you a few weeks to see what you can achieve. Di was trying all sorts of things. Promotions, buying in pallets of cheap stock – the problem is that no one knows we're here.'

'You're a smart guy, right?' I confirm.

'I hope so,' he replies, then he narrows his eyes. 'Why?'

I reach into my bag and pull out the Millennium Falcon of sex toys.

'Can you figure out this thing? It's from one of the pallets.'

I hand the unidentifiable object to Oliver. He holds it as though he's terrified of where it's been.

'It's unused,' I reassure him. 'No one knows what it's for.'

Oliver examines it curiously.

Oliver is (I'd guess) in his late twenties. He's wearing a suit, although he isn't wearing a tie and his top button is undone. I don't imagine he's as uptight as he seems, I think he's just shy. He has dark blonde hair that is longish on top which – combined with his round-rimmed glasses – somehow make him seem extra smart. That said, he looks baffled by the gadget.

'Perhaps it works over Bluetooth,' he suggests as he hands it back to me. 'With an app, maybe.'

'That's one sophisticated sex toy,' I say with a sigh as I return it to my bag.

'So, we're going to try and drum up some more business?' Oliver says hopefully.

'I guess we are,' I reply. 'I'll have a think, see if I can come up with any ideas.'

'Any numbers you need crunching, just let me know,' he says with a smile.

I like Oliver already. He has kind eyes. I don't have the heart to tell him that I have no idea what I'm doing and, in a month, everyone here is probably going to be joining me at the Job Centre.

'I will, thanks.'

I have a lunch date with Dean, so I need to get a move on. Money is his thing – perhaps he'll have some ideas for me. At the very least, maybe he can get this sex toy working. I'll take all the progress I can get today.

13

'I thought you were joking,' Dean says through a cackle. 'You really own an adult shop?'

'I do indeed,' I reply. 'Not the building, just the business – basically the name and the stock.'

'Is it well stocked?' he asks across the lunch table before biting his lip.

I reach out with my foot under the table and lightly caress his leg.

'Right now, I may just be the owner of the world's largest collection of sex toys, lingerie, and adult films,' I joke flirtatiously. 'So if there's anything I can bring you...'

'I'll make a list,' he replies through a grin. 'But, just to be serious for a second, you're seriously going to try to run this business?'

'I don't have much choice,' I reply. 'Obviously, I don't have a job right now, and I need one, but Diana left the place to me, in the hope I would keep it open. The pressure I'm feeling is just... I don't want to let her down, so I need to make it work.'

'Is it making money?' he asks.

I shake my head.

'Losing money?' he checks. 'A lot?'

'It looked like it to me,' I reply. 'Oliver, the accountant, said I could sell it, but I wouldn't get much for it.'

'I'd sell it if I were you,' Dean replies, reaching over the table to take my hand in his. 'I'm sure Diana had deep pockets, when she was running the show. But if it's your company now, and you start racking up debts to try and keep the place afloat... that's not good for you. I don't want to sound harsh, but you don't know anything about running a business, do you? That's not a strong position to be in.'

'Shit, I hadn't really thought about it like that,' I admit. 'I just really, really don't want to sell it – no matter what it's worth. I know it sounds stupid, but I know Diana wouldn't have wanted me to sell it, just like she didn't want the tea room selling, and I couldn't stop her vile kids from doing that – from selling off her legacy – but if I can't keep Diana's open, I don't know, I just hoped I could keep Di's open. You're right, though, I don't know anything about running a business, or a shop, I certainly don't know anything about sex toys. Look at this...'

I take the Millennium-Falcon-looking sex toy from my bag and place it on the table.

'Take this stupid thing, for example,' I start. I'm getting upset now. I can't seem to calm myself down, it's like I'm spiralling. 'I can't for the life of me figure out what the hell you're supposed to do with it, I can't turn it on, I can't open it up, I just...'

I grab my fork and begin to try to pry my way inside the black casing. Perhaps I can get in by force.

'What's that?' Dean asks.

'A sex toy,' I tell him, still jabbing away, like a woman on a mission.

I slip with the fork, scraping lines into the matte black finish on the top. Still, the toy remains otherwise exactly as it's always been. Useless – just like I feel right now.

Dean's eyes widen at the sex toy I just dropped on the table in a busy restaurant. Thankfully no one is looking, everyone is too busy focusing on their own lives.

Still, Dean snatches it up, and drops it in his jacket pocket.

'Bloody hell, I thought it was a piece of modern art or something. I'll have a look at it later, without an audience,' he tells me. 'I'm sure I'll be able to figure it out. I'm no expert but I'm pretty sure that if you don't put them in *something*, then you put something in *them*.'

'Well, be careful, I'm pretty sure I bent the fork,' I say, attempting a joke to lighten the mood. 'I'm sorry, I'm just feeling so stressed out at the moment. It's suddenly being a business owner, it's missing Diana and not being able to believe that she's gone, and, to be honest, it's my housemate.'

'*Ziggy*,' Dean says his name mockingly. 'It sounds like an arsehole's name. Go on, what's *Ziggy* done?'

'He's a nightmare,' I reply. 'Honestly, I don't know how much longer I can stand him. At this rate, I'm going to wind up sleeping on a pile of inflatable love dolls, in a windowless shop down a backstreet in the city centre.'

'Do you want me to come over tonight and sort him out?' Dean suggests. 'I won't say or do anything, I'll just show my face, show him that I exist and that I'm protective of you.'

'That's really sweet of you,' I reply, unsure how intimidating Dean would be to Ziggy. 'But I'm seeing a friend this evening and I'm not sure what time I'll be back.'

'I could come for a late-night visit,' he suggests. 'We could make some noise, drive your housemate wild with jealousy.'

I snort. I'm also relieved he hasn't asked me what friend I'm seeing but I would really rather not lie to him – thankfully he's got other things on his mind right now.

'You're welcome to try,' I say. 'But I can tell he does not like me *at all*. It might annoy him, though...'

'Listen, how about I take a few days off work, and we go stay somewhere – on the coast, or a cabin in the woods? Just the two of us, a roaring fire, a bubbling hot tub... what do you say?'

Dean's suggestion breathes air into my lungs, instantly calming me down.

'Really?' I reply.

'Really,' he says. 'A few days off from this Ziggy and, by the time you get back, he might have settled in and calmed down a bit. You find us somewhere to go, send me a link, and I'll get it booked. Sound good?'

'You're wonderful,' I tell him.

'I get that all the time,' he jokes.

Things might not be going well in a few areas of my life but at least I have Dean. Taking a break with him is just what I need right now and, who knows, if he enjoys taking a mini-break with me then it might just show him that he could stand to live with me. That really would be the answer to my problems.

14

Whenever I arrive home and realise that Ziggy isn't in, I feel this instant wave of relief – although this afternoon I felt emboldened by Dean's offer to take me away for a few days. I walked in like I owned the place, with this confidence afforded to me by the fact that I have options, I can go somewhere else, to get away from Ziggy, even if it is only for a couple of days.

To be honest, I was looking forward to telling him. I was going to just blurt it so casually, in a matter-of-fact kind of way. But he wasn't in, so I made myself a cup of tea, I watched TV, I had a long bath and then I got ready for this evening.

I kept my promise to Lacey, agreeing to meet her in town so that I could set her up with a caterer and tell her where to get a wedding cake from. To strike up a friendship with the ex-girl-friend of the guy I'm seeing would be extremely weird, even if she is about to tie the knot, and with things seeming so great between me and Dean, the last thing I want to do is ruin it by making myself look like a crazy girl. It's a shame, though, because she seems really nice. I need all the friends I can get at the moment.

I met Lacey outside Hades, a super-exclusive nightclub with a list of entry requirements so notoriously wild I probably don't qualify for entry in a handful of different ways. I secretly hoped we might be going in – that Lacey might have connections willing to sneak someone like me in through the back door. I can tell from the way Lacey dresses, from the perfect ends of her hair, and the way her make-up looks so flawless, that she must be quite well off. I'll bet she's allowed in Hades whenever she likes.

I was disappointed when she walked me around the corner – until I realised we were heading into the famous LDS apartment building. Everyone who is anyone (who lives in Leeds city centre, at least) lives in the LDS building. Honestly, the look on my face when we stepped into the lift and I watched Lacey use a key instead of pushing a button to take us to the top floor. I know the look on my face because I saw it in the lift mirror.

'I left my date planner on the coffee table,' she told me. 'But I make a mean espresso martini.'

We've just walked through the apartment door and, genuinely, I am in awe. Unsurprisingly, I've never been in a penthouse before.

The front door leads into a large hallway with white walls. The long corridor ahead has a series of doors, as well as a large, fancy staircase that curls around to the floor above us.

'Right, let's get a drink,' Lacey says, kicking her heels off.

Is this a shoes-off home? I wrestle off my black ankle boots just in case. I wish I'd put nicer socks on, but I'll be fine as long as she doesn't notice the hole on my heel.

Lacey strolls into her living room with such a casual confidence. Her hips wiggle as she walks in a way that I always thought could only be put on. I can't help but try to mirror her walk but I look like I'm waddling, so I quickly cut it out. Some of us were not designed to be sexy.

'Oh, wow, this place is stunning,' I blurt as I enter the living room. 'I've seen it from the street below, shining bright at the top of the building, but I never would have guessed it looked like this inside.'

'Yeah, it's pretty cool,' Lacey says as she searches the kitchen for the things she needs. Well, this is her home, I suppose the magic has worn off.

It's a large living space with a kitchen, then a dining area, and finally a living room. The walls are all white, lined with contemporary lighting. The pops of colour come from artworks and sculptures dotted around the place.

It's amazing, all the time, effort, thought and money that must have gone into creating and acquiring the various works of art in the room and yet the show is stolen by clear glass. The entire south-facing wall of the room is replaced by floor-to-ceiling windows that lead out on to a terrace. I can't resist wandering over, looking out over the city. It's so bizarre, seeing the familiar from a different perspective, places you've seen and visited a hundred times seeming completely unrecognisable. It takes me a moment to locate a landmark and then get my bearings from there, but once I know what I'm looking at, I take a moment to marvel at the array of sights Leeds city has to offer.

'So, you think you can help me with a caterer for the party, huh?' Lacey cuts to the chase as she mixes cocktails for us.

'Yes, well, I know one of the owners at S&J Events,' I explain. 'I thought I could give her a ring – I used to send her referrals all the time when I was working at the tea room, if people wanted something beyond what we offered. They always prioritise referrals over new enquiries so I'm hoping, if I call her for you, she'll fit you in whenever you want.'

'That would be awesome,' she tells me, her hands briefly over her heart. 'I'm really feeling the pressure with this engagement party. Let's just say I've been a little highly strung recently. I have... trust issues, always have done, and I always take them out on whoever I'm with. Now I'm engaged, I need to cut that out, I need to accept that the problem is with me, and just focus on getting married and moving on with things, y'know? Sorry, you're supposed to be helping with my catering, not my baggage.'

I smile.

'That's okay, we've all got things we carry around with us,' I reassure her.

'I know it's all in my head, I really do, but it's still good to talk about things, and half my problem is that I care so much about how everything looks that I don't talk about my feelings with those close to me, I find it embarrassing.'

'No, I get that,' I reply. 'I lost someone close to me recently and I've been trying not to think about it, because I don't really have anyone to talk to about it, and I don't really know what to do with it on my own.'

'Was it a family member?' she asks me.

'Not family, but she felt like it,' I reply. 'It's wild, that someone can be there one day, nothing seemingly wrong with them, making mundane plans for the immediate future – like what they're going to have for dinner – and then suddenly that's it, they're gone. No warnings, no goodbyes, nothing.'

'I'm so sorry,' she tells me. 'Isn't it funny, how it's so much easier to open up to a stranger sometimes?'

'It really is,' I say, fighting back the tears, swallowing hard, recomposing myself.

I can't befriend Dean's ex-girlfriend, can I? Surely that would never work? But what if this could be my chance to make a friend, someone I can talk to, someone I can help?

'I'll call Sara Jane,' I tell her. 'Let's get your engagement party catering off your plate.'

'You're a doll,' Lacey insists. 'You really are.'

I grab my phone and hit call on Sara Jane – one half of S&J Events. Sara Jane is the catering side of things, whereas James focuses on things like live music events and everything involved in throwing weddings apart from the food.

'Hey, it's Serena, how are you?' I say cheerily, shaking off any creeping feelings of grief while I talk to her. I just need to try to keep it out of my mind.

'Hey lovely, oh my god, I was so sorry to hear about Diana,' she says. 'And those rotten kids of hers, selling the place off – have they just let you all go?'

'Yep,' I reply. I don't want to say too much about my situation in front of my potential new friend in case it scares her off.

'That's horrible,' she says.

'I'm actually calling with a job for you,' I tell her. 'Someone came into the tea room looking for catering for her engagement party – I said you guys would help her out.'

'Yeah, no worries,' she replies. 'Although, there is one thing, we are pretty rammed at the moment. I could use an extra pair of serving hands, if you don't have a new job lined up yet. It would just be for events here and there, what do you think? I never know who I can rely on, but I know you won't let me down.'

On the one hand, I do have the shop now. But it doesn't make any money, so it's not like I'm going to get paid for working there. I need all the money I can get right now.

'That would be really great, thank you.'

'So, do you have dates for this engagement party?' she asks. 'I've got the diary here.'

'She's here with me,' I reply. 'I could put her on?'

'Sure,' Sara Jane replies. 'And I'll be in touch about any jobs I need help with.'

I can't help but wonder whether Sara Jane is genuinely understaffed or if she just feels sorry for me – either way, I need to take what I can get right now.

'She wants to talk dates with you,' I tell Lacey, giving her an enthusiastic smile.

'Okay, cool,' she says as she reaches for my phone.

'Can I use your loo, please?' I ask in a whisper.

'Sure,' Lacey replies. 'Oh, but you gotta use one of the ones upstairs, we're doing some work in the one down here. There's one in either bedroom.'

'Okay, thanks,' I reply.

I'm not disappointed that I get to have a nosy upstairs. There was something about the staircase that intrigued me when I passed it on the way in. Perhaps it was the fact that it curves around, not even giving me a glimpse of what lies beyond it, or maybe I just really like that each step lights up. Either way, with downstairs being this cool, I'm intrigued to see what's upstairs.

Even though I have permission to be up here, I feel bad, walking into one of the bedrooms, so I walk purposefully through the room into the en suite – just in case someone is watching me, even though I know they aren't.

I love the bathroom, with its dark grey tiles and modern lighting that matches the rest of the house. This place is just so cool in a way that normal people like me could never achieve. A fancy architect and/or interior designer did this, without a doubt. I wonder what Lacey – or her future husband – does to afford such a stunning apartment because, whatever it is, I could be convinced to retrain. As I wash my hands, I look at myself in the mirror and chew my lip anxiously. I'm out of my mind, wondering if I'll ever be able to afford a home like this, when I'm currently crashing in someone else's house while they're on holiday – and then what? Nope. Now is not the time, Serena. Stop it.

I leave the bathroom, briefly admiring what must be the master bedroom as I pass through it this time. It's so cool, so minimal, so...

The light hits something – whatever it is that is sitting on top of the chest of drawers by the floor-to-ceiling windows. It catches my attention and then I realise that I recognise it. Oh, my goodness... Lacey, you dark horse! She's only got (what I now know is) a sex toy sitting there. It's none other than the Millennium-Falcon-looking thingy that has been terrorising me for a few days. Wow, she must know how to work it then. Would it be awkward of me to ask her, just to satisfy my curiosity? I'm almost certain it would.

I take a few steps closer, to see if there's a remote control or something sitting next to it – any kind of clue as to how you get the damn thing going.

I narrow my eyes as I notice something on the top of it. Is that... no, it can't be.

'Admiring my new sculpture?' Lacey asks me. She's standing in the bedroom doorway, her body in silhouette because it's brighter out there than it is in here. It's like something out of a horror movie – I feel like I'm in a horror movie right now.

I glance back at the sex toy. My brain realises the markings on the top are the ones I made with the fork earlier about two seconds before I look at the framed photo sitting next to it. Lacey smiling widely and a man standing behind her, his arms locked around her waist... it's Dean.

'Who is this?' I ask, nodding towards the photo, trying to sound little more than curious.

'Oh, that's Dean, my fiancé,' she replies.

'Sorry, I thought you said your fiancé's name was Teddy?' I say, trying not to make it sound like an accusation, but I'm sure she did.

'Oh, no, I just call him my teddy sometimes,' she explains. 'Like, he's my teddy, my security blanket, I squeeze him when I'm scared sorta thing.'

I can't help but hold eye contact with the photo of Dean. Fucking Dean! My Dean! The bastard is *engaged*.

'He's cute, right?' she prompts me.

'Yeah, he looks like a nice guy,' I reply, keeping my shit together, even though I want to scream.

'A nice guy who is going to be stoked when he hears all about the engagement party I just booked,' she practically sings. 'Thank you so, so much for hooking me up. This party is going to blow him away, it's going to make him forget about all my wild cheating accusations, about me nagging him all the time, it's going to show him that I'm willing to do whatever it takes. Thank you, Serena, thank you so, so much for helping me. You're a good friend.'

Before I know what's happening Lacey is approaching me and suddenly we're hugging, me still glaring at Dean's photo over her shoulder because I am *in his apartment*.

Oh, my god, I'm in Dean's apartment. He could get home any minute and find me standing here, hugging his ex... I mean, his fiancée. Oh, no, he would think I was absolutely crazy, and he's clearly got this poor girl gaslit into thinking she's imagining all the red flags I'm certain he's raising. She would never believe me over him – not just because he's gaslighting her, but because I haven't been honest. I've known who she was all this time and said nothing. If she knew that, she'd think I was a psycho too.

All I know is that I need to get out of this apartment right now.

'Sorry, I'm not feeling so good,' I tell her. 'I think I need to go home.'

'Aw, hon, are you sure?' she replies. 'We still need to chat wedding things – how about I call you and we rearrange for when we're feeling better?'

'Yeah, that would be great,' I lie. 'Sorry.'

I head downstairs and put on my boots and then I get out of the building as fast as my legs will carry me. As I burst out on to the busy streets of Leeds, I take a sharp breath but the cold air hits my lungs like a thousand tiny knives and I cough and splutter. Most people look at me like I'm diseased. One elderly lady stops to ask me if I'm okay. I thank her and tell her I'm okay but I'm not. I'm really, really not.

As hard as I've been trying to save money, I think now is definitely a time when I can justify a taxi. I grab my phone and book one as I move around the corner, because I don't even know what I would do if Dean arrived home right now.

I'm running on pure adrenaline until I get in the taxi. Once I'm safe inside, with the door closed, and the driver starts moving, I'm like a balloon that someone is letting the air out of. I feel everything draining from my body, making me feel dizzy. I try to think, to process what just happened, but I can't. I just need to get home. Everything will be easier once I'm home.

15

I'm sitting at the kitchen island, cradling a cup of tea. I take a deep breath in and then forcibly push the air from my cheeks. I was not expecting this tonight.

Obviously when you know, you know, but the more than I think about it, the more I can't believe I missed so many red flags.

Suddenly I feel so incredibly stupid. Dean has a good job – a great job, even, in finance. *Finance.* Where everyone is loaded. Why didn't it flag, when he told me he lived with a flatmate? How many men in their thirties have a flatmate unless they need one? It doesn't make sense. A fancy apartment makes sense. Living with a fiancée makes sense. Oh, and, of course, this is why I couldn't stay at his place, and why he always had to work. I believed he was working all the hours he could and I imagine that's what Lacey thinks too – at least now he's convinced her she's crazy for thinking he could be cheating on her, that fucking scumbag.

I feel so gross. So dirty and ashamed. I had no idea, but it doesn't alter the facts, does it? I'm the other woman. Well, I *was* the other woman. Not any more. I never want to see that wanker's face or even hear his name again.

I've got my AirPods in my ears, pumping The All-American Rejects directly into my brain. There's something about the music from my teenage years that I find to be such a comfort in times of crisis. Whether it's because it transports me back to my youth – when things were easier, before I got it all so wrong – or perhaps it's simply because it's so angsty. I always used to fantasise about screaming the lyrics to 'Gives You Hell' into the faces of the boys who weren't nice to me at school. I still think it would be pretty therapeutic.

Oh, speaking of The All-American Rejects, I've just noticed Tyson Ritter's all-English doppelganger walk into the kitchen. Ziggy was watching TV in the lounge (on my night) when I got in. I ignored him and headed straight for the kitchen, not at all in the mood for a confrontation tonight.

He hovers in front of me and gives me a wave, as though he's trying to get my attention. He's shirtless, because of course he is. His slender body is ripped with the kind of muscles you only seem to get from thrashing around on stage with a band – not the kind to impress anyone at the gym, but an annoyingly attractive kind of toned. Of course, he ruins it all with a mess of chaotic tattoos. It's not that I have anything against ink – each to their own but I'm too indecisive to commit to anything for life – but Ziggy has a lot going on. Different styles, colours and themes, all vying for space on his abdomen.

Stop looking at his body, Serena!

I pause my music and take out my AirPods.

I give him a look, as if to ask what's up.

'Dean is at the door,' he tells me.

'What?'

'Dean...' he says again, '...is at the door.'

'The front door?' I ask.

'No, the bathroom door,' Ziggy replies. 'Yes, the front door.'

'Did you let him in?' I ask.

'No, I don't know the guy,' Ziggy replies. 'I'm going back to the sofa, but you can let him in if you want.'

Ziggy grabs a bag of crisps from a cupboard and saunters off again. I'm not far behind him, heading for the front door, with no idea what I'm going to do other than get rid of him.

I stop in my tracks for a second. Obviously I'm not going to have it out with him here, now – not in front of Ziggy, who I can't help but notice is peeping into the hallway from where he's sitting. It's not just that, though, I feel so sorry for Lacey, she deserves better than this man. But it's not like she'll believe me over him, and if I dump him now, he's just going to go back to her and pretend this never happened. I suppose I could just keep out of it but, ugh, that's just not my style, I can't sit back and watch a man treat a woman so terribly. There's only one thing I can do, I need to break them up – it's for Lacey's own good, I certainly don't want him for myself. But for this to work, I'm going to need to get her to dump him and if I'm going to do that then I need to keep Lacey close, but Dean closer. But not tonight. Tonight I need him out of my sight.

I put my game face on and open the door.

'Hey, babe,' he says as he steps inside.

He hands me a bottle of wine before leaning in to kiss me. I pretend I haven't noticed and place the bottle on the sideboard in the hallway.

'It's freezing out there,' he tells me, lowering his voice. 'I didn't think *Ziggy* was going to let me in.'

'He's a strange one,' I reply.

'Well, that's why I thought we could take that bottle of wine up to your bedroom and forget all about him,' Dean suggests flirtatiously.

He places his hands on my waist and pulls me in for a kiss. The thought of kissing him repulses me to the point where I push him away – it's a reflex, but one that isn't going to get me very far, if I want to break them up.

I can't help but glance into the lounge, embarrassed that Ziggy might have seen that. Interestingly, I notice he's on the edge of his seat. He keeps eyeballing me, although I think he's trying not to be too obvious.

'Whoa, what's the matter?' Dean asks. 'What was that all about?'

'Sorry, sorry,' I say quickly. 'It's just... my housemate... is very religious... and he can't be in a house with... premarital relations going on. I promised him I wouldn't, in the spirit of good housemate relations.'

'That guy is religious?' Dean asks me in disbelief, loud enough that Ziggy hears. He gets up and walks toward us.

'Yep, that guy is religious,' I reply. 'He's even got religious tattoos. Ziggy, show him your cross.'

'Get out of my house,' Ziggy jokes angrily.

I can't help but laugh, because I get the joke, but Dean looks confused.

'Jesus Christ, I mean, shit, okay, I'll go,' he babbles. 'I'll call you tomorrow, babe.'

Dean leans in to kiss me. I offer him my cheek.

Once he's gone, Ziggy stares at me for a moment with a bemused but smiley look on his face.

'You're weird,' he tells me. 'That was just... yeah... weird. Thanks for letting me be a part of it.'

'You're welcome,' I say sarcastically.

'That's the guy you're seeing then?' he asks.

'Not that it's any of your business,' I start. 'It's complicated.'

I don't want to tell Ziggy that everything is amazing between me and Dean, but I don't want to give him the satisfaction of knowing what a mess my love life is – and what a gullible idiot I am.

'Well, if you figure it out, perhaps you can invite him to the party,' Ziggy suggests.

'What party?' I ask.

'Our party,' he replies. 'A sort of house-warming party. I thought we could throw one. I was thinking tomorrow night... unless parties aren't your thing? Totally understandable if not. You don't seem like the kind of girl...'

'I love parties,' I insist. I quickly realise that he was probably just trying to goad me into agreeing to it. A party might be just what I need, though.

'Okay, tomorrow night then?'

'Tomorrow night,' I confirm. 'I'm going to bed.'

'Oh, you might need to close your bedroom window,' Ziggy calls after me. 'I don't know what it was, the house was smelling like someone had anti-bac wiped the whole place from top to bottom, so I opened a few windows, I think I forgot to close yours.'

On a cold night like tonight? I bet he did. That's okay, luckily I'm boiling hot with rage over Dean. I'll just have to think of a way to get back at Ziggy – tomorrow night at the party might be a good time for it.

But for now, I'll just have to settle for sneaking into his bedroom and unscrewing all the light bulbs just a little. That will have him chasing his tail in the dark for a little while before he can sleep. It's a small thing but I'm just getting warmed up. Time to do some scheming.

16

———

Working was not something I expected to be doing today.

Truthfully, I'm relieved. Not just because I could do with the money – although obviously that's great – but because it gives me somewhere to go. Somewhere that isn't the house or the shop.

The problem with the house is obviously Ziggy's presence. I can't stand being around him and he's definitely trying to push my buttons. When I went downstairs this morning, to make myself a cup of tea to start the day, I couldn't because the milk was frozen solid *again*. Everything else in the fridge was as you would expect, only the milk was frozen, which doesn't happen without meddling, does it? Not repeatedly, and only with the cow's milk, and never the oat milk.

We're having our house-warming party tonight. Annoyingly, I have no one to invite. Well, who could I ask? Dean? Lacey? Dean *and* Lacey? I suppose tanking the party with the explosive fallout from a love triangle might go some way to convincing Ziggy that he wants to leave. Call me crazy, but it's too important that I help Lacey see for herself that Dean is a no-good, lying, cheating bastard. She'll only be rid of him for good if she decides to end it.

If I make a scene, try to end things between them not on her terms, she'll probably take him back.

The only other place I have to go at the moment is Dirty Di's and I'm finding it really hard to be there too. Aside from the fact that burying my head in the sand is the easiest way to deal with a failing business, I think the reason I find it so uncomfortable there is partly because I can feel Diana's ghost there. Not her actual ghost, more like her footprint. You would think it would be comforting, still feeling her presence, but the Diana that I feel there is like a stranger to me. How did I not know there was this whole other side to her? It makes me feel uneasy, like I didn't know her as well as I thought I did. She knew everything about me. Then again, I didn't have any interesting secrets.

Turning up to a day job – even if it isn't the one I had a week ago – feels good. It feels normal. I might not be in the tea room but I'm in an industry I feel comfortable in. Serving cups of tea and sandwiches makes me feel like myself.

Today's event doesn't feel all that different to working at Diana's for another reason. This is some kind of ladies' society meet-up – exactly the sort of customer you would expect to serve at Diana's, so I've been taking comfort in that too.

It's been a pretty easy day so far, I'm blending into the background. Actually, I'm blending into oblivion, because one of the other servers is a nice young man, and women can't resist a nice young man, can they? They certainly can't resist a nice young man who is as jacked as Al.

I arrived earlier just in time to see Al lifting up one of the large tables while someone else tightened the leg. His muscles aren't just impressive on the eye, they're effective too. If I ever need a car towing or something, I know who to call – Al, who will surely be able to drag it out of the way, and with a smile on his face too.

I'm currently sitting next to Al having my lunch. His arms are thicker than my thighs and the urge to touch them is overwhelming – not in a sexual way, just because I can't even imagine what they must feel like. His limbs must weigh tonnes.

'I used to compete in Mr Macho competitions,' he tells me.

I must not be staring as subtly as I thought I was.

'I just, er... what's a Mr Macho competition?' I ask, moving the conversation along to try and style out my blatant staring, although I am actually really curious now that I've asked.

'You know, sort of like a Mr Universe or a strong man competition,' he explains. 'It's half getting your body looking good, half proving your physical strength – things like pulling HGVs and carrying fridges – I won a few times.'

Wow, Al must be seriously strong. I bet he could throw me around like I was nothing.

'I know what you're thinking,' Al says. 'How did a Mr Macho end up serving tea at a hotel in Morley?'

I mean, that's not what I was thinking at all, but it's preferable that he thinks that, I suppose.

'I've been doing the competitions for a while now, I'm in my mid-thirties, it's time I settled down,' he explains. 'So, I moved back to Leeds, after years living in London, and decided that I'm going to start my own PT business. In the meantime, I'm doing this.'

'Good for you,' I tell him. 'I'm also trying to get my own business going – a shop – and I appreciate how hard it is. I'm living with a stranger, just to have a roof over my head.'

'Me too,' he replies, almost excitedly. 'He's driving me up the wall. Sometimes he acts like he's scared of me and can't talk to me, even though I'm not scary in the slightest and would never hurt a fly, and then other times he's complaining about the stupidest crap. See this.'

Al rolls up his white shirtsleeve to show me his arm.

'See that?' he says. 'See how pale I'm going?'

I hold my arm out next to his. His tan makes my skin look like milk.

'Just stand next to me,' I joke.

'I used to have to tan, for the competitions, and even though I'm not doing them any more, I don't know, I just like the way it looks on me,' he says.

'Hey, you don't owe anyone an explanation,' I remind him. 'You can look, dress or tan however you like.'

'My flatmate doesn't think so,' he replies. 'He's banned me from spray tanning in the flat. I have my own machine for doing it, and I'm saving up for the business, I don't want to waste money paying for spray tans – they're expensive. But Kieran hates the smell, so I'm banned, can you believe that?'

I'm about to tell him that I can believe that, because Ziggy is exactly the same, but then I have an idea.

'Why don't you come to my house?' I suggest.

'Huh?' he replies.

'Come to my house, to do your spray tan,' I insist. 'Hell, I'll help you. You could give me one too, it's been years since I had a holiday, it might look good on me.'

'Really?' he replies. 'Are you sure? It's much easier with an extra pair of hands.'

'Yeah, absolutely,' I reply. 'In fact, what are you doing after this? Because we're throwing a house-warming party tonight. You could head home with me after work, we can give each other a tan, and then you can stay for the party, if you fancy it?'

'You know what, that would actually be really good,' he replies. 'I don't feel like I have any friends here now, we've all drifted apart since I moved away, so it will be nice to socialise.'

Al seems like a genuinely nice guy. Okay, I might only be

offering to give him a spray tan because I know the smell will drive Ziggy insane, but this party will be a good way for him to make connections with more people, and given that I've got no one else to invite, it will probably be good for me too.

'Amazing,' I say with a big smile before draining the last of my tea, almost ready to get back to work, only now I've got an extra spring in my step.

'Can I bring anything?' he asks politely.

'Just yourself,' I tell him. 'And your spray tan machine.'

17

Needless to say, as a former rock chick (who never fully grew out of the fashion), spray tans have never really been something I've considered. Sure, I dabbled with gradual tan lotions when I was in Year 7 or 8, when the height of fashion was Elizabeth Duke jewellery, blue eyeshadows, and a ponytail so high it probably caused damage, but that was a phase I didn't stay in for long.

Getting and maintaining a fake tan is not something I am familiar with, and that's why I wasn't prepared in any way, shape or form for what is happening right now.

'Are you sure you don't want a pair?' Al asks me. 'You get tops in the pack too, so I bought you a set.'

'Oh, I'm fine,' I insist. 'My underwear is black and it's definitely seen better days.'

'Suit yourself,' he says with a smile.

I'm not sure if I've made a mistake or played a blinder. See, I invited Al over to cause a stink – literally – and while that is clearly very much on the cards, something else has popped into my head. My mind is darting back to the other night when Ziggy had his band friends and Kira over, and she was teasing them all about feeling threatened by Daniel Craig's muscular body. Maybe big men do make Ziggy feel insecure, maybe she was just joking – either way, I'm not sure any man wants to compete with a guy like Al.

I love Al's confidence and his relationship with his body. Of course, it would be easy to be so proud of a body that would make a young Arnie sweat, but I still can't believe he's standing here, in the dining room, in a disposable plastic thong – you would think this would make any man feel awkward. Not Al, though. Even when he's getting his arse spray tanned, he still looks like a statue of Hercules.

'Your arse is a work of art,' I tell him honestly. 'You have, like, a textbook good bum.'

'Thanks,' he says through a laugh. 'Squats, squats, squats. You could do some, while you're down there. Make sure you put lots of colour on it.'

For a split second, I can't believe this is my life right now and I smile.

Obviously, Ziggy arrives home and walks in right as I'm crouching down behind Al's bare bum, spraying his cheeks as carefully as I can. Oh, and did I mention I was already in my underwear, because I didn't want to get any on my clothes, and it's my turn to tan next?

I feel a moment of satisfaction when I see his nose twitch, the undeniable pong of fake tan hitting his nose. Then he looks over at us. I follow his eyes as he looks Al up and down. I wait for his reaction, for him to avert his eyes, to look awkward, but his eyes eventually settle on me and he smiles. He doesn't seem uncomfortable at all. In fact, I feel uncomfortable.

'Dare I ask?' he says as he approaches us.

Al, ever the gent, turns to greet him.

'Hello, pal,' Al says, offering him a hand to shake. 'Al. How's it going?'

'All right, Al, I'm Ziggy,' he replies.

Ziggy shakes his hand. I'm shocked when the next thing he does is grab Al's bicep.

'Bloody hell, fella, they're impressive,' Ziggy compliments him.

'Cheers, mate,' Al replies, tightening everything up, striking one of the typical bodybuilder poses.

'How much can you lift?' Ziggy asks curiously, looking him over, like he's a classic car or something.

As the boys chat bodies, I chew my lip. This hasn't exactly worked the way I hoped it would. Al isn't making him feel bad at all, Ziggy is happy for him. Ah well, at least Al is lapping up the attention, and I'm getting a tan out of it so that's something.

'Are you staying for the party?' Ziggy asks him as he taps away on his phone.

'Yeah, definitely,' Al replies.

'Sweet,' Ziggy says. 'I'm off to get changed. It will be party time before you know it.'

Is Ziggy going out of his way to not really acknowledge me? I'm standing here in my underwear and all he's interested in is how much Al can lift, and if Al is staying to hang out.

'Right, your turn,' Al tells me once we're alone.

I glance up at the clock over on the kitchen side of the room. There's still plenty of time before the party.

'Okay, but I only need a light coating,' I insist, probably using the wrong words. 'Just something subtle for me.'

'You got it,' he says.

'I imagine this makes you really popular with the ladies,' I point out. 'A man who can do tans.'

'To be honest, I think muscles probably do the job first,' he says with a sigh. 'Although I think people find me quite boring.'

'You're not boring,' I remind him. Everything he's told me so far hasn't made him sound boring at all.

'I think the fancy package leads people to believe there's something more exciting going on, on the inside, and then I'm just a normal bloke.'

'Well, I think you're great,' I reassure him. 'You just keep being you. I've gone for a much different approach where I make myself seem so undesirable – that way, when someone gets a glimpse of something good, I've got nowhere to go but up. I'm keeping the bar low.'

Al laughs.

'You're great too,' he tells me. 'And you've got a killer tan.'

With no mirror in the room, I look at my reflection in the glass of the patio doors, the dark winter evening turning them into a mirror, although it does little to show my colour. I try to look at my body, like a dog chasing its tail.

'Oh, missed a bit,' Al says. 'Lift up your left arm for a sec.'

I do as I'm told, holding still while Al eliminates my last white patch – well, if you don't count what's going on under my underwear, but I suppose the tan lines will make it seem more natural.

'Oh, shit, sorry,' Kira blurts. 'I didn't realise you were... sorry!'

'What's this?' Benji asks through a snigger. 'Ziggy messaged us and told us the party was starting early. We were just killing time in the pub on the corner. What kind of party is this?'

Bloody Ziggy! He must have messaged Kira, Benji, Koby and someone I'm going to guess is Otto – although we never did meet that day he used my bathroom.

Now I really, really do feel uncomfortable. This situation has really got away from me.

'Well, we're ready to party,' Al says with an enthusiastic clap of his hands. 'I'll just slip into something less comfortable.'

There's no way those plastic pants are comfortable.

Kira ushers me to one side.

'Who is that?' she asks me quietly, nodding towards Al.

'That's Al,' I reply.

'He's like a double Daniel Craig – at least,' she marvels.

I shift awkwardly on the spot.

'I just need to go, er...'

'Oh, yeah, sure, go get ready for the party,' she insists. 'You can fill me in later.'

I smile before heading upstairs, getting dressed in my bedroom, leaving my bathroom to Al, so he can swap his plastic thong for his party outfit. Thankfully the tan only takes ten minutes to dry, so no need to attend the party in my pants.

I slip myself into a fitted gold sparkly miniskirt, and a black roll-neck jumper with a slash across the chest. Even when I try to glam up, I still need to grunge down, just a little, to feel myself.

Al steps out of the bathroom in a pair of tight (or maybe they're just tight on him) jeans and a black T-shirt.

'I meant to say to wear dark colours, because of the tan,' he tells me. 'Good call.'

'Right, let's head downstairs to the party,' I announce excitedly. 'How does my tan look?'

'You're glowing,' Al replies.

I checked it out in the mirror, when I was getting ready, and I must admit, I look strangely healthier.

I feel a bit better, having a friend here. It would have been truly tragic if everyone here was someone Ziggy knew.

I follow the music downstairs. This should be interesting...

18

It's been a long time since I was at a house party like this.

Thinking back, I was probably a student, so I suppose it's only right that I make my return to the house party circuit in Headingly.

I think the beauty of house parties is just how quickly you can make something out of nothing. You don't need to do any planning, all you need is music, booze and people – all of which can be pulled together at the last minute.

So far, it's been a pretty good night, although every time I clap eyes on Ziggy, I feel annoyed. I bet he thought he was so funny, telling people to come over early, disturbing me and Al.

There's delight in his naturally smoky eyes, and you can see his self-confidence in his posture. He's wearing tight skinny jeans and a seriously clingy T-shirt with an oddly low neck – another band I've never heard of. I hate not knowing, it makes me feel old, out of touch, and like I'm dull and mainstream now I'm older.

'You're staring at him,' Kira tells me, nudging me with her elbow before nodding towards Ziggy.

'Oh, no, I'm not, I promise,' I reply. 'Well, not like you think I am, I'm not into him, honestly.'

I'm not about to steal anyone's man – accidentally or intentionally. In fact, moving forward, I'm going to start double-checking with people that they are genuinely single.

'The two of you have been following each other around all night, constantly trying to one-up each other – who can drink the most shots? Who is the better dancer? Who can annoy the other the most?'

'I definitely don't think I'm the better dancer,' I stress.

'Ah, but the other two are true,' she says with a smug grin.

'No, Kira, honestly, just...'

'Okay, okay, chill,' she insists. 'If you two have... something, that's between the two of you.'

'Do you have an open relationship?' I ask curiously. She seems very okay with what she thinks she's seeing.

'What? Me and Ziggy?' Kira cackles. 'Serena, Ziggy and I are not a thing.'

'Oh,' I say simply. 'I thought...'

'Ooh, because of the WAG comment?' she replies. 'No, I was with Benji for a bit, it didn't work out, but I never really stopped being one of the gang. Were you jealous?' she asks me. 'About me and Ziggy?'

'No,' I insist. 'No, no, no. To be honest, he's driving me mad.'

'He's a good guy, you know,' she says. 'But I mean, come on, Al is like a masterpiece. I don't blame you.'

Oh, she must think Al and I are together.

'Right, you two, come on,' Benji insists, grabbing us by the hands. 'It's time to play a game.'

'Ooh, I love games,' Kira sings.

'What sort of game?' I ask at the same time.

A small crowd is gathered around the kitchen island.

'Truth or dare,' Benji announces, with all the creepiness and intensity of someone working the ghost train at the fair.

I take a seat on the stool next to Al.

'Are you playing?' I ask him.

'Yeah, why not?' he replies.

Okay, I definitely haven't done this in years. I wonder if we might be a bit old for this but...

'I love truth or dare,' Ziggy announces.

'Me too,' I add, refusing to budge an inch. If he thinks him throwing a crazy house party is going to convince me to move out, then he can think again.

'So, we like to play by spinning a bottle,' Kira explains. 'Lest we see a repeat of the ugly Otto incident of 2019.'

'They just kept picking me,' Otto says with a distant look of a horrible memory in his eyes.

'The bottle just makes it a bit fairer,' Kira confirms. 'And the less said about that day, the better.'

We go through a few rounds of the usual truth or dare stuff. Kiss this person, who would you most like to sleep with at the table, down your drink, and so on.

'Al, truth or dare?' Benji asks.

'Hmm, dare,' he replies.

'I dare you to do twenty press-ups with one of the girls lying on your back,' Benji says.

Al gives a casual shrug.

'I once dead-lifted a 600-pound car but okay, sure, I'll do a few push-ups with basically no weight on my back,' he teases confidently. 'Come on, Serena.'

'Me?' I squeak. 'No, no. Do someone lighter.'

'Give over,' he insists. 'I just told you I lifted a car.'

'I'm not sturdy,' I protest.

Al assumes the position as a small crowd of people gather round to spectate.

'Come on, we can do this,' he says.

'Go on, Serena, don't be a wuss,' Benji chimes in.

I look over at Ziggy. There's a slight smirk on his face, maybe. I don't want to give him the satisfaction of thinking I'm a stick-in-the-mud.

'Okay, how do we do this, do I sit on you?' I ask.

'You can't do this side-saddle,' Al tells me. 'You need to lie on top of me, face down, on my back.'

'My skirt might be too short for this,' I point out. 'But... okay.'

I somehow scramble onto Al's back and manage to roll onto my stomach. I quickly reach back with one hand to make sure my skirt hasn't wiggled up then...

'Go!' Benji shouts.

Everyone cheers Al on as he goes up and down, up and down, and somehow I can just feel how easy he's finding this. In fact, for the last one, he relies on only his right arm, throwing his left one out to the side. Such a performer.

Al lowers himself to the ground, to the sound of woops and cheers, so that I can hop off easily.

'Piece of cake,' he tells me, giving me a playful nudge.

'You're a beast,' I reply as I playfully grab him by the biceps and give him a shake – not that he budges an inch.

Soon enough, a spin lands on Ziggy. Kira gives him the choice of truth or dare. He picks truth.

'Shag, marry, kill,' she starts. 'Anyone at the table.'

'Well, shag you, seeing as though you're asking – and there are only two girls at the table,' he says, although you can get a sense that he's just playing when it comes to wanting to sleep with his friend/his other friend's ex. 'You know, I think I'd have to marry Al, because I feel like you're a useful chap to have around, and you're the undeniable star of this party. And kill... hmm... sorry, Serena, but if I kill you, then I get the house to myself.'

'Oh, that's fine,' I insist. 'I'd never shag anyone still wearing a JLS-neck T-shirt in 2023.'

My teasing goes down a storm with our audience.

'At least my top isn't ripped on the chest,' he points out.

'At least my top has a chest,' I clap back.

'Okay, okay, calm down,' Benji asks. 'Spin, Ziggy.'

Would you believe it, it lands on me. Not wanting Ziggy to give me something horrible to do, like lick a toilet, or dare me to move out, I choose truth.

'Did you sneak into my room and unscrew all my light bulbs?' he asks.

'What?' I laugh. Of course I did. 'No! I'd never go in *your* room.'

'Is this because I left your bedroom window open?' he asks. 'After you left the house stinking—'

'That's two questions,' I point out, cutting him off as I take the bottle and spin it. I sigh when it lands on Ziggy.

'Truth or dare?' I ask him.

'Dare,' he replies. 'I'm not scared.'

I think for a second. I only know of a few things that he hates (one of them is me, but I don't want him anywhere near me) so I decide to play on his dislike of strong smells.

'Go get one of the onions and take a bite,' I say.

He just laughs.

'You think that's a dare?' he replies. 'Eating a bit of onion?'

'Raw onion stinks, I wouldn't be able to do it,' I point out. 'The smell is gross.'

'Food is never a problem,' he says as he returns with an onion. I cringe as he takes a confident bite. 'Delicious.'

I can feel my nose scrunch with disgust.

Ziggy's spin lands on Al, who takes another dare, this time to down every drink at the table.

'This won't do a thing to me,' he says with a confident smile as he knocks back a beer, a shot, an alcopop and so on.

I smile at him. Anyone who thinks Al is boring is an idiot.

When Kira spins one and it lands on me, she narrows her eyes and smiles.

'Dare,' I say quickly. I know if I choose truth then she'll probably ask me if I fancy Ziggy and, well, you can fancy someone in a sort of abstract way, as the sum of *some* of his parts, but hate their guts otherwise. I don't want anything up for interpretation and I certainly don't want to try to explain myself. I've had a few drinks and I'm not sure I'm making the most sense.

'I dare you to go in that kitchen cupboard until I tell you that you can come out,' she says.

'Okay, sure,' I reply. 'Easy.'

It is easy because it's more like a tiny room than a cupboard, and there are crisps in there.

'...with Ziggy,' she adds.

'Erm...'

I look over at Ziggy. His lips are pursed and his eyes are wide, as though he's waiting to see what I'm going to do. Obviously, I won't be beaten, and I certainly won't back down.

'Sure,' I reply.

While a cupboard full of snacks might have been a delight for one person, it's pretty cramped for two. We both step in and do our best to keep our distance from one another but it's virtually impossible. Our bodies keep lightly touching, much as we're trying to breathe in and keep separate. Would this be easier if we were in total darkness? Probably, it would be easier not having to see his face. The shutter-style wooden door lets small bursts of light in, breaking up our shadowy figures with stripes of light.

'Having fun?' he asks me.

'The most,' I reply. 'You?'

'Yeah, your guy is great,' he tells me. 'This one, that's here tonight, not your other one, who was here last night.'

I smirk.

'I see.'

'It can't be said that you have a type, though,' he points out. 'Last night was a posh boy in a suit, tonight it's a bodybuilder. Wild that you have no one else you can stay with.'

'Kira was telling me you're single,' I say, lacing my words with just a touch of patronising sympathy, not that she fully confirmed it, and not that I'm in a better situation really.

'Would you prefer me to have a conveyor belt of Matcher girls moving through the place?' he asks.

I make a thoughtful face for a second.

'Would it keep you out of the lounge and the kitchen?' I reply hopefully.

'Trying to make the house reek of cleaning products and fake tan, parading your boyfriends around – and I know you swapped out the lounge schedule I agreed to with a new one, because somehow not one of my nights is when Leeds City are playing,' he rants, keeping his voice low so that the others can't hear. I don't even think they're listening, to be honest. It sounds like they're playing the game.

I may have swapped the schedule for a new one, with dates that do not favour Ziggy's desire to watch Leeds City on TV.

'You're trying to drive me out, aren't you?' he says, getting to the point.

'You're one to talk,' I reply. 'You seem to think throwing these crazy parties, filling the house with your friends, hogging the shared spaces and leaving everything a mess is going to drive me away. Not to mention the little stunts you pulled, first of all leaving the windows open to make my room cold, and then inviting everyone over early tonight, so that they walked in on me and Al in our underwear.'

Ziggy raises his eyebrows and shrugs.

'You're going to have to try a lot harder than that, if you think you can get me to leave,' I tell him. 'So give it your best shot.'

Our bodies are touching but we've both been making a conscious effort to keep our faces apart. Of course, both of us leaning backwards like this means from the waist down we're actually pushing ourselves together.

Ziggy brings the rest of his body in line with his legs, then his face. He leans in a little closer to me and exhales hard, in an attempt to project his onion breath in my direction. Unfazed (or seemingly unfazed at least), I slowly lean into it, my nose resting just next to his, my lips only a matter of millimetres from his mouth.

'I'm not going anywhere,' I whisper.

'Me either,' he replies.

It's like we're playing chicken, seeing who is going to pull away first. Thankfully the door opens, causing us both to jolt apart. It's Al, with a big dumb grin on his face.

'Room for one more?' he asks through a chuckle.

'Oh, er...' I laugh. 'I guess?'

Al crams himself in between us. Suddenly it's like there's a wall between me and Ziggy.

'You know, they dared me to join you,' he says in bemusement. 'I can't imagine why?'

I feel like my bones are breaking. I can probably guess why.

'I'm out,' Ziggy says, wriggling his way out from behind Al. He opens the door and steps back into the kitchen. I hear Kira booing him just before Al pulls the door closed again.

'Your friends are great,' he tells me. 'Honestly, this is just what I needed.'

'I'm glad you're having a good time,' I say with a smile.

'One question, though, what's the deal with you and Ziggy?' he asks curiously.

'Nothing really, beyond him being my annoying housemate,' I say. 'Why?'

'I notice things,' Al tells me.

'You notice things?' I repeat back to him.

'I'm a very perceptive bloke,' he insists, shifting his mountain of a body around in this tiny cupboard to make himself more comfortable.

I can't help but let out a squeak as he squashes me again.

'Geez, man, you're like The Thing from the Fantastic Four,' I tell him.

'What, really tanned and built like I'm made of rocks?' he asks. 'Because it's been said before.'

I laugh.

'I just mean that you're really big but... I guess so,' I reply.

'Jokes aside, I think Ziggy fancies you,' he tells me in a whisper.

I scoff.

'I think your head is made of rocks,' I tell him.

'Trust me,' he says. 'I know unrequited love – or lust, at least. I keep catching him staring at you and anytime you're with me, I can see the jealousy in his eyes.'

'That might be for your guns,' I say. 'Because he wishes he had them.'

Al looks thoughtful for a second.

'I can prove it to you,' he says. 'Permission to try?'

'Permission granted,' I say. 'What have you got?'

Al opens the cupboard door and steps out into the kitchen. As

I follow him, I notice Ziggy is sitting back down at the island. He looks at me, then back down at his beer.

I think about Al's theory for a second, but I just can't seem to get a read on Ziggy. I wonder if...

I don't get to mull it over for long before I feel myself rising up off the floor. It all happens in an instant but it takes my disorientated, booze-altered brain a second or two to figure out what is happening.

Al has me thrown over his shoulder in a fireman's carry. I've got to admit, it feels good to feel like I'm so light.

'Right then, gang, we're off to bed,' he announces. 'Good night.'

'Good night,' everyone sings after us.

As Al carries me away, I get to look back into the room and see everyone's reaction.

'Bloody hell, I hope the floor is reinforced,' I just about hear Benji joke to Ziggy.

Is Al right? Can I see something in Ziggy's eyes? There's no smirking, no taunting. Either he has the best poker face in the world, or something is going on behind those eyes. I wonder.

Eventually Al puts me down in my bedroom and slams the door closed behind him.

I feel my eyebrows shoot up.

'Oh, I'm going, don't worry,' he reassures me. 'But I'll slink out, let Ziggy think I'm up here with you all night. Who knows, maybe he's jealous? If he isn't, well, you get a night off from him messing with you.'

I kiss Al on the cheek.

'You're pretty great,' I tell him. 'Thanks for the tan.'

'Hey, thank you too,' he replies. 'Maybe see you on another shift?'

'I'd love that,' I reply.

Al – probably the closest thing this world will ever have to a Marvel-style superhero – sneaks out of my room.

I lie down on the bed, relieved to have left the awkwardness of the party now that my wingman has gone home. God, this room is awful. It's such a bleak space, the old décor really brings you down, and now the weather is getting ever colder outside, my sad little radiator really isn't up to the job.

I take off my party outfit, slip into my pyjamas and my dressing gown and then tuck myself in under the covers.

I laugh to myself. Everyone thinks I'm up here having the time of my life with Al – Benji is expecting us to fall through the floor any second – and the reality is me, in my jammies, scrolling through Google trying to work out where the best, cheapest place to buy a VHS player is (although not having much luck) as I wait for my eyes to grow heavy. I wonder if I could recruit Al to get a little petty revenge on Dean? He's been on and off my mind all night. I'd love to see Al wipe the smile off his face too.

Good old Al. Let everyone downstairs think we're up here together. I don't care if Ziggy is annoyed or jealous or what. If it drives him out of the house then great, I hope it does. If it doesn't, well, it sounds like things are about to get kicked up a gear.

19

I woke up earlier today with a lot on my mind.

There's my immediate problem of the house, Ziggy, and the war I'm pretty sure we both declared last night, then there's the sinking ship of an adult store I have suddenly found myself the captain of, and finally there's the whole Dean and Lacey thing – and that's what I can't stop thinking about.

Dean is a scumbag, pure and simple. He's a liar, he's a cheat – and (not that it's okay) there's a big difference between a one-nighter with a girl you meet when you're drunk and instantly regret, and a full-blown affair where you're lying to both your fiancée and the unsuspecting girl you're dating.

I'm in my thirties, I know my mind, I know what I want, and what I'm willing to do to get it. I went into this – whatever it is – with Dean with my cards fully on the table. I wasn't just looking for a bit of fun, I was dating with intent, trying to find someone I can settle down with. Of course, I made it clear that if that wasn't what he wanted, then no hard feelings, not everyone wants the same things. The problem is that he made me feel like we were on the same page, that we were both seeing how things went, seeing if we'd found the one this time. But I'm not the one for him, I'm the two at best.

I feel duped, but what he's doing to me is nothing compared to what he's doing to Lacey. I feel so sorry for her because she's so sweet and so hopeful. And she's not stupid, she's seen signs and picked up on vibes, but Dean has her convinced that she is the one in the wrong. He isn't some guy thinking with his pants and making a mistake, he's cold and calculated. He wants to have his cake and eat it. He's... here.

'Hey, handsome,' I say brightly.

'Hey, babe,' he replies, kissing me on the cheek.

Now that I think about it, when we're in town, he always acts in a way that could be styled out as platonic, if he needed to. What did I say? Scumbag.

'Are you okay?' he asks me as we take a seat at the bar.

'I'm doing great, how are you?' I ask, squeezing his arm.

'Yeah, I'm all right,' he says. He's smiling, but he looks puzzled. 'I was worried, after the other night, something seemed up.'

'Oh, no, it's just because Ziggy was there,' I insist. 'To be honest, he's driving me mad, so screw what he wants me to do, or not do.'

'Or who not to do,' he jokes, relaxing now that he's confident I seem fine. 'I love the lipstick.'

'Thank you very much,' I reply. 'The shade is called Scarlet Woman. I thought I'd go super bold today.'

'I'm feeling it,' he tells me, his voice getting lower with each word as he leans in closer. 'I can think of a few other places I'd love to see it.'

I smile.

'I got here a little early so I bought you a drink,' I tell him, nudging a bourbon-based cocktail towards him.

I take a sip of my Pornstar Martini.

'Serena, you look great,' Dean tells me enthusiastically. 'Those lips, that strappy dress – and you smell phenomenal.'

Does a particular smell ever take you right back to a time in your life?

I remember, back when I was twenty-six or twenty-seven, trying out Matcher for the first time, hopefully getting dressed up and going on dates with various guys (and ultimately, sooner or later, being woefully disappointed by them in one way or another). It's funny because, for my first date, I would always wear the exact same thing. I would curl my long blonde hair in the same way, wear the same little black dress, the same pair of five-inch heels (top tip: wearing your highest pair of heels is a great way to immediately weed out any crazies, because a good guy won't care, but it's an easy way to spot a red flag, if a guy gets annoyed if you're taller than him), and my make-up would be so similar each time I did it that it could've been applied by a full-face stamp. But there was one other thing I always did in preparation for a Matcher date and it's something I haven't done in years.

There was a product on sale in Lush called a Shimmy Shimmy that was basically a bar of cocoa butter infused with glitter. I would smother my skin in it, before I got dressed, leaving my skin covered with this delicate little shimmer. Of course, we all know what glitter is like, making it almost like a calling card of mine. If there's one way to leave a guy thinking about you, it's to send him home covered with body glitter, even if it's only from hugging you goodbye. That's how I look back at it, at least. I remember telling another girl about it and her suggesting I was doing it to protect myself, leaving my mark on men, tagging them, just in case anything happened to me. I suppose there's nothing as hard to get rid of as glitter, but that's a very bleak way of looking at it. More than anything, I think I just liked the way it made me smell.

Unfortunately Lush discontinued Shimmy Shimmy (potentially I was their only taker), so I kept the one bar I had left, unwilling to waste it. I broke it out today, though, for the first time in years, because it's about time my calling card made a comeback.

I lean over and wrap my arms around Dean, hooking one around his neck and the other across his front.

'You're not looking so bad yourself,' I whisper into his ear.

As I pull away, I subtly but purposefully swipe my red lips across his white shirt collar, hopefully in a place where he won't be able to spot it. Between that, and the snail trails of body glitter I'm subtly rubbing all over him, Lacey surely must notice. There's no way Dean is turning up at home with lipstick on his collar, head to toe in stripper glitter, and she's not going to even ask a question.

'Did you think any more about our weekend getaway?' Dean asks. 'I just want to get you on your own somewhere.'

'I did, I have a few potential places,' I reply. 'But I can't wait until then, I need you... Perhaps we could meet up at your place, to discuss potential getaway destinations.'

'God, I would love to,' he says, and he sounds like he means it, or part of it anyway. 'But you know what my flatmate is like, I can't bend the rules.'

Now that I *know* Dean is lying, I feel like I can push him.

'He works, right? Why don't we sneak in there when we know he's out?' I suggest. 'Imagine how hot that would be.'

'Yeah, well, he's on annual leave for a couple of weeks, so he could walk in any minute,' Dean lies. 'Best we save it for the getaway.'

'Okay,' I say with a pout. 'Well, I'd best get going, it's testing day at the shop.'

'Testing day?' Dean replies curiously.

'Oh, yeah, when the new stock comes in, it all needs quality testing, before we decide it's good enough for the customers,' I tell him.

This is the lie of all lies. I mean, imagine if that were true. I'm not even going to the shop today (I'm still very much burying my head in the sand as far as that goes). Now I've got Big Dean thinking with Little Dean, his guard is well and truly down. In fact, as he does that subtle (but not subtle at all – women can spot it a mile off) manoeuvre to disguise whatever is going on with Little Dean right now (super-apt name, because he's definitely a dick), I notice his sleeve sparkling with a double dose of glitter. I think my work here is done.

'Message me later, yeah? I'm out with the boys tonight, I'll pop over to yours after, say goodnight…'

'Will do,' I lie. 'Have fun.'

I walk out of the bar with my head held high, confident with my plan.

I called Dean earlier to invite him for a quick lunchtime cocktail. The plan was to call Lacey too, to meet up with her later when hopefully she would tell me all about the state her fiancé came home from work in. Luckily she called me first, asking if I was free to talk wedding cakes. I said yes, that I would stop by hers this evening.

That gives Dean time to get home covered in glitter, and me time to dash back to Headingly to wash mine off. By the time I'm back, he'll be out with his friends, leaving me to try to convince his fiancée that he's cheating on her – without incriminating myself.

I suppose the ironic thing is that technically Dean isn't

cheating on her any more, not in a physical way, because other than to deposit glitter and make-up, there hasn't been an ounce of intimacy between me and Dean since I found out.

He still thinks he's cheating, though, and that's what matters, that's what I need to stop once and for all. Because, even if I dump him, he'll just find another me. His bad behaviours will continue unchecked and I can't let that happen.

I may not have entered into this mess willingly but I'm certainly going to do my best to clean it up.

There's something so bizarrely exciting about spending time in Dean's apartment while he's out, oblivious, thinking he's getting away with having his cake and eating it.

Is this why people have affairs, the thrill of getting caught? It's not a good enough reason, I'm just curious.

I've been sitting with Lacey for over an hour now, talking her through the best alternatives to Diana's for a wedding cake. I can tell that something is wrong, she seems quiet, distant. It's as though her heart isn't really in it.

'Is everything okay?' I ask her. 'You seem a bit off.'

'Oh, I'm fine,' she replies. 'I just embarrassed myself again earlier today. Dean stopped by after work, to get ready for his big night out with the boys, and I made a total ass of myself.'

'What happened?' I ask, trying not to give away the fact that I already know.

'I went to greet him with a kiss, as I always do, and I noticed lipstick on his collar,' she tells me. 'Then, when I looked closer, I realised he was covered with glitter too.'

'Oh, my gosh,' I say, trying not to oversell it. 'Do you think he's cheating on you?'

'That's what I thought,' she replies.

'Well, no wonder your heart isn't in looking at wedding cakes,' I say sympathetically – it's a genuine sympathy too. Just because I know, doesn't mean I don't feel terrible for her. 'There's no way I could marry someone that was cheating on me.'

'Oh, he's not cheating,' she replies. 'I made an ass of myself by getting it wrong *again*.'

'Didn't you say he was covered in glitter and lipstick?' I remind her. 'What else could that be?'

'The people at work ambushed him with a cake, presents and a card,' she tells me.

'Why?' I ask in disbelief, struggling to mask my annoyance.

I need to rein it in a bit but I'm livid. That's not even a good excuse.

'For his birthday,' she tells me. 'It's on Sunday so, I guess with it being Friday, his colleagues wanted to surprise him today. He said they were all kissing him, and the glitter was from the card – I felt so stupid.'

'His birthday is on Sunday? This Sunday?' I say – okay, that has to be my last burst of disbelief.

'Yep,' she replies.

That bastard told me his birthday was in September. I suppose it makes sense that he didn't tell me his actual birthday, because he would always be spending that with his fiancée. I wonder if he was planning on just having a fake birthday as far as I was concerned, or if he figured we wouldn't be together for that long so it wouldn't matter.

I still can't believe what he was getting away with. It's hard to tell, with so many men not being all that into posting on social media, just lurking around to look at other people's posts, never allowing anyone to tag them in anything. I'm officially adding a low social media profile to my list of red flags – better safe than sorry.

'Thanks for listening,' she says. 'I feel so much better for telling someone. Now I can focus on finding a cake for the wedding. I can't wait to marry him. It's going to be the best day of my life.'

I get back to the task at hand, but I'm secretly fuming. I can't believe this hasn't worked, it seemed like a foolproof plan.

Ah well, back to the drawing board. I'll just have to come up with something else.

21

It's pushing half eight by the time I get home.

It's my night in the lounge but as I walk through the hallway, I notice Ziggy is in there watching TV. He hasn't said a word to me since we were in the cupboard together. I don't bother him – in fact, I probably won't even ask him to leave the room.

We'd both had a bit to drink last night and things got heated. Perhaps that was just what we needed to do, to de-escalate things. In the sober light of day, perhaps things aren't as bad as they seemed. Maybe I'm making this feud a whole thing by imagining things being much worse than they are. If that's true, I'll be glad, to be honest, because I only have the mental capacity for so many battles at the moment. It would be nice to get this one off my plate at least.

The overwhelmingly strong smell of onions hits me the second I step into the kitchen. Oh, wow, it's so powerful. I dare to go in deeper, but the smell only gets more intense.

'Ziggy,' I call out. '*Ziggy!*'

'What's up?' he asks as he hurries into the room.

'What on earth is that smell?' I ask.

'French onion soup,' he tells me, like it's a perfectly normal thing. 'Sorry, I don't have any leftovers for you, I spilt it everywhere. I did my best to clean it up, though.'

Upon closer inspection I can still see splashes of it everywhere.

'Oh, my god, it's all over the cupboards,' I point out.

'Is it?' he replies, peering over with a childlike curiosity. 'I did my best. I might need your anti-bac wipes.'

He turns and heads back towards the lounge.

He's definitely, without a doubt, done this just to upset me, because he knows I hate the smell of onions. Well, if he thinks this is going to put an end to the battle of the smells, he can think again. I'm going to find a cleaning product so strong, I'm going to need to wear a mask while I use it. This place is going to be operating-theatre levels of clean – something that will be useful if I wind up trying to stab him.

'Oh, I'll deep clean it for you later,' I call after him. 'I'm going to watch a movie now.'

Ziggy stops in his tracks.

'I figured you weren't coming home tonight so I thought I'd be safe to watch the football here,' he replies.

Oh, I'll bet that's what he thought.

'That wasn't very bright, was it?' I reply. 'Perhaps you should've spent less time making soup and more time going somewhere else to watch football.'

I do feel bad, making him turn the football off, when he's already watching it and I'm so knackered I could happily just go to bed but, come on, the man made soup just to stink up the kitchen. We're still very much at war.

'I'll grab my things and take them to my bedroom then, I guess,' he says.

I make myself a cup of tea and a sandwich, my jumper pulled

over my face to try to mask the stink of French onion soup. I grab all of my things and carefully carry it all through to the lounge. Ziggy, ever the gent, hasn't only turned the TV off, he's turned all the lights off too.

I use the light from the hallway to make my way through the lounge and put my things down on the coffee table, but when I head back over to the switch to turn the lights on, nothing happens when I flick it. None of the lamps will work either – the first thing I check is that all the bulbs are screwed in properly. They're all fine, though, and the TV isn't working either, so something more must be going on here.

I stand in the middle of the room, puzzled, because the lights are on in the hallway, so it's not like we've had a power cut.

'Good night,' I hear Ziggy practically sing from the top of the stairs.

Oh, that little shit. *He* did this. And I suppose if he did it, he knows how to fix it. Well, I'm not going to give him the satisfaction of me asking for his help.

I head up to my bedroom and grab a book and a bunch of candles to spread out around the lounge. With my mood lighting in place, I make myself comfortable in the armchair next to the doorway, so that I can read my book by the light from the hallway. I'm going to show Ziggy that, just because he thinks he's stopped me watching a movie, it doesn't mean he's ruined my night. I'll read for a bit, to prove a point, and then take myself off to bed.

I can feel my eyes getting heavy already.

22

'Serena... Serena!'

I must have been dreaming about Ziggy because I wake up thinking about his hands all over me.

It only takes a split second for me to realise that his hands are all over me. He's carrying me, sort of, dragging me from the lounge.

It's on fire!

I cough and splutter as the smoke hits my lungs. Ziggy places me on the hallway floor before grabbing a fire extinguisher – the one that is usually in the kitchen – and putting out the blaze.

I lean over, to see what's going on. The fire is out, and it seems like it was only small, but the damage is very clearly done.

There's an alcove, by the window, with fitted shelves built into it. I remember seeing them on Taylor's Instagram when she had them installed – she was so pleased with them. Well, they're all burned up now, as is the wall behind them. What's left of a burnt curtain dances in the wind coming in from the open window. It's such a mess.

Without saying a word, Ziggy reaches for my hand and pulls

me to my feet. He grabs our coats from the hooks on the wall in the hallway, and our boots from the floor, and takes me to the kitchen. We quickly wrap up before stepping out into the back garden to get some air.

'Thank you,' I tell him sincerely. 'I can't even imagine what would've happened if you hadn't been there.'

'This is all my fault,' he tells me with a heavy heart.

I look at him.

'I caused the fire.'

I furrow my brow.

'Wow,' I blurt. 'I know you want me to leave but trying to murder me is a bit extreme.'

'It was an accident, obviously,' he replies. 'I was annoyed at you, for kicking me out of the lounge, so I flipped the switch for the room in the fuse box.'

That sneaky bastard. I never would've figured out that's what he had done – I didn't even know you could do that.

'I came downstairs, to see if you'd figured it out, and I found you curled up in the chair with your book in your lap, snoozing happily in the candlelight,' he continues. 'So I tried a trick from the old book, and opened the window, to make the room cold. I thought you'd wake up uncomfortable and head up to bed in a mood. Thankfully I stuck around to see the look on your face when you did. I was in the kitchen when I smelt the smoke. The window must've blown the curtain into the candle, which knocked it over on the shelf. Serena, I'm so sorry.'

'Wow,' I say again.

My mind always goes blank at the first sign of drama, like a hedgehog curling up into a ball, waiting for the danger to pass.

'It was an accident,' he says. 'A series of dumb moves that led to something no one could have guessed would happen.'

I think for a second.

'We're both to blame,' I reply. 'All these stupid games we've been playing. Something bad was going to happen sooner or later.'

Ziggy looks taken aback, like he wasn't expecting me to say we were in this together.

I shiver.

'You go to bed,' he tells me. 'I'll make sure the fire is out and that everything is safe.'

'Are you sure?' I reply.

'Of course,' he says. 'I'm... I'm so sorry.'

'It was an accident,' I remind him. Well, it was. 'We'll come up with a plan of action in the morning.'

'Thanks,' Ziggy calls after me as I head inside.

'Thank me when I've come up with a plan to fix it,' I reply.

23

I cradle my cup of tea as I assess the damage in the harsh light of day.

'It's bad, isn't it?' Ziggy says.

'It's, er, not good,' I reply.

I cock my head. As bad as it is, it could have been so much worse.

'The positive news is that, because you had opened the window, the smoke pretty much went straight out,' I say, offering a silver lining.

'And the negative news is that the wall needs repairing and the curtain and the shelves need replacing,' he points out.

'Yeah, I've been thinking about that all night,' I say. 'So, we need a wall guy, to fix the wall. A plasterer, I'd guess. The damage looks bad but it's clearly superficial. As for the curtains, and the shelves, I checked, and Taylor puts everything on her Instagram, and she always tags the person or company she used.'

'Well, that's handy,' he says.

'Yeah, we're fortunate to be of the generation who make Instagram accounts for their houses,' I reply. 'So I know where the curtains are from, what kind they are, and I've got the name of the carpenter who did the shelves – thank goodness there was nothing on them.'

'I'll find us a plasterer,' Ziggy replies. 'Is that it? Is that how we fix this? Surely it can't be that easy.'

'There is one obvious very big problem,' I remind him. 'Paying for it all.'

'Ah,' he replies. 'There is that. I have a little bit saved up – admittedly not much, or I wouldn't be living here. I imagine you're the same?'

I nod.

'But I've got a temporary catering gig, so I'll see if I can get some more jobs,' I say.

'I'm freelance too, so the work comes when it comes, although I do have a gig tonight, which I'm being paid for. By the time it's split four ways, it's not much, but it all helps. We've got a support slot, opening for Chillz, the metalcore band.'

'See, in my day, Chillz were more of a pop band pretending to be a heavy metal band,' I say wistfully.

'You could always tell they were faking it, it was all a bit try-hard,' Ziggy says. 'But don't tell them that, if you see them tonight.'

'If *I* see them tonight?'

'Yeah, I thought you might want to come,' he replies. 'We've got a handful of guest-list spots, I can put your name down with a plus-one. You're welcome to bring one of the guys you're seeing. I'd choose Al, obviously, but it's up to you.'

Ziggy laughs at he says the last part.

'It's the least I can do, for almost burning you alive,' he adds.

I can tell that Ziggy feels awful about what happened last night, and that he believes this is all his fault, but I really do feel like I'm equally to blame. We've been pranking each other, winding each other up, trying to drive one another crazy since pretty much the day we moved in. Something like this was going to happen sooner or later. It just is what it is, that it was one of Ziggy's pranks that went wrong. The only thing that matters, in all of this, is that we make sure we fix it, that Taylor and Tim return to this house in the exact condition they left it. They were so generous, letting us both stay here, we've really let them down by being so childish.

'I'd love that,' I say with a smile. 'Just, you know, for clarity, or whatever. Dean is an ex, one I have a little platonic unfinished business with, and Al is just a friend. I'll ask him if he wants to come, though – I'm sure he will. He keeps texting me, telling me what a great time he had at the party.'

'Oh, sorry, I thought the two of you went upstairs together,' he replies, before quickly backtracking. 'Not that it's any of my business.'

'That was just Al messing around,' I tell him honestly. 'He grabbed his tanning gun and his tiny plastic thong and went home.'

'Oh, okay, cool,' he replies coolly. 'Got it.'

We stand side by side, our shoulders occasionally rubbing as we drink our drinks and stare at the damage.

'We've really stuffed this one up, haven't we?' Ziggy eventually says softly, still frozen on the spot.

'Big time,' I reply. 'But we'll sort it.'

24

I'm spinning so many plates at the moment that it's getting harder and harder to keep them all going. As soon as I start giving too much attention to one plate, I notice another is about to go. That's when I find myself suddenly scrambling to fix things, which is what I'm doing right now. It's the reason I'm at Dirty Di's. But it's not what you think.

Jen seems delighted to see me when I walk through the door, although potentially she's just pleased to see someone walk through the door, because the place is dead, just like it was last time.

'Serena, hello,' she says brightly. 'I was wondering when we'd see you again. Oliver is in the office, he said he was going to call you.'

'Oh, right, well, I'll pop through to see him, but it's actually you I'm here to see,' I reply.

'Exciting,' she says. 'Well, I'll be here.'

I step into the office and close the door behind me.

'You're back,' Oliver points out. 'I was just going to call you.'

'Yeah?'

'Yeah, just to see if you'd thought any more about your plan of action,' he replies.

'To be honest...' I lower my voice. 'I think I'm going to need to sell up. I know, I probably won't get anything for the business, but we might get a bit for the stock. Basically, I need money, fast, and I'll take whatever I can get.'

'Is everything okay?' Oliver asks, concerned, which is touching, although thinking about it, what I just said did sound quite alarming.

'Everything is fine,' I insist. 'I just have some big bills coming up, I need to get the money together for them.'

'Okay then, I'll see what I can do.'

'Thanks,' I reply.

I head back into the shop where Jen is waiting with a big smile on her face.

It's so dim in here – do adult stores have to be this dark? I understand that it's probably not a good idea to have a wall of dildos on display next to a large window, where kids might see the display, and shoppers might feel embarrassed browsing in front of passers-by, but I can't help but feel like this place is not inviting at all.

'So, come on then, what can I do for you?' she asks curiously.

'I need some underwear that will make a grown man's head spin,' I tell her very matter-of-factly.

'You're in luck then, because we have lots of that here,' she replies.

Yep, that's why I'm here, to get myself something so ridiculously sexy that Dean would crawl over broken glass just to get his hands on me.

After Ziggy and I made all the calls we needed to, to try to get Taylor and Tim's lounge back to the way it should be, I realised I had missed calls and messages from Dean, from the night before.

He obviously got boozed up with his boys and then decided to booty call me instead of going home to his fiancée. I suppose it makes sense, to a cheater, might as well nip over and bang the other woman while your missus thinks you're out with your friends. Honestly, he's brilliant. It would be impressive if it weren't so disgusting.

I called him back, to apologise for missing his call, and to tell him about the fire – if there's one good thing about, y'know, setting my friends' house alight, it's the fact that it got me off the hook as far as a drunken Dean coming over to try and get lucky goes. He's lucky I don't murder him.

'A fire?' Dean repeated back to me.

'Yeah,' I replied.

'A fire-fire?' he confirmed, not that him saying the word twice meant anything extra to me. A fire is a fire.

'Yes!' I replied.

'How bad is the damage? What did the fire brigade say?' he asked, concerned.

'We didn't need to call them,' I replied. 'It wasn't a big fire. There's damage but we think we know how to get it all repaired. We were really lucky.'

'Is this about us?' he replied, catching me off guard.

'The fire?' I replied.

'The excuses,' he corrected me. 'I feel like you never want to spend any time with me, you don't show me any affection, we're not having sex.'

'I'm sorry, there's just a lot going on,' I told him – which is true.

'Look, if you want to call it a day, if you're not into me any more, that's fine, just tell me,' he said.

That really wound me up. Imagine that: him, trying to break

up with me. I'm not proud but I'm not stupid either. I knew I needed to do something. Option one would be to agree with him and go our separate ways – it goes without saying I want nothing to do with the man, romantically or otherwise. But if I did that, then Lacey would unwittingly marry him, even though he's a big, dirty cheater, and he would carry on doing this to her forever. I like to think I'm a pretty savvy girl when it comes to men and even *I* fell for his act. So that only left option two: Operation Seduce Dean. Sort of, anyway. Just enough to get him back on the hook, and keep him there long enough for me to burn him to the ground.

So I reassured him that I was still into him and that I would more than make up for it. He bought it, for now.

'Let me get you a selection of things to try on,' Jen says. 'We have a fitting room over in the back corner.'

'Thanks,' I reply.

I must admit, I'm a little nervous. Obviously I've bought underwear before, both sexy and practical, but what I need for tonight needs to be something beyond anything I've ever worn before.

Jen hands me a stack of items.

'So, any of these will do the trick,' she tells me. 'Team any of it with a pair of crotchless tights and you can wear it under any outfit, but be ready to go at a second's notice.'

'Crotchless tights,' I repeat back to her. 'I have plenty of those, in a roundabout way, just from wearing the same pairs to death and them fading away to nothing where my thighs rub.'

'God, I hope that's not your dirty talk,' Jen teases. 'Stick with the pair I'm giving you, they're fully crotchless, plenty of room for accessing all areas, and not sharp, ripped material.'

I laugh.

'Yeah, I'll do that.'

'All the underwear is crotchless too, of course, and I've gone for full-body items, instead of sets.'

I hold up a coat hanger containing what can only be described as a series of skinny straps. I give Jen a look.

'I said full body, not full coverage,' she says through a grin.

Jen laughs. She means this in a 'it's worth a go' kind of way obviously.

'You can take them all for free, I suppose, you are the owner,' she jokes.

I close the fitting room curtain behind me and place my items on the hooks on the wall. I decide to start with the one I'm the least confident with.

'What are you trying on first?' Jen calls out.

'The strappy black thing,' I reply. 'I doubt it will stay on long – I doubt it will go on, to be honest, I feel like I have too much going on, to be contained by all these little bits.'

'Give it a go,' she replies. 'Just obviously keep your own knickers on, when you're trying things on, but definitely don't wear them underneath on the night.'

'That's a shame,' I call back. 'Because this would only look worse if I didn't have my own knickers on underneath.'

It's made from a wet-look black PU leather, with little gold hoops and hooks at the points where the straps meet. It has quarter cups which – for people with larger natural boobs, who are closer to forty then twenty – is a nightmare because things just don't sit how you would like them to. This whole thing just has too many holes generally – too many areas for squishy bits to creep out. I don't consider myself to be a large person but I think, unless everything is relatively flat and hard, something like this is going to be a logistical nightmare. All I can think about is when you tie string around a pork joint, and I imagine how you feel in these things plays almost as big a part as how you look, so I think we can rule this one out.

'Not for me,' I announce.

'Are you sure?' she calls back. 'Do you want me to have a look, see if it's the fit?'

'Erm, my nipples aren't even poking out of the same parts as each other,' I reply. 'I don't need nipple wrangling on my plate.'

'Fair enough,' she calls back through a chuckle. 'Are you comfortable being a little more specific with what you're trying to achieve? Perhaps I can find you something else.'

It's not that I'm retreating but I need to go with what works, so I grab the item that looks like it consists of the most material. It's a red lace bodysuit, crotchless, but with sheer cups instead of peepholes that are – crucially – underwired, so I can make the most of my assets, and try and keep things as symmetrical as possible. It's cinched in at the waist and barely there at the back. The thong isn't exactly sitting right over my own pants but that should be fine.

'I don't imagine what I'm planning is something that people often want things like this for,' I reply as I check myself out in the mirror.

'Try me,' Jen insists. 'We don't judge here.'

'Basically what I need is something so incredibly sexy that the man I show it to is going to want to shag my brains out, but I'm not going to shag him, ever, because he's a lying, cheating bastard, so it needs to be sexy enough that it will keep him interested in me, even though I'm not going to have sex with him.'

I whip the curtain open just in time to see Jen's eyebrows shoot up, and a bright red Oliver scurrying back to the office with a meal deal.

'I said I don't judge, I didn't say things don't surprise me,' Jen points out. 'Wow, look at you, though. I don't know why you want to do what you're planning on doing but this outfit will certainly do what you're wanting it to do.'

'Perfect,' I say with a smile. 'I probably won't even have it on for long, then I'll be back in my ugly undies, throwing on a shirt dress, and going to a gig.'

Jen walks off briefly and returns with something.

'Wear this black corset over your shirt dress,' she insists. 'It goes just under your bust. You need to show that waist off. Plus, a corset makes any outfit look better.'

'I'll do that, thank you.'

'I see a lot of Diana in you, you know,' Jen tells me. 'That must be one of the reasons she was so fond of you.'

'Please don't take any offence from this, because none is intended, but when I'm here, looking around this place, talking to you... I just don't see Diana at all.'

'Perhaps if I tell you a little more about why she opened the shop in the first place,' Jen suggests. 'Then maybe you'll understand why Di kept her two personalities so separate. If you have time, of course.'

'I have time,' I reply. 'Just let me put my clothes on.'

'You put your clothes on, I'll put the kettle on,' she replies. 'Back in a sec.'

Inside the fitting room, I look myself up and down. God, am I really going to do this? Am I going to be able to pull this off? I have to give it a go, I owe it to Lacey to try. I never even knew she existed, so it's not like I planned to hurt her, but that doesn't mean me dating her fiancé won't wound her regardless.

I grab my phone and take a close-up photo of my red-strap-clad shoulder before sending it to Dean along with the message:

Fancy keeping me company tonight?

His reply comes back almost instantly.

Yes!

I change back into my clothes and set aside the things I'm going to take home. I guess that's the perks of owning an adult store – or any store – you get free stuff. I know the financial situation here isn't ideal, but a handful of items won't make a difference.

I join Jen at the counter, where a cup of tea and a plate of biscuits are waiting for me.

Jen takes my things from me and delicately wraps them in tissue before placing them in a bag, just like she does for the customers. It's a nice touch.

'This might surprise you, but Dirty Di's came before Diana's Tearoom,' Jen explains. 'It was the early sixties when Di started selling adult entertainment supplies, before she was even twenty. I used to love hearing her stories about what things were like back then. She always used to tell me that sex toys had existed for decades, we just didn't used to market them that way back then, because obviously *women didn't do that sort of thing*. It was more a case of, you could buy vibrators that were being sold as healthcare devices, but like most things, anything is a sex toy if you know where to put it.'

I laugh.

'Things got better as the sixties progressed,' she continues. 'Di was a champion for women's rights, and a promoter of women's sexuality. When the technology picked up, and society was more accepting of adult stores, the shop really came into its own – no pun intended. Di just wanted to make people happy. Eventually she opened the tea room – with the money from Dirty Di's – but she knew that people would never accept her dildos-and-all, so she split her personality in two. I think she would have liked to open up about it more but, to be honest, she didn't want to destroy the legacy of the tea room, and I suppose she didn't want to make a spectacle of this place.'

'Wow, I honestly had no idea,' I reply. 'She really was amazing, wasn't she?'

'She was,' Jen replies. 'A feminist icon. But it turns out, if you want to make a killing on a cute tea room, then people want the face of it to be a sweet, innocent lady-who-lunches type. She was a feminist, but she was a smart businesswoman. She knew what she was doing.'

'What's it like working here?' I ask curiously.

'Interesting,' Jen replies. 'We're quiet most days but when we were busier – wow. Just after *Fifty Shades* came out – the book, then the movie – business was great. It all went downhill after that, sadly. We have some good customers – some regulars – but a person only needs to come here so often. Sex toys are serious bits of tech these days, people aren't wearing them out – the world would be a better place if we were. I have plenty of stories from over the years. The things people would try and do in that fitting room, the items they would try and return, and the things they would ask for advice about...'

'Do you like working here?' I say, reshaping my question.

'Honestly, I love it,' she says with a sigh. It sounds crazy but her eyes are sparkling while she talks about it. 'I've worked here for over a decade now. Not everyone will appreciate this, but shops like these are an amazing thing to be able to offer to people – I love making people happy. You have to read a person's body language, when they walk through that door, to figure out if they want you to talk to them or if they want you to leave them alone to browse in peace. You don't judge anyone, you help them as best you can, give them advice, help them pick out gifts for their partner – usually guessing a bra size from a photo or a series of hand gestures.'

'That's really nice,' I say with a smile. 'I'd never really thought about the positives of a shop like this.'

Wait, that isn't a sparkle in Jen's eyes, it's tears.

'Look, take this lingerie, I'll put the money for it all in the till myself,' Jen insists. 'Honestly, it's the least I can do. This job means the world to me, and this shop meant everything to Di. She worked so hard to make this a safe space for all genders and sexualities, for people to explore what made them happy. Mostly, though, she gave me a place to feel like I was making a difference. I was terrified you were going to shut the place down, so consider this a thank you gift from me.'

'That's very sweet of you,' I reply. 'But you don't have to do that.'

'I'm going to have to insist,' she says.

'I, er, just give me two seconds,' I tell her. 'I've just remembered something I meant to check with Oliver.'

I hurry into the office and close the door behind me.

'Hi, you know before, when I said I wanted to sell the business?' I start.

Oliver nods.

'Yeah, scratch that,' I tell him. 'I'm not selling it, I'm keeping it.'

'Are you sure?' Oliver replies. 'I thought you said you needed money?'

'It doesn't matter,' I say. 'This place is too important.'

After everything Jen just told me, how on earth could I sell the business now? I'll just have to come up with some other way of finding the money for the repairs.

25

The door is unlocked, the candles are lit (and I'm watching them very closely this time), and Whitney Houston's 'Saving All My Love for You' is currently playing through my Bluetooth speaker – well, it's a sexy-sounding song, and I can't resist a cheeky dig with the subject matter.

And then there's me, standing over by the window, leaning against the wall – no, leaning isn't sexy, is it? Bending? Should I be bending? No, why would I be bending right now? That's stupid.

I try hopping up on top of the chest of drawers but that just makes my dressing gown fall open prematurely, and what I'm going for is a big reveal, but a slow and steady one. What I'm doing right now has more of an Amsterdam vibe.

Ziggy is out, already at the venue – I guess they have to do soundchecks and whatever so the band has to arrive early. Before I left, I told him that Al and I would see him there – Al was over the moon to be invited to hang out with us all again. So, with the house to myself, I told Dean he should walk straight in and find me in the bedroom – I don't care if he thinks the room is a mess now, I'm not bothered about impressing him.

So, the plan was to splay myself in some sexy position but unless I want to look like a dissected frog, or like I've dropped something and I'm trying to find it under the bed, then I'm going to have to go back to the drawing board.

A knock on the bedroom door snaps me from the thoughts, making me jump. Right, okay, come on, Serena. Game face on.

I settle for standing as sexily as I can in the centre of the room. 'Come in,' I call out.

Dean walks through the door all wrapped up in his smart black coat. He's got a smile on his face – of course he has, after the photo that I sent him earlier.

'Hello,' he says.

'Hi,' I reply coyly. Then I slip off and drop my dressing gown. It hits the floor and then, a split second later, Dean's jaw does too.

Is it strange that Dean looking at my body makes me feel so gross? He's seen it before, obviously, before I found out about Lacey. I didn't mind him seeing me then. I suppose it's all about context, knowing what he's thinking, knowing what he's keeping from me.

'Babe, you look so fucking sexy,' Dean tells me as he approaches me. 'I was beginning to think you'd gone off me.'

'Oh, no, no, no, no, no,' I insist. 'Absence makes the heart grow fonder; didn't anyone ever tell you that?'

'It's not my heart that's growing,' he replies.

Gross. So, *so* gross.

'Come here,' he insists.

I walk over to Dean. There's a smile on my face but inside all I can think about is how I can shut this down as quickly as possible.

He takes my hips in his hands and pulls me close for a kiss.

Before his lips get anywhere near mine, I quickly turn around in his grip.

'I want a kiss,' Dean insists as he pushes his body up against mine.

'No kissing,' I insist breathlessly.

'No kissing, eh?' he replies excitedly. 'Is this some kind of sexworker role play?'

Jesus fucking Christ, what did I ever see in this man?

'No,' I reply, gritting my teeth. 'In fact, just a sec.'

I break away from him and dive onto my bed, leaning over it to grab something from my bedside drawer. I pop a tablet from a foil sheet and put it in my mouth.

'What's that?' Dean asks curiously. 'Something I might want to take too?'

'Oh, no,' I insist, kind of casually, as I sip from a glass of water. 'This is just for me. It's the reason we can't kiss.'

Dean had been approaching the bed until I said this. He stops in his tracks.

'Erm, why's that?' he asks.

'I've got a fungal thing,' I tell him. 'A few days on these tablets and I'll be back to normal.'

'A fungal thing?' he repeats back to me, already disgusted.

Truthfully, I have no idea what sort of fungal thing I have, I just felt certain that it would put him off sleeping with me.

I can see the cogs turning in Dean's brain. He's probably trying to work out when the last time we had sex was, and feeling relieved that it was at least a week before the day of Diana's funeral.

'Yeah, just in my mouth, and my downstairs – no idea how that got from A to B,' I say with a dorky laugh. 'But so long as we don't kiss, and we use protection, I'm like 99 per cent certain you can't catch it. And, hey, if you do, these tablets work a treat.'

'Look, if you're not feeling well, this can wait,' Dean says, sounding like he has my best interests at heart, but only thinking of himself. Obviously he can't risk catching anything – even something made up – because how would he explain that to his fiancée?

'Aw, are you sure?' I reply. 'I should be fine in a day or two.'

'Yeah, let's wait a day or two,' he replies. 'In fact, I think I'll go home, let you get your rest.'

My god, he is so predictable.

'We can still hug,' I insist, approaching him with my arms out.

It's not even funny how awkward the hug is. Dean does not want to touch me right now. The feeling is mutual, of course. I'm only doing this to slip a hot pink thong that I picked up at the shop in his pocket. Let's see him try to explain that one away as a sculpture or a birthday gift from his colleagues.

'Rest up,' he says as he hurries out of the bedroom. 'See you soon.'

'Bye, babe,' I call after him before flopping back onto the bed gleefully.

That couldn't have gone better and, with a bit of luck, I won't ever need to see him again. Perhaps the thong will do the trick. Wouldn't that be perfect?

I chew the vitamin gummy I just successfully passed off as, well, whatever you treat fictitious fungal things with, that I only pretended to wash down with water. I'm quite proud of myself – perhaps I should have been an actress?

'Hello?' I hear Ziggy call out.

Shit! Shit, shit, shit.

I grab my shirt dress and throw it on to cover up my saucy underwear. I can hear Ziggy walking up the stairs – it would probably seem pretty sus if I ran over and closed the door in his face, so I do up the important buttons and then, just as he appears in my bedroom doorway, I make out like I'm just putting on my corset over my dress, fixing it in place.

'Oh, hi,' I say coolly.

'Serena, wow, you look phenomenal,' he blurts when he lays eyes on me.

His response isn't all that different to Dean's on paper but, somehow, it couldn't feel more different.

'Thanks,' I reply with a smile. 'What are you doing here? Shouldn't you be at the venue?'

'Yeah, but, long story short…'

Ziggy turns around to show me a huge split down the arse of his skinny jeans. Hey, they don't look unlike what I've got on down there, not that I vocalise that fact, of course.

'Oh, wow,' I say. 'I won't ask how you did that.'

'Nothing fun,' he playfully reassures me. 'Anyway, I've got a pair on the radiator in the hallway, so I'm just here to grab those. Is that you ready?'

'Yes,' I reply, because clearly it is.

'Come on, then, I've got the bandwagon, I can give you a lift,' he suggests. 'We can pick Al up on the way.'

'Oh, you don't have to do that,' I insist.

'It's no biggy,' he insists.

'I might get changed, so I can—'

'What? Don't get changed, you look amazing,' he says. 'Come on, let's go.'

He flashes me a smile as he hovers in the doorway, waiting for me to follow him.

The reason I'm trying to hang back is so that I can literally slip into something more comfortable, as far as my underwear goes, but I don't want to tell him that. If I didn't know better, I'd think he knew exactly why I was hanging back. He couldn't possibly, though.

I grab my over-the-knee black boots from the floor and pull them on.

Ziggy approaches me and leans towards me – no, wait, he's leaning over me.

I don't realise I'm holding my breath until I eventually exhale, when it becomes obvious that Ziggy isn't here for me, he's just leaning over to blow out the candle.

'Right, obviously,' I say. 'I was definitely going to do that, don't worry.'

I follow Ziggy downstairs. He snatches a pair of jeans from the radiator and then heads for the door.

'I'll lock up,' he tells me. 'You get on the bus, it's freezing out here tonight.'

Yeah, tell me about it, mate. You're not the one wearing crotchless tights and crotchless knickers.

'Okay,' I say instead.

I guess I'm wearing this all night then. Great.

Thank goodness I didn't go for the strappy thing instead!

26

Arriving at the Academy with Ziggy meant parking up at the artist entrance and walking in through the back door.

The venue is situated inside a grade II listed Gothic building – seriously cool – but parting ways with Ziggy at the dressing room door meant Al and me making our way down to the door into the venue alone.

As is often the case with these beautiful old buildings, the backstage area is like a labyrinth, with multiple staircases, split levels, doors everywhere, and no real way to tell which way you're going. One minute, we're in front of a door that says 'Chillz dressing room', the next we're at one that says 'Stage door' – we definitely don't want to walk through that one.

'Over there,' Al announces proudly as a door briefly opens, letting in a burst of loud music, leading us towards where we need to be.

'Ooh, Ziggy gave me some earplugs,' I tell him. 'And some for you.'

'Are they that bad?' Al jokes.

'We'll soon find out,' I reply. 'I've never heard them before.'

'We should have looked them up online,' he says.

I laugh and shake my head.

'Ah, well, what better way to experience them for the first time than live?' I reply.

With our ears sufficiently plugged, we head out through the door next to the stage. The big, burly bloke manning it gives us a nod of acknowledgement. I say the big, burly bloke – next to Al, he looks like Captain America's 'before' picture.

'Shall we get a drink?' I suggest.

'Let's do it,' Al replies.

We head to the bar and queue for our drinks. While we're waiting for them, Al spots Kira over at the merchandise table, selling Neon City Split T-shirts and CDs.

'Wow, look at Kira,' he says. 'She looks amazing.'

I chew my lip thoughtfully. At the party I picked up on a bit of a vibe from Kira that maybe she fancied Al. I wonder if he might fancy her too.

'Let's go over and see her,' I suggest.

Kira screams gleefully as she comes out from behind the table to give us both a big squeeze.

'Ahh, I'm so glad you guys came,' she sings. 'How's it going?'

'Great,' I reply. 'How's business?'

'Oh, it's okay, it's just so boring,' she replies. 'Honestly, you date one musician for barely any time at all and somehow that saddles you with the job of merch girl for the rest of your life.'

'Do you want me to keep you company?' Al asks her. 'I could be your minder.'

'I've love that,' she replies, suddenly all wide-eyed and gooey.

Well, I guess that's me on my own then. Neon City Split are playing first, and I am so curious to watch their set, to see if they're any good. Once they're done, Ziggy said they would all head down here to watch the rest of the show.

The music playing through the speakers goes quiet.

'I'm going to head down the front, to get a good view,' I say. 'Ziggy said if we stood in a particular place, on a particular side, we would be under a light and he would give us a wave.'

'Ooh, enjoy,' Kira says as Al squashes his chunky thighs behind the table with her.

'I will,' I reply, unable to hide my chuckle as I walk off.

Al and Kira are definitely into each other, it's obvious for all to see, but they do make a pretty cute couple, and I got the impression from Al that he'd been pretty unlucky in love thus far. Kira might be good for him.

As I make my way through the crowd, I grab at the hips of my underwear through my shirt and give it a wiggle back into place – I think all the stairs backstage made it ride up or down or something.

I locate the spot Ziggy told me to stand in just as lights illuminate the stage to reveal the band. The audience gives them a welcome cheer.

'Hello, Leeds, we're Neon City Split, how's everyone doing tonight?' Ziggy asks the audience, hyping them up.

Everyone screams excitedly back at him.

'This first song is called "A Little Mad" – let's go,' he shouts into the mic.

All at once, Ziggy, Benji, Koby and Otto erupt into a lively, melodic song that sits somewhere between metalcore and punk rock.

I used to go to gigs all the time when I was a teenager – sometimes more than once a week. When I think about the local bands I used to watch, everyone fit into one category, stylistically. Either you were doing the Slipknot, Korn, Marilyn Manson kind of thing – the whole metal works, with mostly black clothing, loads of piercings and haircuts that were frankly a work of art – or you went down the punk rock route, Blink-182 style with baggy jeans, messy hair and skateboards, and if you didn't fit into either of those categories, you were probably more of an indie rock band with a clean, simple look – think Arctic Monkeys or The Killers.

Looking at the styling of Neon City Split, I don't know, this might sound crazy but it's almost as though alternative musicians have got hotter. They have tattoos and stretched ears, but gone are the days of messy, greasy hair, lip piercings and having your boxers on show because your skater-boy chains are pulling your jeans down. Ziggy is wearing a pair of black skinny jeans with a really nice white shirt. He has a pair of black braces holding up his trousers – honestly, they're good-looking boys, and they all look quite smart. This isn't what I was expecting at all.

Ziggy is undeniably the frontman, standing centre stage in front of a microphone, playing his guitar and making it look effortless. He smiles cheekily as he belts out lyrics and, when he isn't singing, he messes around, dancing with Benji, having a blast. I'm not really one for typical angry, screamy heavy metal but I really like the more commercial Bring Me the Horizon, Asking Alexandria kind of sound – and with Neon City Split clearly being so heavy influenced by the punk rock bands of their teens, it makes for such a fun sound.

It's a good song. I can't keep still. Not only is he an awesome guitarist, there's just something about his vocals that I love. He's got a great voice that is spot on for the genre, and there's this sexy, breathy edge to it. It makes my ears tingle.

They finish their song to applause and cheers from the adoring crowd. I imagine it can be a tough gig, opening for a band people have paid to see, when you're not the one they came for, but everyone seems to love them. They certainly know how to work a crowd.

'We're going to slow things down a little, with a cover,' Ziggy announces, wiping sweat from his forehead with the back of his hand. 'This is our take on the legendary Elvis Presley's "Can't Help Falling in Love".'

Ziggy counts the band in.

Credit where it's due, as much as it pains me to admit it, there is something seriously sexy about Ziggy's stage presence. Perhaps it's just a case of all women being genetically programmed to find the lead singer of a band attractive, but I don't think that's all that is going on here.

He's wearing his shirt unbuttoned all the way down. His guitar is hanging down in front of him, but his abs occasionally peek out from behind it, the sweat rolling down the contours of his body catching the bright stage lights.

It's a big move, covering someone as huge as Elvis (and to take on such an iconic song too), but they're taking a classic and putting a new spin on it, giving it a new sound. The timing is pretty much the same but the electric guitars and the drums – along with Ziggy's sexy vocals – separate it from the original. It isn't like karaoke, it's great. It's such a passionate song, something about Neon City Split's louder, heavier sound makes the message seem all the more powerful.

I'm loving watching Ziggy up on the stage. I got to hear his screams and his growls in the first song but, hearing his clean vocals in this song, wow – his voice is just so good. His presence is commanding, all eyes are on him. And I suppose it's really clever, when you're an up-and-coming support act, to perform a cover of a classic because it's an easy way to get an audience on your side, to have them singing along with your performance. Looking around the room, it seems like the crowd can't help falling in love with Ziggy – especially some of the women.

By the time my eyes wander back to the stage, I realise Ziggy is looking right at me, smiling as he sings. A shiver runs down my spine. When all eyes are on him, his eyes being on me was the last thing I was expecting to see. I feel nervous, knowing that he can see me, that he's watching me right back. He did tell me where to stand, so it's not like he picked me out of the crowd just like that, but even so, there's always an expectation that you're anonymous in a crowd, suddenly I feel like I'm on stage in front of all these people too.

With less guitar present in this song, Ziggy has his hanging from his body. He's cradling his microphone between his hands as he sings, then suddenly he winks at me, and gives me a playful little salute.

I feel something in my stomach. I know, it's Ziggy up there, and he's basically my nemesis, but do you know how many times, when I was a teen, I would fantasise about the lead singer of my favourite band picking me out of the crowd, smiling at me, seeking me out after the show before taking me backstage to his dressing room to have his wicked way with me?

He breaks eye contact with me to belt out the last lines of his song. I physically shake myself, trying to shrug him off, to get out from under his spell.

I make my way back to Al and Kira, only to find her with her legs locked around his waist as he kisses her passionately.

When all else fails, I head to the bar. I need a drink – no, two drinks. Whatever is going on in my head right now, I need to snap out of it.

I do *not* fancy Ziggy. I really, really don't.

I catch myself glancing back at the stage.

The show will be over soon and he'll be down here, annoying

me, no doubt, probably trying to get me to move out still, even though we've called a sort of temporary ceasefire.

I take a big drink of my vodka cranberry juice. Suddenly I'm feeling so uncomfortable – and it's not because of the complicated underwear I keep needing to readjust.

27

This is daft, I just need to talk to him. He's Ziggy, he's my annoying Ziggy – well, not *mine*, but you know what I mean. It's silly to be worried about approaching him. He isn't Jon Bon Jovi, he's *Ziggy*.

Now that their set is over, Ziggy is out here mingling. I've avoided him so far, watching him from afar, waiting for my feelings of contempt to come flooding back, but the longer I wait for them, the more I am struggling with how strong they really were to begin with.

He's chatting with a tall guy, with long brown hair. They look friendly, like they know each other, so now feels like my time to ease into the conversation.

'Hello,' I say brightly.

'Serena, hi,' Ziggy replies, clearly still on a high from his set.

'Hi, I'm Dan,' the tall guy says, offering me his hand to shake.

'Nice to meet you,' I reply. 'Don't let me interrupt, I just wanted to tell Ziggy how much I enjoyed his set.'

'You're not interrupting anything,' Dan insists. 'I'm just asking this one when he's going to sell me his sixties Marshall Plexi amp.'

I think he thinks I know what that means.

'It's not for sale,' Ziggy reminds him.

'Come on, I'll pay over the odds,' Dan replies.

Ziggy laughs.

'Mate, you're always asking to buy guitar gear off me, but it's never going to make you as good as me,' he teases him.

'I'll get something off you, one day,' Dan says with a laugh as he slaps Ziggy on the back. 'See you around, man.'

Ziggy purses his lips at me and raises his eyebrows in anticipation.

'You were great,' I tell him again. 'Honestly, I'm surprised, I loved it.'

'Phew,' he says playfully, pretending to wipe sweat from his brow. 'Let's hope everyone else thinks so. I'm going to check CD sales with Kira. Have you seen her yet?'

'Last time I saw her, she was being ingested by Al,' I tell him.

'Oh, shit,' Ziggy laughs. 'Maybe I'll give them a minute then. Are you okay?'

'Yeah, just, one thing,' I start, raising my voice as more and more people return from the bar and the toilets, getting into place to watch the headliner.

Ziggy ushers me to the side of the crowd.

'What's up?' he asks.

'That guy,' I start again. 'He wants to buy a speaker from you?'

'An amp but, yeah, he's always asking,' Ziggy replies. 'If it's not my amp he's after, it's a pedal or even a guitar sometimes. I'm starting to think he wants to be me.'

Ziggy laughs but his face falls when he sees the look on mine.

'Sell him something then,' I suggest.

'Nah, none of it is for sale,' he replies.

'Maybe it should be,' I respond. 'You have assets – valuable assets – and we need money for the repair work.'

Ziggy just laughs.

'Not a chance,' he insists.

'Why not?' I reply.

Really loud, really heavy metal music starts playing, and the audience erupts with cheers, as Chillz take to the stage.

Ziggy is shouting something back to me, clearly trying to explain himself, I can tell by his animated hand movements. But between the music, the crowd and earplugs, I can't hear a thing.

I point at my ears, as if to say I can't hear him. Ziggy appears as though he's trying to raise his voice, but I still can't hear him. He sighs with frustration before grabbing me by the hand and leading me towards the door to the backstage area. He flashes his pass at the security guard who lets us by.

Once we're through the doorway, and up one of the stairwells, we both remove our earplugs so we can hear one another.

'So, if I sell my gear, what personal belongings are you going to sell?' Ziggy asks.

'I don't have any,' I reply with a shrug. 'Nothing that's worth anything.'

'But you still expect me to sell my things?' he says in disbelief.

'Well, yeah,' I reply. 'You were the one who started the fire.'

Ziggy laughs and it's not a happy one.

'You've changed your tune,' he says. 'What happened to this being both our faults?'

'The stupid feud is on both of us,' I correct him. 'The fire was all you.'

'It was your candle,' he points out.

'Yeah, that I left in a safe place,' I remind him. 'You opened a window next to it.'

'I'm not doing this, Serena,' he says, marching off up the stairs.

Am I being unfair? I do feel somewhat responsible for the fire – the circumstances that brought it about, definitely – but at the end of the day, I didn't cause it, Ziggy did. I'm only working with him to fix this because Taylor and Tim should not be the ones to suffer. If Ziggy has all this expensive equipment, why can't he sell some of it to fund the repair work? Surely it's our only option?

Sticking to my guns, I follow him.

'What other choice do we have?' I ask him.

'I told you, I'm getting paid tonight, I'm seeing about some new work gigs, some new gig-gigs, I'm going to try and figure something out,' he replies. 'Just leave it out tonight, please.'

'You're being childish,' I tell him. 'If I'd damaged someone's house, and I had a collection of expensive – I don't know – kitchen appliances, I would definitely sell what I needed to, to cover my bills.'

Ziggy stops dead outside his dressing room door and leans back against the corridor wall. I stand in front of him, leaning back on the other wall while I wait for his reply.

'Since when were you such a goody-goody?' he asks me.

'I'm not,' I reply, standing up straight again. 'I'm just not an arsehole.'

Ziggy stands up straight too.

'Is that what you think I am, you think I'm an arsehole?' he replies.

I shrug my shoulders and my eyebrows in unison, as if to say: maybe.

'That's funny,' he says. 'Because the other night, at the party, before Al joined us in the cupboard, I could have sworn you were going to kiss me.'

'Oh, in your dreams,' I scoff.

'In *your* dreams,' he replies. 'You're the one getting close to me.'

Ziggy moves closer, meeting me in the middle, putting us as close as we were in the cupboard, playing chicken once again.

'Hmm, let's see, you have a bad attitude, even worse tattoos, you always seem to stink of beer whenever I'm physically close to you – which I try not to be. I think you were the one who was going to try and kiss me.'

'Yeah, that checks out,' he says sarcastically. 'The girl who talks at a million miles an hour, always seems to be nagging me about something, who cleans the house incessantly – just to wind me up – and yet somehow stills leaves long blonde hair on every possible surface. I found one in my boxers the other day.'

'Ha! You wish,' I clap back.

We're in another stand-off, neither one of us willing to back down. I feel my breathing quicken and my palms start to sweat. The only thing it makes sense to do is...

I've already made my mind up that I'm going to kiss Ziggy when I realise he's moving in to kiss me. It all happens so quickly, us throwing ourselves at one another right here in the corridor, a blur of hands and passionate kisses. Honestly, it's chaos. The result of every encounter we've had since we met – it's all built up to this. Whatever this is.

I push Ziggy's shirt off his shoulders right before he fumbles to unhook the corset over my shirt dress. Once that's off, he starts unbuttoning my dress. He's starting at the bottom, I can feel his hands knocking against my thighs, so I undo the buttons at the top myself to save time.

Once my dress is open, we break for a second. Ziggy looks down at my body, clocking my underwear, then back up at my eyes. It is as though he briefly wonders why I'm wearing such an aggressively sexy item, but then just decides to go with it.

He pulls me back into his arms, edging me towards the dressing room door. He pushes me against it for a second before opening it so we can go inside. Probably best we don't do this in the corridor.

Wow, I always imagined backstage being more glamorous than this, but who cares right now?

I push Ziggy back onto one of the black leather sofas and sit myself down on top of him, reaching forward to fumble with his zip as we continue kissing.

Honestly, it's like he's pulling me in, now we've started kissing I don't know how to stop. As well as feeling intensely attracted to him, I'm still so mad at him, I feel like I'm taking my anger out on him by kissing him, which doesn't make a tonne of sense, but I can't resist going with it.

I can feel the vibration from the loud music below us buzzing through the floor, the walls, through the furniture even. As Ziggy places a hand on the back of my neck, it feels like my entire body is vibrating too.

I've never disliked someone, been so mad at them, and yet wanted them so badly at the same time. I'm powerless to stop myself. I'll just have to worry about the consequences tomorrow...

28

A grown woman, hiding in her bedroom, how tragic.

Last night was... I don't even know what last night was. I know that it was amazing, mind-blowing, the best sex I've ever had in my life. And it wasn't even that awkward after, I think we were both a bit stunned, but we put our clothes back on and headed back down to the gig in a very civilised manner. I hung around for a bit but then I found myself making an effort to avoid Ziggy, so I decided to make my own way home.

I went to bed long before he got home and I haven't left my room since – except I have to leave now, because I've got a catering gig, and we need all the money we can get. Oh, and because, pathetically, I've needed a wee for like two hours now.

I just... I don't want to see him. I don't know what to say to him, or how to be around him. Whatever we did last night has rattled the anger out of me and now I don't know what I'm left with.

I'm hovering near my bedroom door, all dressed up and ready to go, when I feel my phone vibrate in my hand. I glance at it and see that it's Lacey.

I hope this isn't weird, I know that we haven't known each other very long, but would you like to come to my engagement party next week? Really appreciate everything you've done for me, girl. x

Well, the panties in the pocket clearly didn't make it home with him. How can she be so blind? I know that I didn't realise, at first, but I didn't live with the guy. We were dating, I had no reason to doubt anything he was telling me, nor were we officially exclusive, although I'd hoped we were – ha!

Aww, that's so sweet of you. I would've loved to but I'm working every night next week. Gutted, but hope you have a wonderful time. x

As soon as I hit send, I wonder whether or not that was the right thing to say. In hindsight, I should've asked her when it was, and then told her I was working on that specific day, but I didn't think about it like that because the bottom line is: I can't go to her engagement party, because she's marrying Dean. She can't marry him, she *can't*.

I poke my head out of the bedroom door. I look right, then left – as though I were crossing a road – and then I make a dash for it to the bathroom opposite. After using the loo and brushing my teeth, I psych myself up to make the dash for the front door. Once I flush this toilet, that's it, I'm giving my position away.

I press down the lever then make a run for it. As I walk across the landing, I notice that Dean is calling me. He's the last person I want to speak to – but then I get to the top of the stairs, and notice Ziggy turning to walk up them, so I answer the call.

'Good morning,' I say brightly into the handset.

I catch Ziggy's eye as I walk downstairs.

'Hey, how are you?' Dean asks me.

'I'm good, I'm great, I'm just running late for work,' I tell him, although I'm saying it for Ziggy's benefit, of course.

I give Ziggy a slight wave, and then point at my phone, as if to say I'm on the phone, which is pointless, but I feel like it gets me off the hook from having to interact with him right now.

'At the shop?' Dean asks, flirtation in his voice.

'Nah, a catering gig,' I reply as I walk out of the house.

I'm probably coming across as a bit colder than I should be. I have no feelings (not good ones at least) for the man at all, my reflexes are not friendly ones.

'You're pissed at me,' he says with a sigh. 'Is it because you didn't get any action last night?'

I smile to myself.

'I'm not pissed at you,' I say, lying generally, but being honest about last night, I guess.

'In hindsight, I think I might have been a bit hasty,' he replies. 'You were all dressed up, looking so good, and I was immature. I was just looking at the photo you sent, and thinking about how good you looked, and... I'm kicking myself today.'

Is this guy for real? Wow.

'I'm not mad at you,' I insist, adding a little sparkle to my voice. Now that I know being infected with some mysterious infection isn't going to put him off, there's no point continuing to say I have one. 'It's actually all cleared up now.'

'Tonight then?' he suggests. 'Last night, take two?'

'Ahh, can't tonight, I'm working all day, a long day, a wedding,' I eventually babble out.

'Oh, right, well, if you're not too tired, give me a call and, if you're knackered, maybe tomorrow afternoon?'

'Yeah, I can see,' I reply.

'Actually, shit, no, not tomorrow afternoon,' he quickly says. 'Evening, maybe?'

Interesting. He must have plans with Lacey tomorrow lunchtime.

'I'll keep you posted,' I reply.

'Okay, well, have a good wedding,' he says.

'You too,' I reply. Oops, Freudian slip. 'I mean have a good day.'

Dean laughs.

'See you soon, sexy.'

I shudder as I walk down the street. It's hard to believe I used to fancy him because these days everything about him gives me the ick.

I quicken my steps, making sure I don't miss the bus into town. I've been prewarned that today's party is a kids' party, which isn't going to be the best with a bit of a hangover, but I need the money.

I wonder what Ziggy is doing, to raise his share – a share which should be greater than mine, in my opinion.

Well, even I know you don't play with fire. Hmm, actually, I suppose that's not quite true.

29

I'm absolutely starving, after a hectic day working at a kids' party, so the first place I head when I get home is the kitchen. Fascinating, really, that a level of hunger exists where I'm happy to face Ziggy if needed.

I walk into the kitchen to find him sitting at the island, hunched over a laptop, shovelling crisps into his mouth.

'Hi,' he says before he takes a swig of his beer. 'Good day at the office, darling?'

I can't help but smile.

'Yes, but I'm starving, sweetheart. What's for dinner?' I reply.

It's strange because we're joking, but it's almost passive-aggressive.

I take the cash I got paid today and slap it down on the island next to him.

'For the fire fund,' I say. 'To go with your gig money.'

'You say that like you think I haven't put any in the pot,' he replies. 'But I have. And I'm just applying for not one but two jobs.'

'What do you even do?' I can't help but ask.

'Well, one is a guitar gig, which would be great, but my day job is something techy and serious,' he says proudly. 'There's a Leeds-based start-up in need of an online store.'

'You make online shops?' I say.

'I work in e-commerce,' he corrects me. 'But, yes, one part of my job is creating online marketplaces for businesses. Not expecting that, eh?'

'I wasn't expecting you to be useful to me,' I reply.

Ziggy pulls a face.

Has a potential answer to not one but two of my problems fallen into my lap? No pun intended, obviously, although I can't help but smile to myself for a second.

'I've inherited a sex shop,' I blurt.

'Erm...' Ziggy laughs. 'You've...'

'Yeah, an adult store, I mean, I've inherited one,' I reply. 'It's not making any money, though, and it's a leasehold property, so there's nothing to sell except stock.'

'Ahh, so you think selling online might be the answer?' he replies.

'Don't you?' I say. 'If you work with me on this, this could be how we get our money together for the repairs.'

'I think it's a great idea,' he says. 'And I'm happy to help. Putting together a website with a marketplace isn't a quick job, though.'

My face falls.

'But, while I'm working on it, we could definitely sell on eBay,' he replies.

'I can put you in touch with the business guy there,' I say. 'He can send us details for whatever sells best. How soon can we get online?'

'On eBay, as soon as I get the info,' he replies as he hops to his feet. 'You're a bit of a dark horse, aren't you?'

Oh, god, it's happening again. The tension is building. He's pulling me in.

Ziggy reaches out and places his hand on the back of my neck. Flashbacks from last night fog up my brain. I need to focus.

'You touch me like you think you know me,' I say as I move closer to him.

'I do know you,' he replies. 'Last night…'

'Last night shouldn't have happened,' I say. 'It was a one-off.'

'Oh, yeah?'

'Yeah,' I reply. 'I'm not going to be your F-buddy. We're not even buddy-buddies.'

'No, of course not,' he says with a firm nod.

And we're kissing again, fantastic. The same wild, passionate kissing from last night. Until we hear someone clear their throat.

'Am I interrupting something?' a fifty-something Yorkshire man asks.

'Serena, this is the plasterer,' Ziggy tells me.

'Has he been here this whole time?' I ask.

'I can hear you, you know,' the man says. 'At least wait until I've gone before you start screwing on the worktop.'

He seems almost angry at the idea. I bite my tongue.

'Here's the quote, boss,' he says, bypassing me, handing a piece of paper to Ziggy. 'So, do you want me to do it?'

I raise my eyebrows. He's keen.

'Can you give us a minute?' Ziggy asks him. The man makes a face. 'Only to discuss the quote.'

'Aye, fine,' he replies. 'I'll be in the other room.'

'Right, he seems like a proper weirdo,' I whisper to Ziggy once we're alone.

'A weirdo but the cheapest of the three quotes,' he whispers back. 'And we said we needed to get a cheaper plasterer if we wanted to afford the same carpenter, to put the same shelves up.'

'That's true,' I reply.

'He said he can do it tomorrow, with the quick-drying plaster, and that he would paint it for us,' he continues. 'If he does that, the carpenter can come in a couple of days – his only availability for two months, he's about to start a big job.'

Ziggy is surprisingly quite useful in a crisis. I'm impressed with the organisational skills I didn't realise he was hiding – although I suppose I should have been tipped off by his organised efforts to try to drive me out of the house. At least he's using his powers for good now.

'Okay, fine,' I reply. 'But you can wrangle him. He has crazy eyes and he doesn't seem to be very fond of me. I'm grabbing some food and I'm going to bed.'

'Of course,' he replies. 'I'll go tell him he starts in the morning.'

Ziggy gives me a playful nudge before he goes off to give the plasterer the good news. I turn around and begin making myself something to eat.

I can't believe I kissed him again, what's wrong with me? What's wrong with both of us? And why can't I stop thinking about doing it again?

30

This bedroom has never been all that warm while I've been living here, thanks to the dodgy radiator, but tonight it is beyond freezing.

On what is being dubbed the coldest night of this winter so far, I am genuinely wearing my coat in bed. I tried to google it, to see what was going on with the partially warm radiator and if there was anything I could do to fix it. Some websites said it might need bleeding, others made it sound more like all the radiators in the house needed balancing – not that I really know what either of those things are, and I'm too scared to do anything that might cause the room to flood the lounge below (although that would have been helpful when the fire was blazing).

I get out of bed and drag my duvet over to where the radiator is. I sit on the floor, with my back against it, and pull my quilt up to my chin. I just need to think warm thoughts and see if that helps. Obviously when I'm thinking about things that will get me hot under the covers, my thoughts jump straight to Ziggy, which annoys me, I feel like my brain is betraying me. I resent thinking about our encounters when he's probably up there all nice and warm and cosy in his bed, basking in the heat from the fancy new radiator – and in his en suite with the underfloor heating too. Do you think he'd let me sleep on his bathroom floor?

Hmm, I think I've had an idea... No. No, I can't do that. Can I?

I shrug off my covers and dump them back on my bed before throwing off my coat. My fleecy pyjamas may be the warmest I own, but they're certainly not the most attractive. I have a night-dress – a black strappy thing with lace edging – that I've some-times been able to pass off as sexy. That will do perfectly.

My skin hurts as I take off my pyjamas and pull on my night-dress. The material running over my goosebumps feels like a razor blade. I look in the mirror and run my hands through my hair, then I grab my perfume and spritz my neck and my wrists.

I leave my room and head upstairs, to Ziggy's room, where I hover behind the door for a second. I place my ear on it lightly to see if I can hear anything but it's silent.

Yes, in theory, I'm thinking about seducing him so I can sneak myself into his warm bed, in a roundabout way, but that's not the only reason I'm doing it. That kiss in the kitchen has been on my mind since it happened and I can't help but think I would've ended up in bed with him sooner if the plasterer hadn't been here.

I knock on the door.

'Ziggy? Are you awake?' I ask softly.

'Yep,' he calls back, although he sounds a little sleepy. 'Come in?'

I step into the room, close the door behind me and let my dressing gown fall to the floor.

'Oh,' he says with a smile. 'Definitely come in.'

* * *

I lie back on the bed, certainly much warmer than I was when I came upstairs, so much so I kick one of my legs out from under the covers.

'Well, that was unexpected,' Ziggy says breathlessly.

'Mmm,' I reply, sleepier than ever now.

I roll onto my side, facing away from Ziggy, but I tuck my butt right up into him. He's so warm, like a human radiator. I'm the comfiest I've been since I moved in here.

'Anyway,' he says.

I open my eyes suddenly and roll over.

'Are you hinting at me to leave?' I ask.

'I'm not hinting,' he says plainly. 'You said it yourself, you don't want to be F-buddies. You said we weren't even friends. Any second, you're going to tell me you've made a mistake and... wait a second. This wasn't a mistake, was it? You came up here to sleep with me.'

'Yeah, obviously,' I reply with a frown. 'And you're welcome.'

'No, I mean you literally came up here to sleep,' he says. 'Oh, my god, is this because your bedroom is cold? Is that why you're here?'

I mean, it is and it isn't, but I'm annoyed he's seen right through me.

'Charming,' I blurt. 'You know what, forget it, I don't want to share a bed with you anyway. I just fancied a repeat of last night but, do you know what, without vibration from the metal gig going on in the room below, you're not actually up to much, so... good night.'

I pop my nightdress back on and storm back down to my bedroom. Wow, it feels even colder now I've been in a room that is so much warmer.

I put my coat back on and get into bed, pulling the covers up as high as they'll go – pretty much to my nose. Tears prick my eyes. Everything feels like such a mess.

A few seconds later, there's a knock on my door before Ziggy walks in. He gets in bed next to me.

'We're swapping rooms for the night,' he tells me. 'I had no idea you were so cold down here. I'm not that cold, in fact, I'm usually too warm at night so, go on, you go sleep upstairs.'

'Are you sure?' I ask.

'I'm sure,' he replies. 'You can't be sleeping in a coat, Serena. Go on, take my room, I'm more than warm enough.'

'Thank you,' I say sheepishly.

I grab my phone and ditch my coat.

'You're sure?' I check.

'I'm sure,' he replies. 'I'll see you in the morning.'

I head upstairs and get into Ziggy's bed alone. It smells like his aftershave – oh, god, I'm sniffing his pillow like a crazy person. I wrap my arms around the pillow and close my eyes.

Perhaps he's not all bad after all.

31

A knock on the bedroom door wakes me up.

'Come in,' I call out.

'I thought you might like a cup of tea,' Ziggy says as he enters the room with two cups.

'Oh, thanks,' I reply, pleasantly surprised.

'Jay, the plasterer, is here already,' he replies. 'I've given him the spare key, in case you need to go out today. I definitely need to pop out and I didn't want you feeling like you had to wait in with him.'

I look at my phone through my sleepy eyes. Shit, the sale at Diana's is today. I still have my heart set on getting that vase back, but there's no way they're going to sell it to me, not if Agatha and Andrew are around.

Ziggy sits down on the bed.

'Can we put... whatever this is aside for one second and talk like adults?' he asks me.

'Of course,' I say, taking my tea from him.

'Are you okay?' he asks. 'Like, are you really okay? Because I'm starting to think something might be wrong.'

His kindness and concern floor me. Tears fill my eyes. I quickly wipe them away but there's no way he hasn't seen them.

Ziggy shifts up the bed, sitting on the pillow next to me.

'Talk to me,' he insists.

I rest my head on his shoulder.

'Is it about the shop?' he asks. 'I reached out to Oliver, the one you left me the details for, and he's already sent me over a list of stock to list. They're online already, I've been up for a while. Or is it about that guy? The ex with the unfinished business?'

I swallow hard. I don't know where to begin.

'Let me tell you about my problem,' he suggests. 'You might find yours easier to talk about if you hear how stupid my life is.'

I laugh.

'Try me,' I say.

'I've been playing guitar ever since I was a kid,' he starts. 'Classical guitar was the first instrument I learned, it was only as I grew up that I felt like I needed to do something "cooler" with my talents. Anyway, when I was trying to get started in music, I used to play guitar with a young adult orchestra, mostly made up of twenty-somethings – so we're talking more than five years ago, this wasn't recently, and we mostly just did it for fun, playing local concerts and festivals. Long story short, I upset one of the guys – his name was Mark Willis. When we parted company, he said I was a fuck-up and a liability and that he would never work with me again.'

'Wow,' I say. 'Why did he say all that?'

'In all honestly it's probably because I was a fuck-up, a liability, and not the kind of person you would want to work with,' he admits. 'I had sex with the cellist he fancied, at a party at his house, where I spilt a bright green drink on his light grey carpet.'

'Oh,' I say.

'And then I slept with her a second time, right before a

concert, and broke her cello in the process, so that was a whole thing.'

'I won't ask how,' I say through a slight laugh.

'It's not as bad as it sounds,' he quickly insists. 'But back then I just didn't take anything seriously, I wasn't trying to hurt anyone or anything, I was just young and stupid. Anyway, flash forward to this week, and I've just found out that there's a string quartet doing a string of shows in Leeds next month – no pun intended – and the guitarist accompanying them has had to drop out at the last minute due to illness. I know the person organising it, so I was hoping I might be able to get the job. But the person organising it is...'

'Mark Willis,' I say, finishing his sentence.

'Bingo,' Ziggy replies. 'And I figured, fortune favours the brave, so I just called him to throw my name in the hat and he scoffed at me. I don't know, I didn't like the way he made me feel, and I do really want the job – and I would of course take it seriously this time – so I lied. I told him I was a changed man – that I owned a house, I had a girlfriend, and that if he gave me another chance, I would show him just how much I've changed. And I have changed, I really have, just not *that* much. It turns out he hasn't changed much either because he immediately called my bluff, and asked if he could come and see my house, and meet my partner. I told him I'd check if it was convenient and get back to him but, you know, I was lying, so the whole thing is dead in the water. I'm disappointed but what can I do? All actions have reactions. I can't expect Mark Willis to believe I've changed just because I pinkie promise him that I have. And obviously I've made the whole thing ten times worse by lying.'

'Oh, wow, that's a lot,' I reply. 'My problems are... not as fun.'

'Well, if you want to talk, I'm here,' he says.

'I lost someone,' I say softly. 'Diana, my boss, except she was so much more than a boss to me. She gave me a job, she put a roof over my head – she's the one who left me the business. There's so much going on at the moment, I can't think straight... I'm trying not to think about her. I don't know what to do with the grief so I'm just storing it up, hoping I can deal with it another day, when there's less to worry about.'

'It's hard, losing a loved one,' Ziggy says, taking one of my hands in his. 'Grief hurts but it doesn't have to be a bad thing. Grief is how we keep loving people when they're not around any more. Diana might be gone but you're still loving her – those are feelings you're having. Don't try to squash them, embrace them, miss her, love her like she's still here.'

My eyes well up. I blink the tears away.

'This is going to sound so stupid,' I start.

'More stupid than me breaking a cello during sex?' Ziggy jokes, trying to cheer me up.

'Potentially,' I reply. 'Diana gave me a vase, while she was still alive, something she had painted herself. It offers nothing beyond sentimental value, and only to me, but her horrible daughter, Agatha, decided I was trying to steal it and took it from me. It's being sold today, along with everything else at the tea room. They're selling off her business, which she never wanted to happen, which is why I feel so much pressure to make her shop do well. If Diana's can't live on, then perhaps Dirty Di's can.'

'Not letting you have that vase is horrible,' Ziggy says. 'I'm sorry.'

'The worst thing is that Agatha isn't even the worst person in my life,' I continue. I pause to sip my tea. 'Dean, my ex, if I can even call him that because we were only dating, oh, and because as far as he knows, we still are.'

'Go on,' Ziggy says, clearly curious.

'I found out he was engaged when his poor unsuspecting

fiancée came into the tea room to ask about engagement party catering and wedding cakes,' I say. 'I was shocked and angry but mostly I just felt sorry for this woman who was excited to be spending the rest of her life with the man of her dreams. I would've told her except he has her convinced that she's paranoid, I knew there was no way she was going to believe me.'

'You're trying to help her catch him on her own,' Ziggy chimes in. 'You're setting him up.'

'I'm trying to,' I reply. 'It's not going very well.'

Ziggy thinks for a moment.

'What are you doing today?' he asks me.

'Nothing,' I reply. 'Why?'

'Clearly we both love a good scheme,' he points out. 'I think we might be able to help each other out.'

32

We all have our comfort movies – those films we can watch time and time again, the ones we can't resist flicking on every time we see them on the TV guide, the ones we search for on Netflix at the end of a tough day. Watching a new movie is like rolling the dice, you don't know if you're going to love it or hate it, if you're going to laugh or cry, if a dog is going to die and ruin the whole thing! So we reach for our old favourites for the comfort of the familiar, because you can always count on your favourite movies to make you feel better.

Ziggy's comfort movies, it turns out, are heist movies. He's a huge nerd for all things heisty and is somewhat of an expert when it comes to everything from the classics to the lesser-known flicks.

'I'm beyond impressed with your outfit,' I tell him.

'You've got to look the part, haven't you?' he replies.

Ziggy looks incredible. He's wearing a navy-blue suit – complete with tie and waistcoat – with a long, smart black coat over the top. He's wearing a black trilby hat that comes with peculiar leather ear flaps, and he's carrying a vintage doctor's bag.

'Thanks,' he replies. 'Most of this stuff belonged to my grand-dad, he left it to me when he passed away. He would always say I was an interesting dresser, and that most of his stuff would probably come back into style if I waited long enough. We might not be at a revival of ear flaps just yet, but it's going to help me look the part today.'

'I can't believe your thing is heist movies,' I say with a laugh as I follow him down the street, heading in the direction of Diana's.

'We all have to have a thing,' he says with a shrug and a smile. I love that Ziggy isn't afraid to unashamedly like what he likes – not that there's anything wrong with heist movies, but I love how willing he is to own it. 'Knowing the components of a good heist is going to get you your vase back.'

'Go on then, educate me,' I insist. 'I want to learn.'

'Okay, I'll bite,' he replies, 'even if I suspect you're just going to laugh at me.'

'It's not that I think it's funny,' I insist. 'I'm just amused that you're using what some people might consider movie trivia in everyday life. I'm fascinated.'

'Well, a heist movie is usually split into three acts,' he explains. 'There's the planning, the execution, and finally the aftermath. We have a plan – which I'll run through with you before I go in. As far as the execution goes, a good heist will have a solid plan – and the audience will know how the plan is supposed to go – but problems will arise and that's where the twist will come in. I live for a twist in a heist. Think *Inside Man*, *The Usual Suspects*, *Ocean's Eleven* – no? What about *Snatch*, you must've seen *Snatch*?'

I shake my head.

'Mafia movies are my go-to,' I reply. 'And musicals, bizarrely.'

'You'd love *Snatch*,' he insists. 'We'll watch it sometime, I won't spoil it, but just know that a good heist relies on a twist that the unsuspecting audience isn't privy to – it's the key to victory.'

'Okay, let's get our plan straight,' I say. 'We're almost there.'

'Well, we're only after getting back a vase from the closing down sale at a tea room, we're not exactly stealing an eighty-four-carat diamond, but the stakes are just as high, so I've given this a lot of thought,' he says. 'If we're going to sell this, I need you to tell me anything you can think of, about the tea room, about Diana, her family. That way, if selling myself as an art collector doesn't quite work, I can try and paint myself as a tea room enthusiast – maybe even Diana's biggest fan.'

'She had plenty of those,' I reply through a smile. 'Diana was one of those people who touched hearts everywhere she turned. She knew how fortunate she was to have found so much success with her business, but she didn't hoard her wealth, she splashed the cash left, right and centre on those who needed it. There would always be one sweet treat – a different one each month – where she would promise a portion of the proceeds to various charities she donated to.'

'That's amazing,' Ziggy replies. 'Not many people are willing to do that.'

'That's not all,' I confide. 'Before her husband died – his name was Armand – the two of them would dress as Santa Claus and Mrs Claus and visit multiple children's wards in West Yorkshire hospitals, to give out gifts to the poorly kids. When Armand passed away, you would think she would've stopped but she kept going, every year, doing it alone, telling the kids that Santa Claus was too busy at the North Pole, working non-stop with the elves to get everything ready for Christmas. One of Diana's most admirable qualities was the way she never turned her back on her commitments, no matter what was going on in her personal life.'

'Did you know Armand well?' Ziggy enquires.

I shake my head.

'He died before I met Diana,' I reply. 'She used to talk about him all the time, though, about how wonderful he was – she was always bursting with love for him. She always used to say that, no matter what happened, she would never marry again. That she made her vows to Armand and that she would never break them. To her, the "till death do us part" meant both of them. Then again, it sounds like they were a real dream pairing, and when you have a relationship that's so perfect, how can you ever find anything else that seems worth it?'

'Yeah, I guess,' Ziggy replies.

'That's the beauty of my approach,' I start. 'Staying single for most of my life, breaking the habit for nothing more than absolute scumbags. That way, when I do find someone I want to marry, the bar is so, so incredibly low, the only way is up.'

'Solid plan,' Ziggy says through a chuckle. 'I wouldn't say I've been dating scumbags, but I definitely feel like the only way is up. You might be on to something.'

'Ooh, look, over there,' I say, pointing out the tea room across the street.

It's strange, seeing it without the usual lunchtime queue of people, either hoping to get a table in the tea room or to look in the shop. It's also so bizarre to see the door unmanned. No dapper-looking gentleman pulling open the large glass door by its long, thick golden handles. It was a Diana's trademark, everyone loved being greeted – I wonder if any of them would like a job at Dirty Di's, greeting customers, welcoming them inside. It's probably too different a vibe, though, and lord knows what the uniform would be.

'So, Diana's Tearoom, Yorkshire institution, end of an era,' Ziggy practises. 'I want unique pieces for my collection. One-of-a-kind items of Diana's memorabilia, to commemorate one of my favourite places, and remember one of my favourite women.'

'Perfect,' I reply.

'How long did Diana do the Christmas thing?' Ziggy asks curiously.

'Oh, basically forever,' I reply.

'Hmm, perhaps I'll say she visited me in hospital when I was a kid,' he muses.

'I mean, let's not make up any horrible stories,' I reply.

'Well, she might have,' he insists. 'I spent a Christmas in hospital, when I was a kid. I had pneumonia, I almost died.'

My heart skips a beat. Is it silly that I'm sort of retrospectively worried about Ziggy's health? Imagine if he had died, if we'd never met. We wouldn't be standing here now. There would be a hole in my life – a hole I wouldn't even realise was there. It doesn't bear thinking about. But, look, I know we're not exactly anything in particular to each other, but the thought of never meeting someone special – never meeting my Armand – is a truly devastating thought indeed.

Diana had no regrets, that I know for sure, she was so beautifully proud of her life, her marriage, of all her achievements. She lived every day in a bubble of bliss, refusing to let negativity inside, because she believed dwelling on the bad things or thoughts was the fastest way to rot your happiness from the inside out. I'm trying so, so hard not to feel the devastating sadness that losing her has left me with. I'm trying to remember the good times, to be proactive to save the shop. But first I need to get that fucking vase back. *My* vase. I swear, once I have it, I'll turn my back on negativity, I'll look to the future with my head held high. And the vase, that my late great friend gave me, safely at home in my house. Or whomever's house I happen to be crashing in at the time, obviously.

'I'm okay now,' Ziggy tells me with a smile, clearly having seen the look on my face.

'Oh, yeah, I know that,' I reply, casually shrugging it off. 'Right, I'll stay out here, hiding myself out of the way, while you go inside and work your magic.'

'I'd say wish me luck but I'm not going to need it,' he says confidently. 'It's a heist!'

Calling what we're doing here a heist feels a little over the top, given that we're just going to go in and buy the vase. It isn't even worth anything so no one in their right mind would try to sell it for more than I can afford.

'I can tell the place looked beautiful before but it's starting to look pretty picked over,' Ziggy tells me through his earpiece. Well, it's not an earpiece, it's an AirPod, but for the purposes of the heist, it's an earpiece.

'Maybe it's best I don't see the place being stripped for parts,' I reply, hugging myself.

'So, as far as I can tell from the instructions, you just make offers on items, and they are either accepted or they go to auction to see if they do better there.'

I exhale deeply.

'This is oddly exciting,' I admit. 'I hope no one has bought it.'

'I'm just looking it up in the auction catalogue, I'll let you know,' Ziggy says.

His voice sounds funny, like he's trying not to move his lips while he speaks. I suppose he isn't moving them, otherwise it would look like he was talking to himself.

'Bloody hell, everything is for sale, from the ovens to the chairs to the CCTV – it's all up for grabs today,' he tells me. 'And here is your vase. Lot 2183 with a guide price of £8. I'll offer them £10, to make sure it's a done deal.'

'My hero,' I tell him.

I wait patiently as Ziggy makes his way through the busy tea room. I can't see in the windows from across the road, but I can hear the crowd noise in the background of the call. Everyone wants a little piece of Diana's or, at the very least, a bargain.

'Yes, I would like to make an offer of £10 on lot 2183,' I hear Ziggy say in a well-to-do accent that is not his own.

'Lot 2183,' a second male voice replies. 'Let's see.'

'You want to buy the vase?' a familiar voice replies. There's no mistaking Agatha's voice, I hear it in my nightmares. 'Why?'

'Why, I'm a collector,' Ziggy replies, his accent a bizarre mixture of an old English gentleman and an oil man from Dallas. 'I'm always on the lookout for unique pieces of unknown origin. I'm also a big fan of the tea room and I can't think of a more exquisite piece to keep hold of a little bit of history.'

'You collect random vases?' I hear Agatha reply.

'We all have our interests,' Ziggy reasons.

I hold my breath through the silence.

'Well, perhaps the vase should go to auction then,' Agatha replies. 'It sounds like it might be worth more than I originally thought.'

'I would say ten pounds is a fair price,' someone who is obviously an auction house employee chimes in.

'No, we'll put it to auction,' Agatha tells him. 'And you can tell your friend, if she wants it so bad, she can come in here and bid for it herself.'

Agatha's voice is much louder for the last part of her sentence, almost as though she's leaning into Ziggy's ear to say it. I don't think she knows about the earpiece, but I think she's made him out as someone acting on my behalf and she wants him to know about it.

'Shit,' I say under my breath.

Ziggy eventually finds me outside. He looks so disappointed that the plan didn't work.

'Sorry, I guess she guessed I was there for you,' he says with a sigh. 'It's going to auction now, though. Why don't you go in and bid for it?'

'Is it worth it?' I reply.

'I can't imagine there being much competition,' he replies. 'I only saw the photo but it's not great. No offence to your boss.'

'I'm sure none would be taken,' I reply with a smile. 'She knew crafting wasn't really her thing.'

'Go on, give it a go, see what you can get it for,' Ziggy encourages me. I can tell he's just trying to make me feel better. 'You might even get it for £8 after all.'

'Wish me luck,' I say as I head back inside, alone, on the off-chance that I can pretend I have never met Ziggy, nor did I send him in, I'm just here for the sale, to get something to remember my old boss by.

Wow, Ziggy was right, the place really has been stripped for parts. A chandelier is missing here, and a piece of art is gone from there. It's a horrible sight to see, like watching Diana's Tearoom slowly dying before my eyes. I almost don't recognise the place. The end feels so near.

Over in the main dining room, an area has been set up with a makeshift stage in front of an arrangement of chairs. Bloody hell, it even looks like a wake, except instead of a vicar saying lovely things about the deceased, it's a man with mutton chops talking at the speed of light, breaking only to whack his gavel down in front of him.

There are a few seats free, scattered around, so I take one and wait until it's time to bid for the vase. By the time lot 2183 comes up, I have a rough idea of what I need to do.

'Next up, we have lot 2183, a handcrafted vase,' the auctioneer starts up. He begins running through the details, which I try to listen to carefully, but I'm distracted when someone sits down next to me.

'I wondered if you would show your face,' Agatha says, ever the supervillain. 'I can't believe you're actually going to bid on that piece of junk.'

I look over to see the vase being placed on a podium next to the auctioneer. It looks so out of place, given its general quality (or lack thereof). A few people in the crowd even laugh.

'Well, it is mine,' I remind her with an entirely put-on level of confidence.

'We'll see about that,' Agatha says, waggling her own paddle back and forth.

I narrow my eyes at her. She's not actually going to try to outbid me, is she?

'Do I hear £8?' the auctioneer asks.

I raise my paddle.

'Eight pounds. Any advance on £8?' he continues.

Agatha raises her paddle.

'Ten pounds,' she calls out.

'Ten pounds to the lady next to the original bidder,' the auctioneer replies. 'Any advance on £10? Twelve pounds, anyone?'

I raise my paddle.

'Twelve pounds over there, £12 bid, that's £12, £12, any advance on £12?' the auctioneer replies at breakneck speed.

'Twenty pounds,' Agatha calls out.

Wow, what on earth is Agatha playing at? Is she just trying to drive the price up? To see how much I want it? To make me pay for it and I mean really pay for it.

'Twenty pounds,' the auctioneer replies. 'Twenty pounds bid, £20, come on, ladies and gentlemen, this is a one-of-a-kind item on the block, can I get any advance on £20?'

'Thirty pounds,' I call out.

'I've got £30 over there, any adva—'

'One thousand pounds,' Agatha interrupts him.

The audience gasps. Agatha smiles smugly. Even the auctioneer is speechless, for a moment, at least.

'I, er... one *thousand* pounds,' he calls out, eventually composing himself. 'Any advance on £1,000, miss?'

He's addressing me directly. I have no choice but to shake my head.

'Going once, going twice,' the auctioneer practically threatens. 'Okay, going, going, gone! Sold to the lady over there for a whopping £1,000.'

'But you hate it,' I blurt softly to Agatha, in a state of genuine disbelief.

'Maybe I hate you more,' she tells me. 'You were leeching off Mum for years. I was her only daughter.'

'You know it wasn't like that,' I insist, but she's not listening.

'Have someone throw the vase in the back room with the other items my brother and I are keeping,' Agatha calls out. 'No need to be gentle. If it smashes, just throw it in the bin.'

I can feel my blood boiling inside my body, the muscles in my hands tensing up, pulling them into fists. What a truly horrible individual. Diana would be horrified if she could see her daughter now. Agatha walks off so I take a deep breath, allow my body to relax for a few minutes, willing myself not to cry – at least until I get outside. I head for the door, walk outside and after a short while manage to locate Ziggy.

'How did it go? Did you win?' he asks hopefully.

I shake my head.

'Agatha outbid me,' I tell him. 'That vile, horrible, evil, spiteful, vindictive, nasty, horrible cow.'

'You said horrible twice,' Ziggy tells me as he takes me in his arms for a hug. 'But she is doubly horrible, so that makes sense.'

'She just didn't want me to have it,' I mumble into his chest. 'She knew how much it meant to me, and I'm sure she believes her mum really did give it to me – I think that's why she was so angry about it.'

'It sounds to me like what you and Diana had was unique,' Ziggy replies. 'If her own daughter can't compete, then that's got to hurt, right?'

I pull away from Ziggy to look him in the eye.

'You're so smart,' I tell him. 'Even if your frankly alarming knowledge of heist movies didn't pay off.'

'I told you, a good heist has three parts,' he replies. 'The planning, the execution and the aftermath.'

'Well, there's no one I'd rather spend the aftermath of our failed heist with than you,' I tell him honestly. 'I appreciate you trying.'

'You are forgetting one thing, though,' Ziggy says.

'What's that?' I reply.

Ziggy opens up the vintage doctor's bag he's been carrying around for effect all day.

'The twist,' he announces proudly.

I look down into the bag and see Diana's vase lying on a bed of bubble wrap.

I gasp.

'Oh, my god,' I blurt. 'Oh, my god, what? How? What?'

I practically squeak that last 'what'.

'I told you, there's the plan – and the audience thinks things are going to go down a certain way – but then there's the twist,' he explains. 'With everything you told me about Agatha when we were making our plan earlier, I knew there was no way she was just going to let you take it, not if she was around to see me trying to buy it. So I figured, okay, let the vase go to auction, that way they would bring it out, and you bidding for it would be the distraction while I, you know, good old-fashioned nicked it.'

I'm stunned.

'Why didn't you tell me?' I ask him.

We had a long chat earlier about our problems, the obstacles in front of us, and what we needed to do to overcome them. We outlined plans with one another, but Ziggy never mentioned pulling a stunt like this.

'I needed you to seem genuine, so the alarm wasn't raised, and so you wouldn't be implicated in the disappearance,' he tells me. 'So, yeah, there you go. You got your vase back.'

Before I even know what I'm doing, I'm grabbing Ziggy's face and kissing him. It starts out kind of frantic, a desperate attempt for me to show him how grateful I am, but then it transitions into something slow and sensual. Perhaps it's just the gratitude talking but I can feel something so powerful between us. Something I've never felt before.

'You really are incredible,' I tell him once our lips part. 'Just... unbelievable.'

'Don't be too impressed yet,' he tells me. 'This is just part one of a three-part plan today, remember? Time to get going, if we're going to make it on time for step two.'

'I'll follow your lead,' I tell him with a smile.

You know me, I love a little scheme to try to get what I want, but schemes with Ziggy are just so, so much fun. I can't wait to see what's going to happen next.

33

'Oh, my gosh, hang on a second,' I blurt, grinding to a halt as we make our way through Leeds city centre.

'What's up?' Ziggy asks. 'We've got a schedule to keep, remember.'

'I know, but look at this,' I say.

On the edge of Bond Court there's a pink wooden letter box with a glass door at the front. The sides have been decorated with painted-on flowers and butterflies. It's beyond cute.

'What's that?' Ziggy asks.

'It's a Little Love Letter Box,' I tell him. 'There are a few, dotted around the city, or if there aren't yet, there will be. This is the first one I've seen. They've been in the works for ages – Diana funded them!'

'What?' he replies. 'No way, that's amazing. What are they?'

'The idea was that people who were feeling lonely or wanted to make new friends could write letters and place them in the letter boxes,' I explain. 'People could come and leave a letter, take one, or both, and it would connect them with a local penfriend, someone they could chat to, and hopefully form a real-life friendship with. Diana hated to think of people being lonely.'

'That's such a nice idea,' Ziggy says.

'It's such a shame she never got to see her vision realised,' I say with a sigh. 'Look, there are letters in there already.'

'Why don't we come back and get one?' Ziggy suggests with a smile.

'That would be lovely,' I reply. 'Let's teach Dean a lesson first.'

Timing is everything with step two of our three-part plan.

I knew, when I messaged Dean, that he wasn't going to be free at lunchtime. I also knew, from messaging Lacey, that she was meeting Dean for lunch. I asked if she was going anywhere nice and she said they were going to her favourite place, Baa Bar Blacks, a vegan restaurant and bar. The fact that Lacey's favourite place to eat was a vegan restaurant got me thinking, did Dean always take me to the same two restaurants because they were places Lacey didn't like? Probably. Scumbag.

So, we know Dean will be leaving his office any minute, and we know where he will be going – where he will be meeting Lacey. The plan is to give him a scare, a near miss, to try to convince him that a cheater's life is no life at all. If he feels bad, perhaps he'll come clean?

We're on Park Row, hiding behind one of those mini-billboards you find on the end of bus shelters. We wait until eventually...

'There he is,' Ziggy says. 'Come on, follow me.'

Dean is just leaving his office so we hurry in his direction, seemingly randomly bumping into him in five, four, three, two, one...

'Oh, my goodness, Dean, hello,' I squeak, doing my best to sound pleased to see him, throwing my arms around him before kissing him on the cheek. He feels so stiff and uncomfortable in my arms. I pretend not to notice. 'How are you?'

'Serena, hey, yeah, I'm good,' he babbles.

'All right, mate,' Ziggy says. He also pulls him close to give him a hug.

Now Dean looks even more alarmed.

'Sorry, I'm just on my way to a work lunch,' Dean says, doing his best to keep calm. 'Can I call you later?'

'Yeah, of course,' I reply. 'Have a good meeting, darling.'

'Yeah, thanks,' he replies. 'See you both later.'

'Well, he's rattled,' I point out once Dean has shuffled off.

'Seriously rattled,' Ziggy replies. 'And I know just how to put the boot in.'

'Oh?' I say. 'Do I want to know?'

'You can listen,' he tells me, popping his AirPod in. 'Looks like Dean *dropped* his glove. Back in a second.'

I can tell by the way Ziggy says the word 'dropped' that he must have taken it from his coat pocket.

It turns out it is possible to combine a jaw drop with a grin because I'm doing it right now.

Baa Bar Blacks is just around the corner, which means Dean will be meeting Lacey there any second. Ziggy smiles cheekily before running off after him.

It's hard to tell if he's with him yet because I can't hear anything apart from Ziggy's huffing and puffing from his run.

'Dean, Dean, mate,' I eventually hear Ziggy call out. 'Buddy, you dropped a glove.'

'Oh, my goodness, thank you,' I hear Lacey reply. 'Hon, where are your manners, huh?'

'Sorry,' Dean eventually says. 'Thanks, I didn't realise I'd dropped it.'

'No dramas,' Ziggy replies.

Silence again.

'I'm Lacey,' she eventually says. 'Dean's fiancée.'

'Lovely to meet you, Lacey,' Ziggy replies, sounding like everything is fine and this is a perfectly normal meeting. 'Dean and I have a mutual friend. We just bumped into him, actually.'

'Babe, go tell them we're here, so we don't lose our booking,' Dean instructs Lacey.

'Okay, hon,' she replies. 'Good to meet you.'

'Yeah, you too,' he replies. 'She seems great.'

'Listen, pal, you can't tell Serena about this, okay?' I hear Dean say in hushed tones. 'It's not what it looks like.'

'It kind of looks like you're cheating on your fiancée with Serena,' Ziggy replies. 'I'd love to know what else it could be.'

'Come on, you've been living with Serena, you know what she's like. Serena knows I'm engaged,' Dean lies.

Oh, my god, just when I think he can't get worse.

'Hey, it's none of my business,' Ziggy replies.

'Cheers, pal,' Dean says with a sigh of relief. It sounds like he pats Ziggy on the back. 'Don't mention that you saw me with Lacey to Serena, though. Not after I lied and told her it was a business lunch. Serena gets so jealous and I just need a little time, to break things off with Lacey properly, you know? I don't want to break the girl's heart. You understand that, right?'

'Oh, totally, buddy,' Ziggy replies. 'Keep up the good work.'

Ziggy can't help but add a little sarcasm to his voice, but Dean seems so relieved to have found an ally that I don't think he's even picking up on it. He really is a piece of work, that man.

'Cheers, pal,' Dean says again.

Oh, suddenly he's his pal.

Ziggy eventually finds me back where he left me.

'What the hell is wrong with that guy?' Ziggy asks me in disbelief. 'Does he have no shame at all?'

'Clearly not,' I say with a shrug. 'I mean, I know you know that I know about Lacey being his fiancée, but Dean doesn't know that I know that, so to tell you that I do know is just the dickhead move to end all dickhead moves.'

'That's one of the most confusing things I've ever heard,' Ziggy says through a laugh. 'But I know exactly what you mean. I'll tell you one thing, though, if the plan today was to make Dean feel so guilty he stops cheating on his fiancée, or at least like he's so close to being figured out that he should call it quits while he's still ahead, then it's safe to say we failed. He ramped up his lying, stuck with it, he even tried to get me in on his lie too. I figured the best thing to do was to let him think that he had succeeded, that I was on his side and happy to keep my mouth shut, while you worked out what you wanted to do next. What do you think you'll do next?'

'You know, I'm starting to feel less and less like this is my fight,' I admit. 'I'm wondering whether or not it's my job to try and change him, to make him do the right thing, or to help Lacey catch him 100 per cent bang to rights, so she has no choice but to believe that he's a lying, cheating arsehole.'

'Well, you wouldn't be the first woman to think she could try to fix a broken man,' he replies with a sigh. 'Don't be so hard on yourself for trying.'

'Yeah, well, unless you've got another brilliant scheme up your sleeve,' I reply. 'Your schemes really are brilliant, by the way. I couldn't be more impressed today.'

'Why, thank you,' he replies playfully. 'It was worth a shot. It was also a lot of fun. You'll be surprised how infrequently, as an adult, you get to execute little schemes like this, guilt-free, without screwing over anyone innocent. Agatha deserved to have that vase taken from her and Dean deserves to squirm like that. Amazing that, at one point, a guy like that had two girls.'

'I honestly don't know what I ever saw in him,' I admit. 'Now that I know who he really is, it's all I can see when I look at him. But enough about that tosser, because it's time for part three of our three-part plan, and this one is mine.'

'And I am very excited to learn all about it, seeing as though this is the one that hopefully benefits me,' he replies.

'Trust me, I've got this one in the bag,' I insist. 'The first thing we need to do is go shopping.'

'Well, that I am good at,' Ziggy says with a smile.

'And seeing as you saved me the fortune it would have cost me to buy back my vase, it's all on me,' I announce.

'I like your scheme better already,' Ziggy replies.

We head back in the direction of the shops. After everything Ziggy has done for me today, I owe him, I need to absolutely smash this one out of the park.

Wish me luck.

34

I never thought I would say anything like what I am about to reveal but, my gosh, I am officially in love with this kitchen.

I know, that's probably not a very cool thing to say, but from the hose tap to the island to the USB sockets, I really feel like I'm living it up in Taylor and Tim's kitchen.

Now that I've used it a few times, I sort of float around it like a butterfly, from A to B to C, using all of the gadgets, making the most of all the space. Oh, and having two ovens is absolutely game-changing, because it means I can make two things at once. I feel like a proper little housewife.

I push the little button on my AirPod.

'Call Maël,' I command.

'Calling Maël,' Siri dutifully replies.

'Hello there, stranger,' Maël answers in what I'd imagine is supposed to be a Scottish accent. 'Top of the morning to you.'

'Erm, that's definitely Irish,' I point out.

'I know,' he says in hushed tones. 'I'm doing it to wind Martyn up.'

I laugh.

'How are things?' I ask. 'How's your Scottish holiday/new life trial going?'

'I am loving Edinburgh,' he admits. 'And there are lots of jobs on offer in the kitchens of some amazing restaurants. I didn't think I was going to like it here but, I have to admit, life here might not be so bad. Obviously we're not letting Martyn know I'm as enthusiastic as I am – I'm in the other room now so we can talk freely – because he's being excessively nice to me, I'm enjoying that more than anything.'

'Your secret is safe with me,' I reassure him.

'Otherwise, you know life, it's been generally uneventful since the Atwood twins paid everyone to leave Diana's immediately so they could sell up,' he says with a sigh. 'How's your life? Boring too?'

'Erm...' I laugh. 'Not exactly, no.'

'I am the most interested in anything I have ever been in my life, you've got a real spring in your voice, Serena, consider me intrigued and tell me everything,' he insists.

Wow, Maël must be bored, if he's begging to know what I've been up to while he's been away.

'Okay, what's the noise?' he asks me suspiciously.

'It's cake batter,' I say with a laugh. 'I'm just giving it a mix, before I put it in the oven.'

'What kind?' he asks.

'Only your famous white chocolate and red velvet layer cake,' I reply. 'I was thinking about you as I made it, so I thought I'd give you a call, see how you were.'

'Yes, I always think of people as I infringe their copyright,' he jokes. 'So, go on, who are you pulling all the stops out for then, hmm? Is Dean getting the cake of all cakes? He hasn't finally popped the question, has he?'

'Dean and I are over,' I say plainly.

'And you don't sound the least bit bothered,' Maël points out. 'Hmm, I would've sworn you were making this cake for a bloke, you sound like you're smiling.'

'I am,' I practically sing.

'You're just going to have to tell me,' Maël insists. 'Come on, I can tell you're itching to tell me everything.'

'Oh, I am,' I confess. 'I just don't know where to begin. I'll just start talking and see what comes out. First of all, that day when I left the tea room for the last time, a girl was there looking for a wedding cake and it turned out she was Dean's fiancée.'

'No!' Maël says. 'That slimy bastard. I hope you told her – and killed him.'

'I did not tell her, and I haven't killed him,' I admit. 'What I've been doing is far worse, although it hasn't really got me anywhere, and I'm probably going to give up on it soon because of *something else* that I need to tell you.'

'This is like drama porn,' Maël says. 'Out with it immediately.'

'I kept seeing him – not *seeing him* seeing him, things stopped happening between us right away – but I started trying to do things, leaving little hints, so that his fiancée would catch him out. At the same time, I was talking to her, trying to get her to see what kind of man Dean really is.'

'And that didn't work?' Maël replies in disbelief.

'It turns out that he's an irredeemable scumbag and she is somewhere between fully gaslit and totally oblivious. There's no helping them.'

'You've got to feel sorry for her but, if she won't listen to reason, what can you do?' he replies. 'So, who is the new guy?'

'His name is Ziggy, he's my new housemate, while I'm crashing at my friends' place,' I tell him. 'And tonight, I'm making a special dinner – and one of your fabulous desserts, as best I can – to serve at a dinner party for a potential new employer of his. And he's going to introduce me as his girlfriend.'

'You're already playing house with the guy?' Maël blurts in disbelief.

'Well, playing house is exactly how I would describe it, because I'm not his girlfriend, and this isn't our house, obviously,' I confess. 'But we're going to put on one hell of a wholesome show to try and bag him the job he wants. And I do owe him, because earlier today he helped me steal back the vase that Diana gave me, that Agatha stole from me as I was leaving.'

I hear Maël exhale so powerfully the phone line crackles.

'That's... a lot,' he says. 'It's a shame you're only pretending to be a couple, though. You sound like you're into him. And, to be honest, he must be into you, if he's playing your odd little games with you.'

'We have slept together,' I confess. 'He's gorgeous, funny, great in bed.'

'I am suitably jealous,' Maël says. 'So you're all dolled up, with an apron on, playing the doting girlfriend character?'

'I am indeed,' I reply. 'I've made a chicken pie and all the trimmings, I've bought wine – I'm going to knock their socks off. I'd better go soon, actually.'

'Okay, well, before you go, any other wild stories about your life since I left, or is that it?' he says sarcastically.

'Actually, now that you mention it, you can keep a secret, right?'

'You know I can't, but that I'm willing to make an exception for you,' he replies.

'Diana left me a business,' I tell him.

'Not the tea room?' he replies with a gasp.

'No – I wish,' I reply. 'That went to her awful children and they picked its bones today ahead of the sale. She left me a shop.'

'I didn't know she owned a shop,' he replies. 'What did she sell, stuff from the tea room?'

'It's an adult store,' I say simply.

Maël starts choking.

'What? No!' he replies. 'You're joking?'

'It's true,' I reply.

'Oh, that dirty girl,' he says playfully.

'The place is genuinely called Dirty Di's,' I admit with a laugh. 'Honestly, though, the place might not be worth much – although I am starting to make a killing selling bits online – but it sounds like she led some sort of post-war sexual revolution for the women of Leeds.'

'She was a cool old bird but I never knew she had a dirty side,' he replies. 'Is that everything?'

'That's everything,' I reply.

'Okay, well, I'll let you go back to playing house,' he says. 'Have fun. And send me pictures of the cake so I can tell you how shit it looks compared to mine.'

'Of course,' I reply. 'Speak to you soon.'

I can't help but smile after telling Maël all about everything. It's amazing how quickly you can turn things around when you're in the shit – although not without a lot of love and support, I must add.

I place the cake in one oven before opening the other to check on the pie. Our guests should be here any minute and I've played a blinder with the timing of the food. I'll take the cake out when I serve dinner and leave it to cool for later, when we have coffee and dessert.

'Wow,' Ziggy blurts. 'Look at you.'

'Oh, this old thing?' I say, holding my apron out on one side while I curtsy.

'You look adorable in the apron but I'm talking about the dress,' he says. 'Just... wow.'

I'm wearing a long black figure-hugging dress. I've styled my hair up, which I rarely ever do, but Diana always used to wear her hair like this and she always looked so classy. Along with a pair of heels and a seriously muted version of my make-up, I am my version of dressed to impress.

'I feel like a proper grown-up, darling,' I admit. 'And look at you, don't you scrub up well?'

'This is my funeral suit,' he confesses. 'And my wedding suit. It's my one good one, I'm getting some serious mileage out of it.'

'Well, you look seriously handsome,' I tell him. 'Your hair looks nice and neat – and I don't know if you usually wear a sneaky bit of eyeliner, or whether you're just wearing concealer today, but you look good. Not gothy at all.'

'Thanks,' he says with a laugh. 'No make-up necessary but I'm glad I've scrubbed up well. The food smells unreal – who knew you were such a good cook? And oh, my god, is that the cake?'

'Yes, but don't open the oven door, or it will dip in the middle, I want it to be perfect,' I tell him.

'You look so at home in this kitchen,' he tells me. 'And you really, seriously look the part. You'd make someone a lovely little wife one day.'

He says this playfully, but I feel my cheeks blush, just a little, anyway.

'Thanks,' I reply. 'Taste my pie first, then we'll talk.'

We both laugh at my terrible choice of words. Our smiles both drop when we hear the doorbell ring.

'Okay, are you sure you're ready for this?' he asks me.

'As I'll ever be, darling,' I reply. 'Hey, if I can fake it for a bastard like Dean, pretending to be in love with you should be a piece of cake.'

'A very valid point,' he replies. 'Let's do this.'

I follow Ziggy to the front door. Once it's open, I wrap my arms around his waist and smile widely.

'Hello,' I say brightly.

'Mark, hello,' Ziggy says. 'Come in, please. This is my girlfriend, Serena. Serena, this is Mark.'

'Hello,' Mark says, offering me a hand to shake.

Mark must be in his mid-to-late thirties. His reddish-brown hair is parted in the middle and falls down on either side of his head just past his ears. He has a round face and big brown eyes. More than his appearance, though, is the way he looks, if you know what I mean. He looks at Ziggy with something somewhere between disgust and suspicion. That's good, though, I think, it means that he's entertaining the fact that Ziggy could have changed. I don't suppose he would be here if he wasn't.

'This is Pearl, my wife,' Mark tells us.

Pearl is a stunner. Tall, slim, shiny brown hair to her waist. Mark gives Ziggy a look, as though he hasn't quite ruled out the idea of Ziggy trying to steal her right here, right now.

'Nice to meet you,' Ziggy says, offering her a hand to shake.

'Hi,' I say warmly, reaching out to do the same.

It's a tiny bit awkward. I just need to snap into action.

'We're so pleased you could both join us for dinner, Ziggy has told me so much about you,' I tell Mark.

'I hope you've done the cooking and not him,' Mark replies. 'He once made six people ill with beans on toast.'

'A mystery to us all,' Ziggy says with a laugh. 'But don't worry, Serena is phenomenal in the kitchen, you're in for a treat.'

'I appreciated you asking in advance if there was any food we were allergic to or didn't like,' Pearl tells me. 'People rarely do that, they just serve you up whatever they're making, and you have to politely go along with it, no matter what is.'

To be honest with you, when I was working at Diana's, it was standard procedure to ask everyone, when you went to take their order, if they had any allergies or intolerances. I suppose it's just stuck but, also, I did want to check I was making something they would both like – I'm out to impress, remember.

'It's the least I can do,' I say with a bat of my hand. 'Ziggy, why don't you go check on the food, I'll show Mark and Pearl the lounge.'

'Of course,' he says, kissing me on the cheek. 'Back in a second.'

'Oh, wow, what a stunning lounge,' Pearl says. 'I love the colour palette – it's simply divine.'

Both Mark and Pearl sound like they were brought up in well-off families, there's just something about the way they speak, the way they carry themselves. Pearl is clearly from the West London area and Mark has no detectable accent at all. My West Yorkshire twang feels harsher than ever when I'm around people who don't share my accent.

'Thank you,' I reply.

'What are you doing over there?' she asks curiously.

'Oh, we're having some reclaimed wood shelves installed,' I reply. 'And we have new curtains arriving too – I fear we may have taken the previous ones down somewhat prematurely.'

Why am I suddenly talking like that? I need to nip that in the bud immediately. I'm probably inwardly panicking because obviously it's the previously fire-damaged wall they're talking about.

'Serena, sweetheart, can I borrow you for a moment?' Ziggy asks me, poking his head around the door.

'Of course, darling,' I reply. 'Make yourselves comfortable, I'll be back in a moment.'

As I approach Ziggy in the doorway, I can see a bead of sweat running down his temple and a tightness in his jaw. Oh, shit. This can't be good.

'What's the matter?' I ask him quietly as I follow him into the kitchen. 'The pie smells great, is it ready?'

'The pie is the matter,' Ziggy tells me quietly, through gritted teeth.

I walk around to the other side of the island and there's my chicken pie, lying on the floor in a messy pile. The empty pie case is on the worktop.

'I'm so sorry, it just fell out,' Ziggy tells me. 'I've fucked it, haven't I?'

Think, Serena, think!

'Okay, here's what you need to do, take the bandwagon, drive to one of the restaurants in Headingly that do takeaways, and get whatever is fastest,' I say. 'I'll stall them – I'll give them a tour of upstairs. Pearl seems like she's into decorating and stuff, so I'll show them the rooms.'

'Can you stall them for long enough?' he asks.

'I'll do my best,' I tell him. 'Just text me when you're back and the food is plated up. But, before you go, pick up the pie mess, and take the cake out of the oven, yeah?'

Ziggy puffs air from his cheeks as he runs a hand through his hair.

'Can we pull this off?' he asks.

'We've got away with worse today,' I reassure him with a smile. 'This is the twist, right?'

'It's one hell of a twist,' he calls after me quietly.

I hover in the hallway for a few minutes, killing some time, giving Ziggy a chance to clean up the mess before he dashes out via the back door. I take a deep breath and head back into the lounge.

'Right, well, I'm leaving the last bits of dinner prep to Ziggy –

and the dessert, but don't worry, he's learned a lot about cooking while we've been together,' I explain.

'I'm expecting nothing less than restaurant quality from him,' Mark insists.

Mark is going to get exactly what he's wished for.

'I was thinking, Pearl, you seem like you have an eye for housey stuff, why don't I give you guys a quick tour of the work we've done so far?' I suggest. 'I would love to get your opinion.'

'Oh, I would love that,' she replies.

'Okay, let's do it,' I insist, nodding towards the hallway with my head.

'I do love these hallway tiles,' Pearl tells me.

'Thank you so much,' I reply. 'I wasn't sure whether or not Ziggy was keen on them at first, but I think they've grown on him now. He actually compromised and said I could have them, because I wasn't the biggest fan of the ones he chose for the en suite.'

'Well, that's a good compromise,' Pearl says.

'To be honest, just between us, I do really quite like the tiles in the en suite, but when Ziggy picked them, I realised it was my chance to negotiate for the hallway tiles that I wanted.'

'Oh, you are terrible,' Pearl insists, clearly charmed by me.

What? Taylor did tell me to write that one down.

'So, the hallways are done, as you can see,' I say, leading them up the stairs.

Once we're on the landing, I'm able to kill a little time by explaining to them that, between doing the rooms downstairs and the new bedroom and bathroom, we haven't quite got around to doing the rooms on the first floor yet. Frankly, even I am impressed by how long I am able to waffle on about it.

'It's just incredible to have made so much progress,' Pearl says.

'With all the challenges of the previous years. Materials are so much harder to get these days.'

'Oh, so much harder,' I agree. 'But we're really happy with the progress we've made. And I'm somewhat of an interiors expert now.'

'Me too,' Pearl replies enthusiastically.

'Ooh, have you renovated your house too?' I ask curiously.

'Only five or six times,' Mark chimes in. 'And hundreds of other people's houses. She's an interior design specialist.'

Fuck. Fuck, fuck, fuck. I have no idea what I'm talking about and it's her actual job – not just her job-job either. She's a fucking specialist.

'Well, that's amazing,' I force myself to reply. 'I wish I'd known that sooner. Known you sooner, I mean.'

I seriously need to keep it together.

'I love the gallery wall,' Pearl says, admiring all the framed pictures. 'I love that it's a mixture of photos and artwork.'

'Who is this?' Mark asks, pointing out a framed photo of a man in an army uniform.

'That... is... my granddad,' I tell him.

'He fought in the war?'

'Yes, the Falklands,' I reply.

'But this is a World War II uniform, isn't it?'

Is it? I have no idea. I don't know anything about any wars. History was not my strong suit at school and, to be honest, I don't even remember being taught about anything but World War II, so in hindsight I should have gone for that one, but I figured if I didn't know anything about the Falklands War, perhaps they wouldn't either, so I wouldn't have to answer any questions.

'Yes, yes, it is,' I reply. 'He fought in both.'

'Your grandad fought in both World War II and the Falklands War?' Mark asks in disbelief. 'The Falklands War took place in the eighties, that would have made your grandad in his sixties, at least?'

'Oh, don't worry, he didn't do any fighting,' I insist. 'He just made the tea and stuff.'

Good lord, what the hell am I saying?

'Anyway, let me show you the bedroom, and the en suite,' I say as I lead them to the other staircase. Best we just gloss over that one.

'Oh, my goodness, stunning, simply stunning,' Pearl tells me as she takes in the bedroom. 'It's very chic. Oh, and these wardrobes – wow.'

I smile.

'Are they the ones you lightly press and they pop open?' she asks.

My smile drops. The only way I'm going to know that is if I open one.

I press the door and not only do I thankfully get the right side, but the door does pop open as Pearl described.

'Yes,' I say victoriously.

My victory is short-lived, though, when we all look down and see what has fallen out. It's a bra – a bralette, specifically, that is clearly way too small for me. Obviously it's one of Taylor's bras – she probably threw it in there as she was packing for the airport, getting it out of Ziggy's way. Pearl and Mark look at me for an explanation. The only thing this could possibly look like is that Ziggy is cheating on me. Unless...

'Well, this is one I don't need any more,' I say as I pick it up and chuck it back in the wardrobe. I lower my voice before I say: 'I've just had them done.'

I subtly nod towards my chest.

'Good for you,' Pearl says. 'They look so good – real, in fact.'

'Oh, thank you,' I say as sincerely as I can.

Mark clears his throat. Pearl takes that as her cue to change the subject.

'I love the paint – what shade is this?' she asks me.

I don't imagine me replying with 'green' is going to cut it. Paint colours are always kind of creative, aren't they? Well, there's only so many ways you can say green. I just need to make something up, the first thing that pops into my head will probably sound right.

'Nice pear,' I blurt without really thinking it through.

An awkward silence. Why did I have to say 'nice pear' right now?

'Can we look in your bathroom?' Mark asks, clearly hoping to steer the conversation away from breasts.

'Of course,' I reply. 'Go ahead.'

I am so, so lucky Ziggy has been keeping it tidy up here.

I've been carrying my phone with me, waiting for Ziggy's message to say that he is downstairs with the food. He's here. Wow, that was fast. Seriously fast. He must have got lucky.

'Shall we head down for dinner?' I suggest. 'Let's get it while it's hot.'

'Let's,' Mark replies. 'I'm starving.'

Heading downstairs, the house still very much smells like gravy. It's a good smell but potentially confusing, depending on what we're actually having.

I walk into the kitchen first and go to give Ziggy a kiss on the cheek.

'I've put it in the oven,' he whispers quickly.

'Great,' I reply softly.

'Sweetheart, why don't you pour some drinks, and take a seat at the table with Mark and Pearl?' Ziggy suggests. 'I'll serve the food and bring it right over.'

'You're an angel,' I tell him. 'Come on, guys, take a seat. I bought the wine Ziggy said you liked best, I'll pour us all a glass.'

'Another photo of Granddad,' Mark says as he sits down at the table, clocking another photo of the army man I would guess is a grandparent of either Taylor or Tim.

'Oh, yes, I'm so proud of my grandad,' Ziggy replies.

I hold my breath.

'Your granddad?' Mark replies, raising one eyebrow.

'No, no, he's my granddad,' I insist. 'Ziggy just calls him his granddad because, well, because...'

'Because he's going to be my granddad too, because we are, in fact, engaged,' Ziggy announces.

'What?' Pearl squeaks giddily. 'When did this happen?'

'Only yesterday,' I reply. 'And we haven't had the chance to tell our families so we're keeping it under wraps for now.'

'Congratulations,' Pearl insists as I take my seat next to her.

'Yes, congratulations,' Mark adds. 'I never would've thought that the Ziggy I knew would be the kind to get married, or buy a house, but it looks like you're both really happy together. Perhaps you have changed.'

'It means a lot to hear you say that,' Ziggy replies. 'I don't think the old me would even recognise the me standing here before you today.'

I'm sure that's true.

'Well, I am in a pinch time-wise, but presuming you can still play as well as you used to, you might just be the perfect guitarist to accompany the quartet,' Mark says as his face softens. 'And it all hangs on whether or not this pie is any good.'

'Yes, we're so hungry,' Pearl replies. 'When Mark told me Ziggy had a girlfriend – well, fiancée – who could cook, I made a point of skipping lunch.'

I know it's cheating to serve them restaurant food, but at least it's guaranteed to be good. Ziggy might just have landed his job.

'Well, dinner is served,' Ziggy announces as he places a plate down in front of Pearl first.

Oh, my god, he's been to Domino's!

To be fair, he gets points for presentation. He's laid three slices out on a rectangular plate along with a small bowl of the vegetables I prepared to go with the pie.

Pearl looks down at her plate.

'Oh, I thought you said we were having pie?' she says.

'Yes, well, pizza pie,' I say, freestyling.

'It's got an interesting finish on it,' Mark says as Ziggy puts his plate down in front of him. 'The brown, almost caramelised-looking finish on the cheese.'

Something which, if you've ever had a Domino's, you will recognise instantly.

'I've eaten pizza all over Italy and yet I've never seen anything like this,' he continues. 'How do you get it like this?'

By some miracle, it turns out neither of them has ever had a Domino's pizza!

'It's grilled,' Ziggy informs them.

'Grilled pizza?' Pearl replies.

'It's a Yorkshire expression. They aren't fully cooked under the grill, just finished there,' I say, because that makes slightly more sense.

'It's a common misconception that pizza came from Italy,' Ziggy tells them. 'Here we eat grilled Yorkshire pizza that originated in the hills of Oxenhope.'

'And is this... vegetables and gravy?' Mark asks.

'A Yorkshire side salad,' Ziggy tells them. 'Locals dip their crust in the gravy.'

'I am always more than excited to try new things,' Pearl announces happily.

'Yes, I'll give anything a go,' Mark adds. 'It's good to broaden your culinary horizons.'

We're certainly all doing that this evening.

Mark takes a bite of his pizza.

'Wow, this is really good,' he announces.

Of course it is, it's Domino's.

'Ziggy, I think this job might be yours,' Mark announces.

Ziggy reaches out, takes my hand in his, and gives it a squeeze.

I allow myself to breathe a subtle sigh of relief. Now I can just sit back, pretend to be in love with Ziggy, and enjoy my Domino's pizza. Suddenly, not one part of that feels all that difficult.

35

I slept with Ziggy last night. No, not like that. Well, actually, yes, like that at first, but then we cuddled up in the master bedroom's glorious super-king bed and we slept like that all night.

I'm lying with my head on his chest and my arm draped across his body. His body always smells so good, it's addictive. *He's* addictive. I snuggle in deeper, if that's even possible.

'Are you awake?' he asks me softly.

'Yes,' I reply. 'Good morning.'

'Morning,' Ziggy says, leaning forward to kiss me on the head. 'I have good news. The curtains are arriving today, the shelves will be fitted by the end of the day, and the few things we put on eBay have not only made enough money to cover the bills, but there's at least £20 left in the pot, if you fancy getting a pizza and watching a movie later.'

I sigh with relief. Thank goodness we've been able to sort the jobs so quickly. With Taylor saying us being here would mean they could send tradespeople in to work while they're away, I was terrified of news about the damage getting back to her one way or another. I've been feeling so incredibly guilty about it – especially every time I've walked past it – so it's going to feel like a huge weight has been lifted to know that everything is as it should be.

I'm also smiling because of Ziggy's suggestion. Regardless of what we are, pizza and a movie sounds a lot like normal couple stuff to me. I'm not getting carried away, I promise, it will just be nice to be with someone, in a normal way, with no strings, secrets or scams.

'A chilled-out day is just what I need,' Ziggy says as he squeezes me. 'Is there anything you need to do today?'

'Yeah, I think I'm going to break up with Dean,' I reply.

Ziggy laughs.

'That's an objectively funny thing to say when you're in bed with another man,' he points out playfully.

'That's true,' I reply. 'But perfect for him.'

'Is that what you think is for the best?' he asks. 'You're not doing it for me, are you? Because you know I understand what you're trying to do.'

'No, I know that,' I reply. 'Although I am doing it because of you, potentially. I've been hung up on the fact that I was part of the problem – even if it was unwittingly – but if Dean wasn't cheating on his fiancée with me, he would be doing it with someone else. This isn't my problem to fix, I don't need him, or any of this, in my life.'

'For what it's worth, I think you're doing the right thing,' Ziggy says. 'It's about time the two of us went straight.'

'Well, there's no one I'd rather do it with,' I reply.

I roll over and grab my phone from the bedside table. I just need to get this over and done with.

Morning. I need to talk to you – when are you free?

Is that too blunt? I guess it would be if this were a normal break-up, but this is nothing more than a formality. And he is a lying, cheating scumbag. In fact, some might say it was too polite.

I can be there in 10 minutes babe.

'Oh, crap, he's coming here,' I babble as I jump out of bed. 'Now.'

'I hope you weren't planning on writing a speech,' Ziggy jokes as he pulls himself up onto his elbows. 'Are you going to call him out?'

'I've thought about it,' I say. 'But, thinking about it, if the cheating is the reason I want to break up with him, it starts a conversation. He'll try to excuse it, or he'll apologise – he might even try and convince me I'm wrong, like he did with Lacey. There's nothing he can say to change my mind so I'm thinking better I just tell him it's not working.'

'Again, I think you're doing the right thing,' Ziggy replies. 'You don't need the aggro.'

'I'd rather not do it right now. I'd better go get some clothes on,' I say.

'I'm right up here if you need me,' he replies.

'Thanks,' I say. 'I just need to get this over with.'

You don't exactly need to dress nice to break up with someone, do you? In fact, I'm pretty sure the only thing I need to be is clothed, and the only thing I own that I shouldn't wear is that underwear.

If I were a different person, and Dean were a different man, you might be able to make a case for getting all dressed up to show them what they would be missing, but with Dean, the last thing I want is to give him any reason at all to try to change my mind.

I manage to get unenthusiastically dressed, downstairs and the kettle on before he arrives.

I open the door to find Dean, all suited and booted in his usual work gear, looking pleased to see me.

'Hello,' I say, neither bright nor blunt. Something vague in the middle is my plan for basically every word I'm about to say. He can't fight indifference.

'Hi, babe,' he replies, stepping through the door. 'I was actually coming to see you when I got your message.'

He pulls out a bunch of flowers from behind his back and I feel bad, but only as a reflex, only for a microsecond.

I stare at them. They're not immediately obvious in letting me know that they came from a supermarket but they're not exactly a florist's finest. As he hands me them, I can see that he's picked a label off. I place them down on the table next to me.

'To say sorry for the other night,' he explains. 'I was insensitive.'

To find a man who knows when he has been insensitive and when he should apologise is to find a good one. It's just a shame that this one isn't sincere. Even if he really does believe he did the wrong thing, and this is a heartfelt apology, it hardly matters. It's not exactly his greatest crime this year, is it?

'You're still mad at me,' he points out. 'I can tell, even if you're trying to hide it from me.'

He really can't because, if he could, he would've known I'd been mad at him for some time now.

'I don't think we should keep seeing each other,' I say, cutting to the chase.

'You don't think we should?' he replies.

'I don't want to,' I say more concisely. 'We're not right for each other. I haven't been feeling happy.'

'What was the other night about?' he asks. 'You seemed happy enough then.'

'I was trying to make it work,' I lie. 'But, look, we haven't been seeing each other that long, we gave it our best shot. I'm sorry it's worked out this way, but you're not the person for me.'

Wow, break-ups are actually really easy when you feel absolutely nothing for the person you're breaking up with.

'People don't go off people just like that,' Dean insists. 'We've got a good thing going on, I don't understand why you would want to finish just like that. Did *Ziggy* say something to you?'

'No,' I reply firmly. He must think he reported back to me what he saw yesterday.

He approaches me, wraps an arm around my body and pulls me close.

'Come on, you know we're good together,' he insists.

I wriggle in his embrace, trying to work myself free, but he keeps me in place for a second.

'Serena, come on,' he says softly. 'You *know* we're good together.'

Staring into Dean's eyes, thinking about the good times we had together, those seemingly perfect first dates where we would drink cocktails and laugh and find any excuse to touch each other... We *were* good together at the start. It was never real, though, he was with Lacey the whole time – I wonder if he even thought of her while he was with me?

'Hello.' I hear Ziggy's voice from behind me.

'All right, mate, just give us a minute,' Dean replies.

'Are you okay, Serena?' Ziggy asks me plainly.

'She's fine,' Dean replies. 'This is none of your business.'

'Actually, I think now it might be,' he replies as he stands next to me, his arm brushing mine so subtly, but Dean's eyes home in on the physical contact and he finally lets me go.

'Wait, you and him? He's the reason you're breaking up with me?' Dean asks me accusingly.

'Dean, come on, we're over, can you just go?' I reply.

'Oh, believe me, I'm leaving,' he says angrily. 'You two have a great life together, won't you?'

'Okay,' Ziggy replies simply with a casual shrug. He turns to me once we're alone. 'That's solid advice.'

I puff air from my cheeks and then laugh.

'There we are, done,' I say proudly.

'He'll be fine,' Ziggy tells me as he wraps his arms around me. 'His fiancée can comfort him.'

'He doesn't deserve her,' I say. 'But I'm glad to be rid of him. Thanks for stepping in.'

'Ah, you didn't need me,' Ziggy replies. 'I just really wanted to piss him off.'

My phone vibrates in my pocket.

'It's Dean, already,' I tell Ziggy.

'Ooh, let me read it,' he insists.

I hand him my phone and brace myself.

'Okay, let's see,' he says as he opens it. His eyebrows shoot up when he does. '"Now I know where you got that infection from – thank god I didn't shag you on Saturday when you were begging for it. I never thought you would turn out to be a cheat, Serena. Don't come crawling back to me when that loser dumps you" – oof.'

'Ha! The audacity of the man!' I practically cackle. 'Him having a go at me for being a cheater.'

Ziggy is staring at my phone. He seems to almost shake off what he just saw before locking my phone and handing it back to me.

'You okay?' I ask him.

'Yeah, yeah, I'm fine,' he insists. 'I just… I saw the photo you sent him, I didn't go looking for it, it was at the top of the screen. I recognise the strap and – Dean mentioned Saturday night?'

'Ah, yeah, but it's not what it seems like,' I insist. 'And I know it seems really, really strange – but needless to say, I don't have any kind of infection. It was all part of the plan and…'

I sigh. Why does it have to be drama, drama, drama all the time? And why do men have to be so fragile?

Ziggy takes my face in his hands and kisses me.

'Hey, you don't owe me any explanation,' he insists. 'But I get it. It's okay.'

'It's okay?' I reply. 'This isn't going to be a thing?'

'Why would it be a thing?' he asks through a laugh.

'I don't know, just thinking about my life recently, everything has been a thing,' I explain.

'Not every month is going to involve trying to break up an engagement, inheriting an adult store, and a mini-heist,' Ziggy reassures me.

'I would say that's good,' I reply. 'But I don't think I've ever had so much fun.'

36

'I used to hang out here all the time,' Ziggy announces, almost embarrassed, as we walk past the Corn Exchange.

'Did you?' I reply in disbelief, although I'm not sure why it surprises me.

'Oh, yeah,' he replies. 'Every Saturday without fail.'

'Me too,' I squeak excitedly. 'I wonder if our paths ever crossed?'

'Remind me to show you some photos of me from back then,' he replies. 'I wanted to be Kurt Cobain so badly. I grew my hair, and my mum bleached it blonde for me. It didn't look good.'

'Wow,' I blurt. 'If you'd looked then like you do now, then I definitely would've noticed you. You look like every super-sexy, dark-eyed, dark-haired, tattooed rockstar I had on my bedroom walls.'

'What did you look like?' he asks curiously.

'Long purple-black hair, about twenty times as much eyeliner as I'm wearing now, baggy jeans, fishnet tops, a backpack covered in badges and topped off with a Korn doll,' I reply. 'Usual stuff.'

'You sound like you were cool,' he replies. 'I like to think I would've talked to you, if we had met, but there was no way I was brave enough to talk to girls back then.'

'And look at us now, heading to the adult store together,' I joke. 'Here it is.'

'I can tell your first problem right away,' he starts. 'It's dark, creepy – kind of seedy. It's 2023, you don't want people to think they're going somewhere shady. I get that some people might want privacy, but there are ways to get that and let light in. Some fun window displays would go down a treat too.'

'Where have you been all my life?' I ask with a sigh.

Ziggy just laughs.

'I'm just saying, this place looks like somewhere designed to make me believe I shouldn't go there,' he continues. 'And that's not the case these days. Lean into it, own it, get some fun, colourful displays going on, a clean and bright new sign – we can match the website to the new branding.'

'Yes,' I blurt. 'Yes, yes, yes. Do you really think it can be that simple?'

'I didn't know this shop was here,' he says simply. 'So we need to increase visibility in all ways.'

'Do you want to look inside?' I ask.

'Yeah, sure,' he replies. 'Okay, this is kind of cool.'

The old Polaroid pictures on the wall have caught his attention.

'Now, is this a customer who just happened to walk in at the same time as you, or are you two together?' Jen asks nosily. She smiles, as though she already knows the answer.

'We're together,' Ziggy says.

Together as in, in the room together, or together as in a couple? Say more things, I want to know.

'Well, let me show you the new stuff we've got in for couples,' Jen insists. 'Satisfaction guaranteed.'

'I'll show Ziggy the shop first,' I tell her. 'He's here to help try and get the business back on track – he's got some great ideas.'

'Oh, you're our eBay boy,' Jen says through a smile.

'That's me,' he laughs. 'It's a cool place. There's so much potential you're not tapping into.'

'There certainly is,' Jen replies. 'You know what? I think Di would've loved you.'

'I think so too,' I say with a smile.

Diana was a really good judge of character. I always thought she was just being a protective mother-type figure when it came to my relationship with Dean, but her instincts were clearly right.

'I wish I could've met her,' Ziggy says. 'She sounded cool.'

'Well, I can tell you all about her,' I reply. 'And if I ever find anyone who owns a VHS player, you can watch my video of her with me.'

'Your video?' Jen asks curiously.

'Yes, Diana left me a video message, I've been carrying it around in my bag since the solicitor gave me it – it turns out no one has a VHS player any more,' I explain. 'And they're not just like a thing you can walk into a shop and buy these days.'

'These kids and their DVDs,' Ziggy teases.

'We have one,' Jen informs me.

I whip my head in her direction.

'What?' I say in disbelief.

'Yeah, we have one here,' she replies. 'We use a DVD player now, obviously, but we used to have one for playing sample videos on. It's still in the back room and the TV over there isn't new – you could connect it back up right now if you want?'

I feel frozen on the spot. I've been wondering how on earth I've been going to play this video, and the plan was to watch it sooner or later (even if I have been happily letting the lack of a VHS player stop me) but I'm in no way prepared for it right now.

'Do you want to?' Ziggy asks me quietly.

'I do,' I reply without a moment of hesitation. It's the chance to see Diana again (or the closest thing I'm going to get) right now. I can't pass that opportunity up.

Ziggy heads to the back room to retrieve the old VHS player before connecting it to the old TV with that knack people either have or don't have for setting up tech from any era.

I take the tape from my bag and pop it inside the player before we all take our places, standing in the middle of the adult DVD aisle, ready to watch. Ziggy takes his place next to me and intertwines his fingers with mine.

My heart beats double time when Diana pops up on-screen.

'Hello, my lovely,' she says brightly, seemingly staring straight into my eyes as she addresses the camera.

I can't help but mouth the word 'hello' back at her.

Diana, looking as beautiful as ever, so full of life and warmth, is right there, just beyond the screen, seemingly only just out of my reach. Her long, shiny grey hair is neatly swirled up on the back of her head – a style that was sort of her trademark – and she's wearing one of her beautiful two-piece outfits in a gorgeous shade of sage. She was such a classy lady, she somehow radiated sophistication.

'If you're watching this, my lovely, I'm sorry to confirm something you will already know: I've snuffed it,' she says, rather casually given what she's saying, through a smile. 'You know me, I've never been one for looking backwards, dwelling on things when I could instead focus on the future and all the good I could do.'

Diana always felt so passionately about helping people. Whether it was those she loved or strangers in need, she did everything she could and then some. It was one of the things that helped her keep moving in life, no matter what she was going through. I would do well to try to be more like Diana.

'If you're watching this video, then you'll know my secret,' she continues, her eyes widening with delight, playfully dropping her jaw for effect. 'And you will know that I have left the place in your very capable hands – I'm sure you have lots of questions about why. Hopefully I'm going to answer them now.'

'Wow, it's so surreal, seeing her again,' Jen says softly as tears escape her eyes. 'I was in no way prepared for this today.'

'Same,' I reassure her.

'I'm under no illusions as far as my dear children are concerned,' Diana says with a knowing smile. 'They will no doubt be liquidating my assets as you watch, but that's just their way of dealing with things. They were the same when their dad died, they didn't like to talk about him, they didn't like to see his things around the house. Some people hide from grief while others dive straight into it. The tea room business was always for my family, to give them a comfortable life, to support them. I knew Agatha and Andrew would never keep Diana's alive, but tea rooms are ten a penny. Dirty Di's, however, is the business that means the world to me. It's more than just a shop, we've changed people's lives, allowed them to be themselves, to express themselves in whatever way they wanted. I know the business isn't doing as well as it used to, now there are more mainstream high-street equivalents that people pass every day, but the shop is my original baby. It means the world to me. Serena, my lovely, that's where you come in. You've made sacrifices for the ones you love, you've known hardship because of those tough choices. I know that if I can leave my shop in the hands of anyone, it's you.'

My bottom lip starts to bounce uncontrollably.

'That first day you came in for an interview, inspired by everything, you were such a bright, positive light,' she continues. 'I saw a lot of myself in you. Giving you a job and a place to stay was so much more than me helping you out in your time of need, you helped me out too. I saw someone who reminded me a lot of myself. Someone I could perhaps one day trust with the thing that meant the most to me. That's why this business is for you, because I know you won't just sell it off to the highest bidder, I know you'll do right by it, and keep my legacy going for as long as you can. So, please, if you are able, take the reins and see if you can do what I have been struggling to do in recent years. Get the shop back to its glory days.'

Ziggy lets go of my hand but only so that he can wrap an arm around me and squeeze me tightly.

'Of course, you know me and my attention to detail,' Diana says with a cheeky glint in her eye. 'Even on the off-chance my children aren't selling Diana's, I did consider that perhaps they might not be so keen to keep a tenant upstairs. So, my gift to you, if you continue to run Dirty Di's for me, is the apartment above it, which has been fully refurbished and is just waiting for someone to move in.'

I cock my head curiously and turn to Jen. She nods, as if to confirm there is in fact an apartment upstairs.

'Serena, I like to think that this is all a waste of time, and that I will have found a way to let you in on my secret with you before my time comes to an end,' she continues, pausing to smile to herself for a moment. 'But it's just been too delicious a secret to share.'

The tears are still streaming down my face, but I allow myself a smile. Diana looks so happy, so pleased with everything she's achieved. That's all you can ask for in life, right?

'Before I go, I just want to say one last thing, because I know how upset you'll be feeling right now, but I want to remind you of what I told you when you lost your mum,' Diana continues with a warm smile. 'Grief is the cost of love. If you feel a lot of sadness to have lost someone, they must have given you a hell of a lot of love while they were alive. And I do love you, my darling. Never forget that. Until we meet again...'

Diana blows me kisses with both hands before waving. Then the video ends.

Ziggy squeezes me again.

'Well, I understand why you loved her so much,' he tells me. 'What a beautiful, thoughtful, loving woman.'

I sob. Not just because I miss her but because I can't believe I almost sold this place.

Jen sniffs hard.

'The apartment?' I ask curiously, trying to style out my sobbing and focus on something else. 'Is that real?'

'Yes, the apartment,' she says, trying to recompose herself too. 'Diana just had it all refitted with swanky appliances and new bathrooms – with the permission of the building owner, of course – it's been empty for a while, I guess now we know why.'

'Can I see it?' I ask.

'Sure.' Jen searches through a drawer behind the checkout. 'Here's the keys. I'd better not leave my post. Well, maybe just for five seconds, to blow my nose, hey?'

Ziggy follows me up the stairs where we find a door. I unlock it and... oh, my god.

'Shit,' Ziggy blurts.

'Look at this place!' I squeak. 'It's amazing.'

Light floods in through the big windows, even on a winter day like today. It's an open-plan space with a modern grey and white kitchen and lots of space for things like sofas and a dining table. A quick search behind the other doors reveals a swanky bathroom with white marble patterned tiles, along with not one but two bedrooms.

'I think you have a flat,' Ziggy informs me through a laugh.

'I think I do,' I reply through a big, stupid grin.

I can't believe this is what Diana had in mind all along. Not only leaving the shop to me because she knew I would carry on running it for her but a shop with an empty flat upstairs too. I always used to joke that she was my guardian angel. It's never felt more true.

'Oh, Jay the plasterer is ringing me,' Ziggy says. 'That's odd.'

'Put him on speaker,' I suggest, half curious, half worried.

'Hello?' Ziggy answers.

'What do you think you're playing at, lad?' he asks accusingly.

'Er...'

'You've not paid your bill,' Jay replies.

'Are you sure?' I chime in. 'I sent the money myself.'

'You left off the VAT,' Jay scoffs.

'The invoice didn't mention VAT,' I reply. 'Just one number.'

'Everything has VAT on it, you silly girl,' he ticks me off.

I know that, I'm not an idiot, but I assumed (because he didn't mention it) that it was factored into what he asked us to pay him.

'Right, okay, well, we'll get that to you,' Ziggy reassures him.

'Today,' Jay says firmly.

'We don't have it right now, but if you can wait a day or two,' I start. We don't have the money right now – after paying Jay, the carpenter and buying the new curtains – but a couple more days on eBay and we should be sorted.

'Today,' Jay insists.

'Be reasonable, mate,' Ziggy tries to reason with him. 'It was an honest mistake.'

'I've still got your spare key,' Jay says menacingly. 'If you want it back, then you'll bring me my money. If you don't, well, I'll sleep well tonight knowing the last thing I did was come round your house and destroy that lovely fresh plaster.'

'Can we have until midnight?' I ask.

'Fine, midnight,' Jay says. 'Otherwise, I'll be round in the morning.'

'You'll have it tonight,' I promise.

'I'm interested to hear how we're going to pull this off,' Ziggy says after hanging up. 'What's the scam?'

I laugh.

'Not a scam,' I reply – although I suppose none of our scams are scams, they're more like schemes. A creative means to morally appropriate ends. 'Quite the opposite, actually.'

37

'An honest night's work,' Ziggy muses. 'That's the big plan?'

'That's the big plan,' I reply. 'You look great in the outfit.'

I'd already agreed to work tonight, serving at an event for Sara Jane, but the money wasn't anywhere near enough to pay Jay. It was, in fact, just about half enough, so I called up to see if she needed an extra pair of hands and gave Ziggy one hell of a reference.

I'm not blowing smoke to try to butter him up, Ziggy really does look good in his smart black trousers and his white shirt – I'm wearing the same thing but I don't look half as good.

'I'm happy to do it,' he insists. 'I just have zero experience.'

'If I can do it, anyone can,' Al points out. 'Although I did just smash a champagne flute by holding it too hard.'

'Well, that can't be helped,' I laugh as I watch him carefully set down a tray of empty glasses. 'Just don't hug Kira too hard and pop her.'

'It's a struggle,' he replies. 'I'm obsessed with the girl. She's so cute, I can't help but squeeze her.'

'Why don't you squeeze me?' I tease Ziggy.

'I'll squeeze you right now if you want?' he replies.

'Maybe after I've handed out these appetisers,' I say. 'Come on, I made sure you're working the same section as me, so that I can keep an eye on you.'

Ziggy and I grab trays of fancy tempura prawns and head out into the main room. We're at the Manson hotel in a pretty big function room. Everyone is dressed in their best, and when you get a job like this and it is stressed to you that you must be smart, neat and clean, it usually means the clients expect a certain standard. Ziggy probably would've been better easing his way into the industry with the chaotic kids' party.

But it's just a one-off, just for tonight, just to get the money for Jay. It's easy money too. I've been doing these jobs since I finished at Diana's and it's tiring, but it's not complicated.

I should have known things were going too well before Jay called, but I'm not going to let it take away from the positives. Things are looking up – at work, with Ziggy, and I might even have my own place to live.

'So, you just carry the tray around and, what, do people come to you, do you approach them?' Ziggy asks.

'Just walk around and if anyone comes to you, let them take one,' I reply. 'You can offer them to people but don't interrupt them. Use day-to-day manners and you should be fine. Well, a normal person would be fine, at least.'

He laughs at my teasing.

'I'll do my best,' he replies.

'You take that side, I'll take...' My voice trails off.

'What?' he asks.

'Over there,' I say, suddenly in a whisper, even though they're too far away to hear me. 'Is that... that's Taylor and Tim.'

Tanned and dressed in their best – I'm sure of it.

'Fuck, it is,' Ziggy replies. 'Did they tell you they were back?'

'No, they must be back for this party,' I reason. 'I mean, if they know we're living in their house, then they're not going to kick us out to sleep there without telling us. But that's not to say they won't pop in tomorrow to see how things are going...'

'...and if Jay has been in and fucked up the wall,' he continues, 'then we're fucked.'

'It's going to be fine,' I reassure him as we head back to the kitchen. 'We just need to finish this shift, get paid, pay Jay and it will all be okay. The wall is fixed, it looks perfect. We sort Jay, we sort everything.'

'Yeah, you're right, we just need to finish the shift,' he replies. 'Can we avoid them?'

'Al,' I call out. 'Can Ziggy and I swap sections with you and whoever you're on with?'

'Er, yeah, sure,' he says. 'Dare I ask?'

'We've just seen someone we know and Ziggy doesn't want to ruin his street cred,' I lie.

'We're too poor to be proud, brother,' Al says as he pats him on the back. 'But, yeah, I'll tell Alice we're swapping. You guys are on drinks, pick them up at the bar near the toilets.'

'There we go, crisis averted,' I reassure Ziggy. 'Come on, let's serve the drinks. It's basically the same as serving the food except you have to carry it a bit more carefully and make sure you don't give any to children.'

'You're good in a crisis, you know,' Ziggy says as we walk through the crowd, careful to avoid Taylor and Tim. 'Right now, when we had the fire – you just seem to know what to do.'

'I've had to put out a lot of fires in my time,' I reply. 'Although last week was the first actual fire.'

'And technically I put it out,' he jokes. 'And started it. What is it about you, Serena? There's just something about you. Something that makes me want to run into this – whatever *this* is –

head first. I should probably slow down but I can't stop, and if I fall... to be honest, I think I am falling.'

Wow. I wasn't expecting him to say that. I've been feeling it, of course I have, but... wow.

'Do you know what our problem was to start with?' I say. 'We were so alike – too alike to not be on the same page. But now that we're a team, it just feels right. Maybe I'm crazy, and potentially the new main thing I look for in a man is him not having a fiancée, but I feel the same way. I might be falling too.'

'Will we still get paid if I give you that squeeze now?' Ziggy asks through a big smile, his dimples deepening as his grin grows wider. 'I want to kiss you, but that might be too far while we're working.'

'I'm sure we can get away with a squeeze,' I reply.

Ziggy stops in his tracks and wraps his arms around me, pulling me in and holding me tightly.

'I'm pretty happy right now,' he says into my ear.

'Me too,' I reply. 'And I didn't think I would be for a long time.'

As Ziggy gives me one big final squeeze, just before he releases me, we stumble into the young couple standing next to us. We bump them but that's about it, thankfully. Still, as the servers, we need to apologise.

'So sorry,' I say.

'No harm done,' the man replies as he hooks his arm back around his partner's waist.

I freeze.

'Serena?' the woman says. 'What are you doing here?'

'Shit,' Ziggy says under his breath.

I need to say something – anything – but my brain is empty, my lips won't move, my ears are ringing. The only sense I have that seems to be functioning properly right now is my sight, as it eventually clocks the banner on the wall that says:

Happy Engagement Dean & Lacey

Dean stares at me, until he realises Lacey knows my name and then he stares at her.

'What are you doing here?' she asks me again.

'Working,' I eventually manage to blurt. 'When I connected you with the caterer, she asked if I would help out with some jobs.'

'I see,' she replies. Then she looks at Ziggy.

'Hello,' he says, with no idea what else to contribute to the conversation.

'Hi,' she replies, but then: 'Something isn't right here.'

I make a dumb face, as if to ask: what?

'Do you guys know each other?' she asks Dean.

'Er, no,' he replies – he doesn't even sound like he believes himself. As for how he looks, I don't know, I can't look at him.

'Are you sure?' Lacey asks him.

I feel Dean turn to face me, so I look back at him out of nothing but reflex. I keep my face blank, but Lacey must surely be able to see the panic in my eyes. I can see it in Dean's.

You know when you watch a movie and a character forgets something, so they pat their pockets, pull a face, and begin looking all over – to really show the audience that they have lost something. Well, Dean narrows his eyes at me and cocks his head theatrically. It's too much.

'No, I've never met her before in my life, babe,' Dean insists.

'Oh, honey, but you have,' Lacey corrects him. 'You've been screwing her for months.'

Oh shit.

'Wh-what?' he replies in stunned disbelief. 'How do you know that?'

'Do you think I'm stupid?' she replies. 'I've known something was off. But your mistake was giving me your old iPad when you bought a new one. Suddenly all your messages were coming to me – messages from *her*.'

Lacey looks at me with so much hate and disgust. My god, how has she been keeping this a secret, all this time, since we met?

'I could see her name and it didn't take long for me to figure out where she worked – where I could find her,' Lacey continues, not exactly keeping her voice down, attracting a slowly growing audience. 'So I went to see her. I thought perhaps if she knew we were engaged, that we were serious and we were happy, then perhaps she would back off.'

Lacey turns to me, to address me directly.

'But then I met you and you didn't seem worried or scared. You genuinely seemed like you were quite happy for me,' she explains. 'I started to wonder if you even knew who I was. You were helping me sort a caterer – hardly the actions of the "other woman". Then you saw the photo of me and Dean in our bedroom.'

'You were in our bedroom?' Dean asks me accusingly. 'Are you some kind of psycho?'

'You were shocked,' Lacey continues, not giving me the chance to respond to Dean. 'I felt sorry for you, assuming you didn't know, and that you would probably back off. But you didn't.'

'Babe, I can explain,' Dean tells her, switching from being angry at me to grovelling to her, now it seems like perhaps she might forgive him, given that she's known all along.

'I don't want you to explain, I understand you,' she tells him, disgust in her voice. 'I want to understand her.'

'Shall we take this somewhere else?' Ziggy suggests quietly.

'This is none of your damn business,' Lacey tells him. 'Unless you didn't know, the two of them have been sleeping together – even only a matter of days ago. I saw his messages to Serena, he thought she was cheating on him with you, so she was definitely cheating on you with him. The goddamn party is over, I want an explanation.'

She turns back to me.

I look over at Ziggy, hoping he doesn't believe I've done anything wrong, or behind his back. He looks at me, then at his watch, and then he walks off. Great, perhaps he does believe her.

I turn back to Lacey.

'Listen, I caught Dean looking at a photo of you and he told me you were his ex,' I explain. 'I was shocked when you came to my work but when you told me you were getting married to someone called Teddy, I felt like I knew I didn't need to worry about anything between you and Dean. I was happy for you – and me – but then when I was at your apartment and I saw that photo of the two of you, believe me, that was the moment when I realised *I* was the other woman.'

'So why not break things off?' Lacey asks. 'A real woman would've broken things off.'

'You had just been telling me how Dean pretty much had you gaslit into thinking you were paranoid,' I explain. 'I knew what I needed to do, I needed to get you to dump him on your own.'

'You really are a psycho,' Dean says angrily. 'That's sociopath behaviour.'

'Yes, you're the expert on model behaviour,' I tell him sarcastically.

'So you're on some moral crusade?' Lacey continues. 'Do you not think it's gross to keep having sex with him? How could you do it?'

'Obviously, once I found out, I didn't even kiss him,' I tell her honestly. 'Our relationship ended the second I realised what was going on.'

'I've seen your messages,' she reminds me. 'How do you explain that photo?'

Wow, this sounds so much worse than it is.

'Can we go somewhere private and talk?' I ask her.

'Yes, I think that's for the best,' Geri, our manager, tells me, interrupting us.

'Sure,' Lacey says in a huff. 'This party is definitely over. You, outside.'

She's talking to me.

'Geri, it's a weird one, but are Ziggy and I going to get paid?' I ask her quietly.

Thank god this hasn't turned into a slanging match, and that Taylor and Tim are at the other side of the large room still. I wonder for a second about why Taylor and Tim are even here, but then I remember that I met Dean at one of Tim's work events. Taylor was telling him he needed to kiss more butts at work – I suppose attending an engagement party is a good way to do that.

'You're absolutely not getting paid,' Geri tells me. 'Needless to say, you're both sacked.'

I sigh. There goes the plaster.

Lacey takes me by the arm and begins to drag me.

'What shall I do?' Dean asks her.

'Tell everyone here to fuck off,' she replies. 'And then do the same.'

Lacey leads me into the public hotel bar and sits me down on a Chesterfield sofa in a quiet corner.

'Lacey, I'm so sorry,' I insist. 'I only had your best interests at heart.'

'You're going to have to make this make sense,' she tells me, taking a breath. 'Those messages, that picture...'

'I didn't think you'd believe me,' I explain. 'It seemed like Dean had you so convinced. I knew I needed to get you to discover him on your own, to break up with him on your own terms. That's what I've been doing this whole time, trying to give him away. I put lipstick on his collar and glitter all over his clothes. The photo was just to try and keep him interested, so I had time to expose him, because he was starting to realise I didn't want to be intimate with him, and I knew he was going to end things with me. Then I never would've been able to help you and he would've just found someone else to cheat with. I didn't touch him, I swear, I didn't want to. He honestly repulses me, and you're so nice. I just wanted to help you.'

Lacey sighs.

'Look, I believe you,' she eventually says. 'Knowing Dean, I should've known. Every time you backed off, I would relax again, and think that maybe we could make it work, that I could change him, and then right away you'd be tempting him back and he wouldn't be able to resist...'

'To try and expose him,' I say weakly. 'I really did want to be your friend.'

'I wanted to be yours too,' she replies. 'At the start, when I thought you didn't know, before things got so messy. Maybe in another life, huh?'

'Maybe,' I reply through a slight smile. 'Are you okay? Do you know what you'll do?'

'It's pathetic but I was willing to forgive and forget if he just stopped – or even if he had come clean about it and said it was a mistake – but I can't do that now, I'll never be able to trust him again,' she says. 'This party only went ahead because I saw from his messages that the two of you were over. Pathetically, I thought I'd won, that it was all finished, that the life we had spent years planning together didn't have to be ruined because of one affair. I thought this could be our fresh start, a chance to give it another go and hope he didn't do it again but...'

Lacey exhales heavily.

'You need to do what's right for you,' I tell her. 'And I need to do the same. I need to go and find Ziggy.'

'Sure,' Lacey says. 'I hope I haven't messed up things for you.'

I smile and head for the door.

See, this is what happens when you get cocky, and you think everything is going your way. Life goes out of its way to laugh in your face, and show you just how bad things can be.

38

I walk up to Jay's front door – the place where he told us the money had to be delivered by midnight, or else – without a plan. You know me, I love a good scheme, a plan of action that will make everything okay, but I have no idea what I can do now.

It's cold out tonight. I'll bet my bedroom is freezing. I doubt Ziggy will want me in his bed tonight, and I can't see him offering to trade with me. He must have been so mad at me, to walk off like that. Perhaps I didn't do as good a job of explaining what was going on with me and Dean (or not going on, as the case was) or maybe Lacey was just far more convincing – after all, she wasn't lying, she believed every word she was saying.

I understand if he's mad at me, if he feels like I've betrayed him in some way, or even if he thinks I'm drama and doesn't want a thing to do with me. But what has shocked and upset me is the fact that he's abandoned me with the Jay problem. I know, I'm not exactly the pinnacle of morality, but I thought we were in this together, no matter what.

I take a deep breath before reaching out to knock on the door. Hopefully the words will come to me when I need them – maybe

I can appeal to Jay's better nature? Perhaps I can sweet-talk him? Or maybe I can offer to pay him in some other way but unless he wants paying in butt plugs and edible thongs, then I doubt we'll be able to come up with some sort of arrangement that way.

The front door opens before I have chance to knock on it, and out walks Ziggy.

'Oh, hello,' he says casually.

'Erm, hi,' I reply.

'I'm guessing we didn't get paid for our shift?' he asks.

'We did not,' I reply. 'Shocking, isn't it?'

'Nah, I had a feeling,' he jokes.

'Is he dead?' I ask, nodding back at Jay's house as we walk away. 'I'm not saying you killed him. Maybe you found him that way.'

I follow Ziggy's lead with the joking. I can't read him right now.

'He isn't dead,' Ziggy replies. 'But I did pay him, so you don't have to worry about him any more. How did the party play out?'

'Not ideal,' I say. 'I think the engagement might be off. I feel like Lacey understands everything I did, and I'm really hoping you do too, but before we get into that – how on earth did you pay Jay?'

'I sold some guitar gear to Dan,' he explains. 'That's why I rushed off, to get it done tonight, to get the cash in time to get it to Jay.'

'Ziggy, no, that's the last thing you wanted to do,' I say, stopping in my tracks. 'You shouldn't have had to do that. This is all my fault.'

'I should have done it the first time you suggested it,' he replies. 'But I didn't do it because you told me to. It was the right thing to do. You paid for most of the work, with your shop sales. I needed to contribute more. Don't worry, though, I didn't sell Dan anything rare, and it won't make him as good as me – as much as he thinks it will.'

'I'm so sorry it's come to this, but I appreciate what you've done so much,' I tell him. 'Taylor and Tim would have been devastated, to find out they left their house with us, and we trashed it with our stupid rivalry.'

'I totally agree,' he replies. 'We're on the same page. But what I want to know is this: why were Taylor and Tim at Dean and Lacey's engagement party?'

'Last year, Taylor roped us into attending some charity thing Tim's work was throwing,' I explain. 'I met a colleague of his, one he didn't know yet, and that was Dean. I guess they're closer now.'

'Did they see you at the party?' he asks me.

'Amazingly, no, they didn't,' I reply.

'That's good,' he replies. 'Because I just got a message from Tim, saying they're back in the country for the night, staying in a hotel, but asking if they could pop in and see us and check their post and things in the morning.'

'We should offer to make them breakfast,' I suggest. 'Just because it's a nice thing to do, I feel guilty as hell, and if we keep them in the dining room, they hopefully won't notice the faint whiff of paint that's still lingering in the lounge.'

'Good plan,' he replies. 'Nice to know we've still got one in us.'

'I have other plans,' I say. 'But first I need to ask you some questions.'

'Sounds serious,' Ziggy replies.

'I'm just going to cut to the chase, even though I know it's not cool to ask questions like this so early on but, if you don't ask, you don't date someone who is actually single, so I'm trying to learn from my mistakes.'

'Smart,' Ziggy replies as we walk down the dimly lit street. Thankfully we're only a couple of streets away from the house.

'Did you run off to sell your guitar gear to Dan, because Lacey told you all that bad stuff about me and you believed her, or a little bit of both?' I ask.

Ziggy stops and turns my body to face his.

'Serena, you don't need to worry,' he insists. 'You're a grown woman, you can do whatever you want, sleep with whomever you want – if you slept with Dean the day we first got together, well, I don't think either of us was expecting anything to happen between the two of us...'

'I was,' I confess. 'I couldn't stop thinking about it.'

'Same,' he replies through a smile. 'As long as the things you did, you did for the right reasons – and not for other people, but for yourself.'

'Nothing happened between me and Dean,' I tell him anyway. 'It was all part of the act. Lacey understands why I did what I did, even if she doesn't agree with my methods.'

'We're a new start,' Ziggy tells me. 'Anything we did before now – be it trying to catch a cheater by any means necessary or breaking a cello with your arse...'

Ziggy notices the look on my face.

'Needless to say, I broke it by sitting on it by accident, and absolutely nothing else,' he quickly insists. 'But, my point is, we're all good, Serena.'

'Well, hang on a minute, don't get carried away, I need to do my checks too,' I tell him. 'Do you have a fiancée?'

'Not yet,' he tells me. 'But maybe I'm working on it.'

Ziggy takes my chin between his thumb and his finger and pulls me close to kiss me. It's a sweet, gentle, reassuring kiss. It tells me everything I need to know.

'See, funny you should say that, but I do have a proposal for you,' I start. 'You know how, between us, we almost destroyed Taylor and Tim's house?'

'Fond memories of that,' Ziggy jokes.

I hook my arm around Ziggy's as we continue walking down the street. It's quiet out tonight. No students staggering home after an Otley Run, no shady characters, no dog walkers. I haven't even seen a car in a few minutes. It's just me and Ziggy and absolute calm. The perfect climate for taking a deep breath, closing my eyes and taking a leap. It's like Ziggy said earlier, I don't mind if I fall doing it because I'm already falling. I might as well grab on to him on my way down.

'How would you like to destroy a flat together?' I ask through a smile.

Ziggy's eyebrows shoot up.

'Serena, are you asking me to move in with you?' he asks.

'Only sort of,' I reply. 'I'm asking you to move in next to me. It's a two-bedroom flat. I thought we could take a room each. There are strings attached, though. You have to help me with the business, I want to be on the guest list for all your gigs and – on a cold night like tonight – I need to be able to climb in next to you and put my cold feet on you.'

'I think I can agree to your terms,' he replies. 'But do you think you can live with a guy who has a bad attitude, even worse tattoos, and always stinks of beer?'

'I'm sure I can,' I insist. 'Because underneath those terrible tattoos, there's a good heart, we have far more in common than we don't, and – for some odd reason – you seem to like me just the way I am. The girl who talks at a million miles an hour, always seems to be cleaning just to annoy you, and who leaves blonde hairs everywhere.'

'You talk a lot because you're a passionate person, I know the flat will always be clean while you have anti-bac wipes in your cupboard and fire in your heart, and I'm kind of into the blonde hairs everywhere – it's like a calling card,' he replies. 'I feel like

I've known you a lot longer than I have. Who knows, maybe we did meet outside the Corn Exchange all those years ago?'

'Maybe we did,' I reply through a smile. 'Perhaps that's why you feel like the missing piece of a puzzle.'

Ziggy smiles.

'Right, come on, you, I need to get you home right now,' he says sexily.

'Oh, yeah?' I reply.

'Yeah,' he says. 'Because if Taylor and Tim are dropping by in the morning, then I'm going to need to let you loose with the cleaning wipes so that the place is nice and clean for them. But, if you do the cleaning, I'll do the tidying, and I'll let you get a head start on putting those cold feet on me. What do you think?'

'Sounds perfect,' I reply.

39

'How does everything look?' I ask Ziggy as I lay the final item on the dining table.

'Potentially suspicious,' he replies, wrapping his arms around my waist from behind me. 'This is the best breakfast spread I've ever seen – excluding hotel breakfast buffets. If someone made this for me, I'd be suspicious.'

'I think Taylor knows that I'm simply much nicer than you, and that this is how I'm showing my gratitude for her letting me live in her lovely home rent-free,' I tell him.

'And I think Tim knows that I'm kind of a liability, and that this is how I'm showing my guilt over almost burning his house to the ground,' he says.

'Then we'll say it's my idea,' I tell him through a laugh. 'I'll make out like I forced you into it.'

'Please do,' he jokes. 'I have a reputation to think about. It would be terrible for my image, if people thought I was just doing nice things for no reason.'

'Noted,' I reply. 'Now go put the kettle on, they should be here any minute.'

Ziggy does as he's told while I put the finishing touches on the breakfast table. There are pastries, crumpets and rolls, along with an array of spreads and fillings – everything from Nutella to marmalade to cheese (although I don't recommend having them all at once). I've also put out fresh fruit, cereals, and yoghurts. Basically, just as much delicious breakfast food as we could afford with whatever was left over after we paid Jay.

I keep thinking about how Ziggy sold off some of his guitar gear to make the money back. I'm hoping that, when we shift some more stock on eBay, and eventually get the shop making more money, I'll be able to pay to replace whatever he sold plus more. He deserves it, for making a sacrifice like he did. He might not like to think he's a good person – that it's not cool or whatever – but he really, truly is.

A knock at the front door jolts me from rearranging the order of the jugs of fruit juices for the fifth time. I look at Ziggy.

'Are we expecting anyone else?' he asks.

'Not that I know of,' I reply.

I head for the front door and open it to find Taylor and Tim standing there.

'Did you just knock on your own door?' I ask with an amused grin.

'I told you, this is your home while we're away,' Taylor reminds me as she greets me with a hug. 'We would never just walk in on you.'

Information that would've been useful to me yesterday.

'How is your tan better than mine?' she asks accusingly. 'We've been in Sierra Leone, sunning ourselves every day on Tokeh Beach.'

'You look beautiful,' I tell her. 'I can't believe you guys are back so soon.'

'It's only a flying visit,' Tim replies as we head through into the kitchen. I'd be lying if I said I wasn't relieved when they both walk past the lounge door without so much as a glance. 'I'm working with a new team at work and one of the guys invited me to his engagement party. I'm trying to kiss the corporate arse more so we figured I should go. We were planning on going somewhere else soon anyway, may as well fly via LBA.'

'It was such a freak show,' Taylor says as she hooks an arm through mine. 'It was all big and nice and swanky. I got a bit of a Patrick Bateman vibe from him, and she looked like she'd accidentally chewed on a wasp and desperately didn't want anyone to realise. You know the type.'

I really, really do.

'Anyway, we were having a great time, eating prawn balls and chatting away to one of the serving staff,' she continues. 'Then, all of a sudden, it's everyone go home, the engagement is off.'

'That's such a shame,' Ziggy says. The ease with which he lies explains so much. It's funny, though, I don't worry about him lying to me.

'No, she got over it,' Tim explains. 'She took a whole tray of prawn balls up to the room with us. She would have filled a bag, if she'd had more than one of those little flat sparkly ones with her.'

'And I'm going to do the same here,' she says, her eyes wide – her jaw too, as if she's getting ready to eat. 'Holy moly, look at this spread!'

'We just wanted to treat you, to say thank you for letting us stay here,' I say.

Tim gets Ziggy in one of those playful manly headlocks I'll never understand.

'Go on then, which toilet have you broken?' Tim teases him. 'Is the lounge flooded?'

Wrong element, buddy.

We all take a seat at the table together and dig in.

'Well, we've been dying to know,' Taylor starts, a curious yet somehow knowing grin spreading across her face. 'How are you two getting on? You're still alive, so that's a good sign.'

'We wanted to murder each other when we first lived here,' Tim admits. 'I started to think the house might be possessed, that an evil spirit was telling me to do despicable things.'

'But it turns out there's nothing that makes you want to kill each other like house renovations and decorating,' Taylor adds.

Okay, well, I certainly know that to be true. Ziggy must be thinking the same thing because he flashes me a look and gives me a cheeky little wink while no one is looking. Or so he thinks.

'Whoa, wait a second,' Taylor says, dropping her crumpet dramatically. 'Are you two...? Are you two?'

Somehow, the second time she says it, we all know what she means.

Ziggy puts half a croissant in his mouth and holds his hands up in the air.

I just smile and sort of shrug my shoulders.

'Oh, my gosh, I knew it,' Taylor says with a victorious clap. 'I know it now, I guessed it while I was on holiday, and, to be honest, I just picked up on this vibe the day you guys met, and I like to think that's why I encouraged you to live together. I can't believe it. I'm so, so happy for you, though, and I hope you continue to enjoy many lovely months together in our home.'

'We're moving out,' I blurt.

'Separately or together?'

I say 'separately' at the same time as Ziggy says 'together'.

'Both,' I clarify on behalf of the two of us. 'I have a lot to tell you but, to give you the quick version, my boss left me a business in her will, and it turns out that business has a two-bed flat just sitting empty above it. So we're going to move in there, take a room each, and work on the shop together. See what we can do.'

'What kind of shop is it?' Tim asks Ziggy, making conversation while he eats his Coco Pops.

'It's an adult store,' Ziggy replies, like it's no big deal.

Tim laughs until he realises he's serious.

'Really?' he says. 'Crikey, what do you sell?'

'All right, pervert, shut up and eat your Coco Pops,' Taylor teases, but she's clearly half joking, in that funny way wives often send words of warning to their husbands.

'We're going to brighten it up a bit, make it more accessible and inviting – you guys will have to stop by when you're back.'

'We will,' Taylor says.

She smiles at me and gives me a bit of a nod. I'm grinning so hard, my face aches.

'The two of you have honestly been so, so generous letting us stay here,' I insist sincerely. 'And hopefully it goes without saying but, even if we move out, we'll hang on to a spare key and let in any tradesmen or whatever you need.'

'Thanks,' Taylor replies. 'Sorry, I just can't stop cooing over the two of you. It's almost as though, while you were playing happy families, you sort of became a real one.'

That's a really nice way of looking at it – a positive spin on the two of us basically terrorising each other, only to fall for one another in the process.

It's funny how things work out sometimes.

40

---

3 JANUARY 2024

'Happy New Year, gorgeous,' Kira practically squeals as I greet her at the door, giving me one of the most intense hugs I've had since, well, the last time I saw her.

'Happy New Year,' I reply. 'You too, Al.'

I lean over (and stretch up) to give him a kiss on the cheek.

'Do you like my sexy dungarees?' she asks, placing her hands in the pockets, rotating her hips to show them off. 'Look at all the pockets! I might start wearing these all the time.'

'They look fabulous,' I tell her. 'And I love the headscarf.'

'Thanks,' she replies. 'It's actually the land girl outfit I wear to the 1940s weekend in Haworth every year, so I need to make sure I don't get paint on it.'

'I did warn her it would be messy,' Al says with a knowing laugh.

'First up, you're just jealous you couldn't get any dungarees in time, because you have to buy all your clothes off the internet,' Kira reminds Al. 'Also, stop acting like you know about these things, because you keep saying you didn't know painting parties were a thing.'

'I've never been to a painting party,' Al tells me. 'And I've been to some weird parties. I accidentally went to an Eiffel Tower party once, not knowing what it was.'

The look on Al's face changes and his eyes glaze over, almost as though he's suddenly looking through me.

'Judging by the look on your face, I'm going to kindly ask that you don't tell me what an Eiffel Tower party is, please,' I quickly insist.

'Whereas I am going to google it,' Kira says excitedly. 'Is everyone through there?'

'Yeah, head through, I'll get you a drink,' I say, right as there's a knock at the door. 'I'll catch you up.'

I open the door to see Taylor and Tim clutching bottles of wine and paintbrushes.

'Ayy, the guests of honour,' I say with a cheer.

'How are we the guests of honour at your party?' she asks through a laugh.

'Because you're the most qualified to be here,' I point out.

The last twelve months have been one hell of a rollercoaster. Sometimes I think that, when you're going through a difficult time, you don't realise just how tough things are while you're going through them. It's almost like you can't think about it because, if you were to let yourself dwell on how unbearable things seem, the problems you were facing would seem impossible to overcome. But if you keep moving, you keep your head up and your eyes forward, you'll be through it before you know it.

It's amazing what a difference a year can make. From crashing in Taylor and Tim's fixer-upper to buying my own. Well, *our* own. It's nothing short of incredible how much things have taken off with Dirty Di's – it turns out, when you extend your consumer base from people who wander down the backstreets of Leeds to the entire internet, business really booms.

'Now this is a scam,' Ziggy says, pulling me in close, kissing me on the cheek. 'We buy a house, but then we get other people to help us decorate it. It's genius.'

I laugh.

'I know you think it's a scam but asking the people who love you to help you paint your walls, and them agreeing – *because they love you* – is not a scam,' I inform him.

'I love you, but you told me I wasn't allowed to paint any more,' he reminds me.

'Yes, because...'

I open the door on the downstairs loo. Ziggy was so excited when we got the keys, he wanted to do something immediately. He had seen all these cool WCs on Instagram – really quirky rooms – with dark walls, wallpaper with bold prints, weird and wonderful gold light fittings with monkeys hanging off them, framed typography prints that say 'Please don't do coke in the bathroom' (which, frankly, some of Ziggy's musician friends do probably need reminding of). Ziggy wanted so badly to turn our downstairs loo into one of the cool rooms... but then he spilt an entire tin of dark green paint all over the floor, closed the door, and has been pretending it isn't there ever since.

'A problem for another day,' he insists, closing the door, running his hands all over my body, kissing me on the neck to try to get me to forget about it again. I've been pretending it isn't there too.

'Come on, let's go help,' I tell him, much as I would love to stay here and do this.

'Just a minute, before we go,' Ziggy starts. 'I know I've said it before, in bits and pieces, but I want to say it again. I am so, so proud of you. Your business is booming, you're making so many people happy, and this house that we're standing in is all because of you. You did all this.'

Ziggy can't hide his pride. But credit where it's due, I couldn't have done this without him and his help to make the business not only pick up, but start doing really well as an online market-place. It was the icing on the cake when we picked up this bargain of a house. The mortgage is intimidating – especially to a previously cashless first-time buyer like me – and it needed the world doing to it when we bought it, but we've made a start, at least.

'We did this,' I remind him. 'Without you, I'd be sat crying in a dark room full of dildos.'

Ziggy raises his eyebrow and opens his mouth to speak. I know exactly what he's going to say.

'Don't,' I playfully tick him off. 'Come on, let's go help.'

At the back of our house, the previous owners had started an extension on the back of the original kitchen and dining room, to create one nice big open-plan room. But then they ran out of money, so it's been up to us to finish it. The builders are gone now, though, throwing the last of the blocks up like they were Lego before the windows went in and the roof went on – it's amazing how much you can get done when you know which tradespeople to use, and which ones to avoid. It's just a shell of a room, though, and the rest of the house is still pretty much as it was when we moved in (the classic floral bedroom and avocado bathroom combo). Now it's time for us to get to work on decorating and furnishing it. This is just the beginning.

Al is standing at the back of the room, holding a box containing a 65-inch TV in his arms like it's a piece of paper.

'Where do you want this?' he asks. 'And am I only here for all the heavy stuff and the high stuff?'

'You're here because we adore you,' I tell him. 'But it's great that you're really strong and really tall.'

'Move out of the way, you big lump,' Kira commands.

As Al pulls his body out of the way, he elbows the wall, damaging the plasterboard.

'Jesus Christ, I'm dating the Hulk,' she says with a playful sigh. I'm sure it has its perks.

'Guys, I am so sorry,' Al insists. 'Can that be fixed?'

'Al, don't worry about it,' I reassure him. 'Sometimes smoothing over the cracks works.'

'Yeah, don't feel bad, fella,' Ziggy tells him. 'Feel guilty, and do all the manly jobs I can't do.'

Al laughs.

'Our plaster guy is great,' Tim chimes in.

'He's great, but he's a bit strange,' Taylor adds. 'I don't think I could recommend him based on that alone.'

'Oh, boy, why is that?' I ask curiously.

'We had him over to finally tackle the guest room,' she says – ahh, my old room. It's the end of an era. 'But he went into the lounge and started banging on about one of the walls, asking us why we'd had it replastered, what was wrong with his work, why we were lying about it – it was really intense.'

'That is... very strange,' I say.

Ziggy subtly gives my hand a squeeze. No matter what, it's so good to feel like we're always in it together. It may have started out as a terrible year – I would say things couldn't be better but, I don't know, I've got a good feeling about 2024.

I'm trying to think positively these days, to look forward instead of backwards, but it's worth remembering where you've been on your journey into the future. More than anything – and this is what I try to remind myself every day – is the fact that no matter what your situation is like today, no matter how bad things seem, it's never too late to turn it around. I had no family, no job, my friends felt few and far between, Diana was gone, I had a failing business dropped onto my lap – oh, and Ziggy was a royal pain in my arse. But look at me now, everything has changed, and so has my outlook.

Things might be great now, but I don't doubt that there will be hard times in the future. I'll be ready for them, though, with whoever is by my side, whatever my situation is.

And if all else fails, I do love a good scheme.

ACKNOWLEDGMENTS

It's so fantastic to be publishing the twelfth novel (of more than twenty!) that I have worked on with the fantastic team at Boldwood Books. Massive thanks to my brilliant editor Nia and to the rest of the incredible team who make my books so great.

Huge thanks to my lovely readers – without everyone who reads and reviews my books I wouldn't be doing this. It means so much to me that you keep picking them up.

Thank you to the wonderful Kim, the lovely Aud, to James and Joey for all their support – and a special shout-out to Darcy for always being there for me.

Finally thank you to Joe, my own leading man, for being so wonderful, so supportive, and most importantly for being the love of my life. It's so easy to keep writing romance (and jokes, to be honest) with you around, fella.

MORE FROM PORTIA MACINTOSH

We hope you enjoyed reading *Your Place or Mine?*. If you did, please leave a review.

If you'd like to gift a copy, this book is also available as an ebook, digital audio download and audiobook CD.

Sign up to Portia MacIntosh's mailing list for news, competitions and updates on future books.

http://bit.ly/PortiaMacIntoshNewsletter

Discover more laugh-out-loud romantic comedies from Portia Macintosh:

ALSO BY PORTIA MACINTOSH

One Way or Another

If We Ever Meet Again

Bad Bridesmaid

Drive Me Crazy

Truth or Date

It's Not You, It's Them

The Accidental Honeymoon

You Can't Hurry Love

Summer Secrets at the Apple Blossom Deli

Love & Lies at the Village Christmas Shop

The Time of Our Lives

Honeymoon For One

My Great Ex-Scape

Make or Break at the Lighthouse B&B

The Plus One Pact

Stuck On You

Faking It

Life's a Beach

Will They, Won't They?

No Ex Before Marriage

The Meet Cute Method

Single All the Way

Just Date and See

ABOUT THE AUTHOR

Portia MacIntosh is a bestselling romantic comedy author of over 15 novels, including *My Great Ex-Scape* and *Honeymoon For One*. Previously a music journalist, Portia writes hilarious stories, drawing on her real life experiences.

Visit Portia's website: https://portiamacintosh.com/

Follow Portia MacIntosh on social media here:

[f] facebook.com/portia.macintosh.3

[twitter] twitter.com/PortiaMacIntosh

[instagram] instagram.com/portiamacintoshauthor

[BB] bookbub.com/authors/portia-macintosh

Boldwood

Boldwood Books is an award-winning fiction publishing company seeking out the best stories from around the world.

Find out more at www.boldwoodbooks.com

Join our reader community for brilliant books, competitions and offers!

Follow us
@BoldwoodBooks
@BookandTonic

Sign up to our weekly
deals newsletter

https://bit.ly/BoldwoodBNewsletter

Made in the USA
Middletown, DE
04 March 2023

26193876R00156